BEFORE
THE
STORM

Books by James D. Shipman

TASK FORCE BAUM

IRENA'S WAR

BEYOND THE WIRE

BEFORE THE STORM

Published by Kensington Publishing Corp.

BEFORE THE THE STORM

JAMES D. SHIPMAN

KENSINGTON
PUBLISHING CORP.

www.kensingtonbooks.com

This book is dedicated to Serge and Beate Klarsfeld and all the other Nazi hunters, for their tireless and courageous dedication, in the face of so much adversity, to bringing these men and women to justice.

Chapter 1
Krystallmorgen

Monday, October 4, 1948
8:47 a.m.
West Berlin, Germany

Swastikas and shattered china. Sara tiptoed through the wreckage of the antiques store. The space was not large, no more than five meters wide and ten deep. Broken porcelain covered the ground, some of it pulverized into dust. The walls were a jumble of smashed shelves. Crooked hooks and nails jutted out of fractured plaster. She glared at the angry red words painted on the windows: *Juden raus!* Jews out.

"You people let this happen," said a voice from behind her.

Sara jolted, dropping her clipboard and pen. She turned to find a man glowering at her. He was in his late thirties, a sunken scarecrow of a man swimming in a brown sweater and worn cords. A wool cap sat at a jaunty angle on his head, tufts of salt-and-pepper hair poking out. He stared at the clipboard, his eyebrows furrowed. He took a half step as if he was going to retrieve them, but then he stopped. "You Americans let this happen," he repeated. He was speaking English, but with a thick German accent.

"I'm one of you," Sara responded in German. "And don't blame the Americans. They are here to help."

The man spat on the ground. "It's the 1930s all over again. I thought the war was over—that the madness was finished. Now this." He took another step toward her, raising his arm to point a finger. "You're supposed to be protecting us."

Sara was startled and a little afraid. She wasn't supposed to be here alone. Where were Mr. Varberg and Jeffrey? A second figure appeared in the doorway, but it was not either of them.

"Now, now, enough of that, Karl. Can't you see you're scaring the poor girl?" The second man smiled at her. He looked a bit like the first, but younger and more attractive, as if God had taken a second stab at improving the original. He was better dressed, and he scratched a few days of beard with fingers attempting to cover a smile. "I have to apologize for my brother," he said, moving into the store and gingerly stepping among the broken china. "He's always been a little short on charm. I'm sorry if we've startled you." He took another step into the store, moving slowly around Karl until both stood only a half meter away from her. He put his hands out. "Don't worry, my dear, you have nothing to worry about from us." He looked down. "May I pick this up?" He bent down and fetched the pen and clipboard. He held them out for her.

Sara stared at the two of them. She was all alone. It was daylight, but this part of Berlin was still rebuilding, and there were few people about. She could feel her heart fluttering like a startled sparrow. He still held her clipboard out for her. Taking a breath, she raised her hand and took the end of the board. The man whipped his other arm around toward her hand.

She gasped and jerked away, but he didn't move toward her. He held up his fingers, twirling her pen. He laughed again.

"Have we frightened you?" he asked. "Well, that would be a

first. A German afraid of a couple of Jews." He reached his hand out. "I'm Max. And of course you've already met the charming Karl."

She took his hand briefly, not looking into his eyes as she did so. "You didn't scare me," she said, not really telling the truth. "It's just early, and I haven't woken up yet."

"Yes," said Max, turning his head to look around. "Our friends, whoever they are, must work the night shift. Now we all have to get up plenty early to try to tidy up after them."

"Is everything a joke to you?" said Karl, scowling even more.

"If I didn't laugh, I'd only be able to cry," said Max softly. Deep pain and sadness rippled across his features, but just for a moment. "Again, you'll have to forgive my brother. He's been through a lot, and we thought all of this unpleasantness was behind us."

"I told you they'd never leave us alone. That these Americans wouldn't be able to protect us."

"She's a German," said Max. "So settle down. Although I assume that our guest works for the Americans, and that they'll be along any moment." He turned to Sara. "Am I correct in this assumption?"

"Yes," she said. "I work for the Office of Public Affairs. I'm the secretary for the head of the department, Mr. Varberg. We received a call from the German police this morning and came down right away. He and Mr. Scott, his assistant, just stepped out a few minutes ago to check on the rest of the neighborhood. I was expecting them back by now."

"For what purpose?" said Karl. "To gloat about the end of our store, our livelihood?" He turned to his brother. "We don't need their help. We can take care of ourselves."

"You'll have to forgive my brother," said Max. He hesitated. "We've had rather bad luck with government officials in the past."

Sara blushed. "I . . . I know you have. I'm sorry about all of that. We are all sorry. All of us Germans."

"Not all of you," said Karl, spitting again into the powdery mess. "Not by a long measure."

"We suffered too," she said, showing a hint of anger. The Jews always assumed they were the only victims of the war.

Karl's face mottled with red. "Tough war for you then? Did you have to cut your calories back? Was your house bombed out by the Americans because of the war *you* started? Are you sad because you didn't win after you set the world on fire? Didn't have enough time to kill every last one of my people?"

"I didn't . . . we didn't—" she stuttered.

"I'm sorry, Max," said Karl, turning away from her. "But I'd rather listen to American excuses than German ones. I'll be in our flat. Come get me when our *saviors* arrive." He stalked out of the store without another glance at Sara.

Max turned to her again. "Truly, I do apologize." He put his hands up again, as if to quiet the broken space. "We had a difficult war. I'm sure you did as well."

She nodded, still stunned by Karl's anger. The two brothers were so different. Still, perhaps Karl's fury was more just, after what the Germans had done to them. "I am truly sorry," she said. "I didn't mean to upset him."

"Don't consider it another moment," said Max. "I'd love to hear more about your own experiences in the war." He glanced at his watch. "I wonder if—"

"Ah, Miss Sturm," said a new voice in English, the tone lilting and nearly joyful. "Have you collected one of the owners for us then?"

Sara turned to the door to face her boss's number two, Jeffrey Scott. She blushed again. "Yes, sir."

Jeffrey leaned against the frame, his head scraping the top of the jamb. He scrutinized the two of them, a tight grin on thin lips. "Whatever do we have here?" he asked. "Have you begun the interview already, Miss Sturm?" He shook his head. "I'm not sure Mr. Varberg would approve. You were to watch the shop while we looked for other vandalism; we didn't ask you to run the investigation."

"Miss Sturm was the perfect host," said Max, his English excellent. "She informed us immediately that you and Mr. Varberg were on the way."

"*Us?*" asked Jeffrey, stepping forward and extending a hand.

Max took the offered grip and it seemed to Sara the two men were sizing each other up. "Yes, us. My brother Karl was here for a few minutes, but he excused himself to go back to our flat until you and Mr. Varberg arrived."

Jeffrey glanced at Sara. "Interesting." He reached into the inside of his overcoat, retrieving a pen and a leather-encased notebook. "You are the victim of vandalism here, correct?"

"I would say it is a bit more than mere vandalism," said Max. "But yes."

"Why the swastikas?" asked Jeffrey.

Max looked to Sara for a moment as if he was confused.

"Mr. Scott is still brushing up on his German and his Germany history," she explained.

"Ah, I see. Well, my brother and I are the owners. We are Jews. The words painted out there," Max said, pointing toward the windows. "That says *Jews out.*"

"I know what it says," said Jeffrey, his tone a trifle irritated. His expression didn't change except to show a hint of concentration as his fingers scribbled away furiously. "And how long have you operated this shop?"

Max cocked his head. "Let me see. We came to Berlin in . . . May of 1947. I guess we started up our store in about October."

"And you sold dishes?"

"Yes, but not ordinary ones. Porcelain, china, antiques."

Jeffrey scanned the destruction, whistling. "Well then, this must have represented quite an investment."

"Everything we had, and everything we could borrow."

"Do you have insurance?" asked Sara, smiling at Max.

He nodded. "Some. But payment will be slow, and we won't have any revenue coming in until we can replace our inventory. This may be the end of our hopes and dreams."

"Maybe you made a mistake," said Jeffrey.

"Pardon me?"

"You know. Staying in Germany," said Jeffrey. He snorted. "I mean, not to be rude, but they made it relatively clear during the war that your kind are not welcome here. Wasn't this to be expected?"

"Jeffrey, stop it," said Sara.

His face twisted into a scowl and he turned on her. "I almost forgot you were here, Miss Sturm. Mr. Portnoy and I have delicate things to discuss."

"But sir—"

"And you just heard him. I doubt he wants a German around right now."

"Not at all," said Max. "Miss Sturm has been nothing but polite this morning."

Jeffrey dismissed the words with a shrug. "In any event she's not needed." He reached into his pocket and pulled out a few Deutschmarks. "Here, Miss Sturm. After our earlier visit to the store, Mr. Varberg was called back to the office to meet some guests. Grab a cab and get back there. He may have dictation for you."

Sara's blood burned at this dismissal, but there was nothing she could do. She turned to Max. "It was a pleasure to meet you today," she said. "I'm sorry for your loss. For everything you've been through."

He smiled at her. His eyes were a stunning blue. "I appreciate your thoughts, Miss Sturm."

She turned to leave.

"Oh, and Sara," said Jeffrey.

"Yes, sir?"

"Be a good girl and fetch my cleaning on the way back to the office, will you?"

Sara dashed out of the store, fighting back tears. Reaching the sidewalk, she observed Karl returning to the store. He marched right past her as if she didn't exist. She tried to wave at him but he pointedly ignored her. She knew she was blocks away from a main thoroughfare, the only place at this time of the day she had any hope of hailing a cab. She cursed Jeffrey under her breath, and for good measure, Karl. Finding a taxi a few minutes later, she directed the driver back to her office. She headed directly there. Jeffrey could pick up his own damned clothes.

Sara arrived back at her workplace a half hour later. The building was situated on Peter-Strasser-Weg, not far from Templehof Airport. The structure was four stories and had been rebuilt after the war from the nearby rubble. The Americans and British had bombed this part of Berlin down to the stones, and there were still colossal mounds of brick dotting the landscape in every direction, serving to remind everyone that a terrible conflict waged here just three short years before.

Sara thought about the war as she exited the cab, what the people of Berlin had endured. She was proud of her people, what they had survived, how they were rebuilding their lives, even as their nation was divided into four parts, controlled by the Soviets, English, Americans, and even the French.

A rumbling in the sky drew her attention. A flight of C-47s were angling in for a landing, bringing in supplies and food for the city. The alliance between the Soviets and the United States hadn't lasted long, she thought. And now, the war clouds were massing again. East against west as it always was. But this time there was no German army, no Wehrmacht to save the West from the Soviets. She shook her head. That was her boss's problem, and part of why this vandalism of a Jewish business meant so much this morning . . .

She hurried into the building and up three flights of stairs to their office—a tight, no-frills space facing the alley on the top floor. There was a foyer where Sara's desk guarded the inner sanctum. Jeffrey had an office directly behind her and Mr. Varberg the corner office to her left. There was a small kitchen/office supply space to her right, with a door at the opposite end that led to the largest space: the records room. All the furniture was US government issue, meaning steel desks, uncomfortable chairs, and stark décor. A portrait of Harry S. Truman loomed over Sara, keeping a close eye on her work.

She could hear voices in Mr. Varberg's office. That was odd; he didn't have any appointments on his schedule today. She settled into her morning routine, brewing some coffee in the break room and then sorting through the messages from yesterday to prioritize them for her boss. She was halfway through the pile when the door opened behind her.

"Ah, Sara, you're back," said Mr. Varberg. "Have you had a chance to make some coffee yet?"

"Yes, sir," she said. She glanced back at him. He was tall, taller even than Jeffrey. He wore a blue suit with white shirt and a red tie. A walking US flag, she thought. His hair was close cropped and the face beneath was chiseled. He was forty, and had arrived in Berlin only a few months before, with orders to start a new agency office here for purposes of keeping up US public relations during the blockade. She remembered their interview—an opportunity for a job she wanted, in competition with so many others—how thrilled she had been when she was offered the position.

"Sara, just checking in, you going to get us some coffee?" Mr. Varberg asked. His eyes sparkled and danced. She had been daydreaming and her face flushed.

"Sorry, sir. Right away I will." She hurried from her desk

and dug through the cupboards, looking for a tray and a carafe for the coffee. She finally found what she was looking for and prepared the service, carefully walking to Mr. Varberg's office. She knocked and entered.

There were two men at Mr. Varberg's desk. They both had brown hair, looked to be in their early thirties, and wore identical blue suits. What was it with Americans and blue suits? Had they not heard of brown or gray? She brought the coffee in and looked around for someplace to put it. Her boss's desk was covered in papers.

"Ah, let me help you with that, Sara." He rose and moved a jumble of documents out of the way, clearing a space on the desk. "This is Mr. Phillips and Mr. Clark. They are visiting businessmen from the United States. They are thinking of opening a business in Berlin. I had them convinced to do so, before they caught wind of this bit of unpleasantness this morning."

"Yes, it was awful," said Sara, setting the tray down.

One of the men, the taller one, leaned forward. "Good morning, Miss . . ."

"Sturm," she said.

"Good morning, Miss Sturm. You are a German woman, living in Berlin, I take it?"

She nodded.

"What do you make of this Nazi propaganda?"

"The war is over," she said. "I don't know who did this, but it was an aberration. My people don't feel this way anymore. Perhaps . . . perhaps it was even just some kids."

Mr. Varberg slapped the desk. "That's exactly what I said." Sara glanced at him and he gave her a wink.

Sara thought it might be more serious than that, but their job was to promote American interests in Germany, and uncovering a lurking Nazi movement in their midst could hardly do that. "I don't think you have anything to worry about," she said, smiling at the two men.

"Thank you, Miss Sturm."

She nodded again and left, closing the door behind her. The men stayed for another hour and then departed. As soon as they were gone, Mr. Varberg invited her into his office. She started to clear away the cups but he motioned her to sit down.

"Is Jeffrey back yet?" he asked.

"Not yet."

Mr. Varberg leaned forward. "What did you think of the Portnoy brothers?" he asked.

"The men from the store?" she asked. "I feel very sorry for them."

"I do too, Sara, but I'm not sure all Germans feel the same way. I don't understand this ongoing hatred. The Soviets have the city surrounded. They are literally trying to starve West Berlin into submission. Why bother with the Jews?"

"Some things die hard," Sara said. "There is still a lot of bitterness out there about the war. Plenty of people want to move on, but not everybody."

"Do you think we should help them?" he asked.

"Help who?"

"The Portnoy brothers, of course."

"How would we do that?"

"I have a budget. When I talked to them this morning, before you arrived, they said they didn't have enough insurance money to bring the store fully back. But I could assist them."

Sara thought of Max, his determined face, his humor in the face of tragedy. "That would be kind of you, sir," she said.

"No, that would be a colossal mistake." Jeffrey's voice chimed in from behind her. "We need them to fail—and fail now."

Sara turned her head. Jeffrey was looking at her, wearing the arrogant mask paraded through the day. "How can you say that?" she asked.

"We are in charge of public affairs. Of the public opinion of how the Germans in our part of Berlin view the job we're doing."

"And we just let a blatant act of anti-Semitism happen right under our noses," said Sara.

Jeffrey turned to Mr. Varberg. "Why am I even having this conversation with a secretary?" he asked. "Miss Sturm, would you excuse us?"

"Not just yet," said Mr. Varberg, leaning forward. "I'd like to hear her opinion."

"Most of the people here won't approve of what just happened," she said. "If you help rebuild their store, you will be showing the population that you will not tolerate the old ways—but that you're here for the people—all the people. In this difficult time, with the blockade and everything, I think that will be a source of comfort for them."

"I couldn't disagree more," said Jeffrey.

"Why is that?" asked Mr. Varberg.

"Because it will happen again. Perhaps Sara might be right, that helping rebuild would also help general morale. But what about when the store is attacked a second time? And again after that? That will force our hand. We will have to assist them each time. We don't have the money for that. We might have to get the army involved, to guard the store day and night. When we do that, we put a spotlight on Nazism at the moment we can least afford it. And, worse yet, we show ourselves to be incapable of protecting the people—when it is critical that they have the utmost faith that we can do just that."

"You're speculating all of that will come to pass," said Sara.

"It *will* happen," said Jeffrey. "And truly, if I wanted the opinion of a woman, I would write to my mother. She has at least a scrap of brains."

"I've more brains than you!" Sara shot back. "You'll reward the Nazis for this bullying! Right here in the American zone!"

"Enough!" shouted Mr. Varberg. His eyes were fire but his face as calm and cold as granite. "Thank you, Sara. I value your input. If you could clear away the tray here. I need to talk to Mr. Scott for a bit, in private."

Sara caught the look of triumph on Jeffrey's face as she rose. She turned away and fumbled with the cups, her eyes filling with tears. Without another look at either of the men, she stormed out of the room, slamming the door behind her.

Dropping the tray into the sink, she violently scrubbed the cups, the tears flowing now. She closed her eyes, forcing herself to breathe deeply. She had to keep her composure. Now was not the time. She had fought too hard for this position. Counting to ten, she felt a little calmer. She finished up the dishes and returned to her desk. Continuing to take deep breaths, she inserted a sheet of paper into her typewriter and worked on a letter Mr. Varberg had dictated to her before the close of work the evening before.

She was halfway through when the door opened. She glanced up. Jeffrey was staring at her again, a smirk on his face. "Where's my laundry?" he asked.

"I didn't have time to pick it up," she said.

"No matter, you can fetch it during your lunch hour."

"Miss Sturm," Mr. Varberg called from his office. "Could you come in for a moment?"

"Yes, sir," she replied. She already knew what the news was. Jeffrey had won him over. There would be no relief for the Portnoy brothers. Their store would close, and a little part of Berlin's uncertain future would die with it.

Chapter 2
The Past

Monday, October 4, 1948
10:42 a.m.
West Berlin, Germany

Nicholas Varberg sat for long moments before he spoke. He tapped absentmindedly on the top of his pipe, turning it over to fill it with tobacco again. He lit the top, drawing in a few quick breaths until the end burned brightly and a rich, fragrant smoke filled the air between them.

"I imagine you've already figured out what I'm about to say to you."

"You're not going to fund the store," she answered.

His eyes glinted. "Always the quick one, aren't you, Sara?"

"That's why you hired me, isn't it, sir? If there isn't anything else, I've that letter to attend to." She started to rise.

"Sit back down," he said gently, waving his hand downward as if willing her to remain. "You're angry, I take it?"

"I think we should help them."

"I know you do, Sara, but we have to consider all of the issues."

"You have to consider the issue of helping Jews being persecuted? In Berlin?"

He took another puff of his pipe. "It's not as simple as all that."

"I think it's exactly that simple," she said.

"Nothing is ever that easy. That's your next lesson." He leaned forward. "Look, if we were only addressing this problem, of course it would be the right thing to help them, but we aren't. We are facing a fight for our survival with the Russians. We're surrounded, Sara. You don't see the reports, but I'll tell you a secret. We are barely holding on. We can't supply this city forever with airplanes alone. If the Soviets keep this up, we'll have to pull out, and then where will any of these people be? Right now, we need the support of the German population. We need them to hang on, to believe in us. Rubbing their noses in the past isn't going to help that."

"Broken glass? Nazi symbols and hate-filled words? Whose nose was rubbed in what?" asked Sara.

"You're right. Of course you're right. But this is two people we are talking about. And we aren't going to stop them from having a future. If they can rebuild, then so be it. But we can't provide the resources for them—at least at the level that they want us to. The issue is simply too sensitive."

"Says Jeffrey."

"I agree."

"You agree because Jeffrey convinced you."

Mr. Varberg's eyes flared. "I think we're done here." He reached into a desk drawer and pulled out an envelope. "I'll give this to you before you leave today."

"What's this?"

"I told you I couldn't fund them at the level they might want, but I can give them a little bit. This is some money to get them started. It's not much, but it should give them some breathing room. I thought you might take it to them."

"Thank you," she said. He wouldn't look at her. She had never seen him angry. He'd always treated her with respect. She felt like she'd crossed a line with him. "I do appreciate what you're trying to do here," she said.

He looked up. "Thank you, Sara. I wish we could do more on this case, but we need less attention on this, not more."

"I don't agree, but I understand."

"Will you take it now?"

"After work, I think."

"Well, leave a little early then. We can't have you working for free, can we?" He was joking now. She'd stayed after work many times without receiving additional pay.

Sara worked the rest of the day, typing up letters and catching up on her filing. She liked to have all her work done each day before she left. She smiled to herself, wondering why. She rarely did anything in the evenings and the work could usually wait until the next day. Still, she liked to feel she had finished everything and could relax for the night and enjoy her apartment. Her dreary flat was drafty and small but it was all hers—a veritable luxury in these times. Thanks to this job, she could afford enough coal to keep herself warm, and she could keep herself fed. Not very many Berliners could say the same.

A half hour before the end of the day, she could hear Mr. Varberg rustling around in his office, and a few minutes later he emerged, briefcase and umbrella in hand, his overcoat slung over his left forearm. "Well, Miss Sturm, as promised, I'm closing us up for the day. You've still got that package for the Portnoys?"

She nodded.

"Ah, good. Please give them my best, and apologize for me that we can't do more."

"I will."

"Do you want a ride there?"

She smiled at him. He was always so thoughtful. "No, thank you, I can manage."

Mr. Varberg rapped his knuckles on her desk. "Well then. I'll see you tomorrow."

She waited until he departed and then started to put her things away for the day. She was just rising to leave when she heard a voice.

"It's not time for work to end yet, Miss Sturm." It was Jeffrey. She glanced behind her. There he was, his head poking out of his office, a smirk galloping across his face.

"Mr. Varberg said I could go early because—"

"Mr. Varberg isn't here," said Jeffrey. "Besides, he's not your only boss. I've got several dictations I need you to take. I'm afraid it's going to be a late night."

"But I'm supposed to take this package to the Portnoys," she said.

"Ah yes, the Portnoys. The younger one caught your eye, didn't he?" Jeffrey's stare bored into her and she felt her face flush. He smiled. "That's what I thought. Well, your extra-curricular activities are going to have to wait. I have important letters to send."

She spent the next two hours with Jeffrey, who perched on the edge of her desk, dictating communications to several government officials. Sara became aware immediately that there was nothing emergent about these letters and that Jeffrey was intentionally taking up her time. Her anger grew but she held her tongue. She checked her watch. It was nearly seven. He was looking over her last letter, tapping it against his wool slacks as he hummed to himself.

"Well, it's not perfect, but I guess good enough for you." He looked down at her, but she refused to meet his glance. She had paper ready in the typewriter, hands at the keys. She gave no indication of anything but a willingness to continue this all night. She wouldn't give him the satisfaction of knowing how frustrated she was with the game he was playing.

"I suppose you want to go," he said.

"I'm fine."

He stood and moved around behind her, and placing his hands on her back, he began rubbing her shoulders. "I'm sure you're sore from a long day of typing."

Her body rebelled against his touch but she kept her head facing the paper. "No, I just want to head home now."

"It's not that late," he said. "Perhaps we should get some dinner? I know you don't have anyone to go home to."

"Thank you, that's . . . very kind of you, but I'm just going to go home and do a little bit of housework." She started to rise but he held her down.

"So it's still a *no*, is it?" he asked.

She didn't answer.

"And now you have the little Jew to keep you busy. I thought you Germans despised them. Well, no matter, there are more attractive women than you waiting at the bar. Younger and prettier. I don't need to waste my time on you." He removed his hands from her shoulders. "Go on," he said. "Go chase your little friend. I'm done with you for the day." He strode into his office, threw his coat on, and marched out without another look in her direction, which suited Sara just fine.

She waited a few minutes at her desk, her eyes closed, breathing deeply in and out, erasing his fingers from her back. When she felt able, she rose and hurried out, locking the door behind her and fleeing the building. She started toward her flat but then stopped herself. What the hell, she thought, it was probably too late, but she wasn't going to let Jeffrey ruin her night. She hailed a taxi and gave the address she'd memorized this morning. She whisked away into the darkness. She was surprised to find herself crying a little. *The bastard.* No matter, he wasn't going to win.

* * *

The angry red paint still scowled from the Portnoys' store-front. She'd been certain before she arrived that the lights would be out, and the brothers gone for the night. To her relief, the space was still illuminated. She could see Max and Karl in-side, bending down and collecting bits of porcelain that they were tossing into a stainless-steel garbage can in the middle of the shop. She hesitated. Perhaps she was intruding? But then she thought of Jeffrey. No, she was going to see Max tonight no matter what. Besides, she had the package from Mr. Varberg.

She tiptoed up to the entrance. The door was ajar, letting the frigid night air into the dusty interior. She knocked on the jamb. The brothers were both startled, looking up sharply be-fore they recognized Sara. Karl gave her a grim, distrustful glare but Max was all smiles. He motioned her in.

"Fräulein Sturm," he said in German. "*Was machen Sie heute Abend hier?*"

"I wanted to check in on how you are doing," she re-sponded. She looked around. The space was much better al-ready. More than half of the store was already clear. The shelves were back in place and the floor well swept. But the swastikas and the hateful words on the window remained. "You've made wonderful progress," she said, stepping farther into the store. "You'll have everything cleaned up in no time."

"We'd make better time without interruptions," grumbled Karl.

"Hush now," said Max. He turned to Sara. "You'll have to excuse my brother. He's had a long day."

"I'm sure you both have," said Sara. "How long will it take to replace what you've lost?"

Max shrugged. "Some time. Cleaning up, as you can see, is no great matter, although I haven't figured out how to get that nasty red paint off the windows. I started scraping at it but it just won't seem to come off. I suppose we may have to order new ones. That's a good month of sales by itself. For now, we will board them up. But that's not the real problem. These antiques are in high demand with our American friends, but also very expensive for us to purchase and keep in inventory. We don't have nearly enough money to replace our inventory. But we've some savings. We'll be able to buy at least a quarter of what we had before. Then it's just a matter of selling and saving. We should be back to the same inventory level in a year or so." She could see the sadness in his eyes, despite the hopeful smile he wore.

"I have something for you," she said, and reaching into the pocket of her coat she retrieved the envelope from Mr. Varberg. She handed the package to Max.

"What's this?"

"Some money from the agency."

Max drew a pocketknife from his pocket and cut open the top of the sealed envelope with a deft motion. He thumbed through the notes. "That's very generous," he said.

Karl stepped over and sniffed at the notes. "Hah! A pittance! What do you expect us to do with this? Buy some dinner?"

"Now don't be rude, Karl," said Max. "These are difficult times. I appreciate the US government coming to our aid, in whatever form."

Karl spat on the ground. "I'll not waste my time thanking the Americans for a cookie. I've more important things to do, and so do you. I'll be at the flat." With that, Karl stormed out of the store, without saying goodnight to Sara.

A storm passed over Max's features, but he composed himself. "I'm sorry again for my brother. As I said before, we've been through a lot. He appreciates this, even if he can't bring himself to say so. And I do also."

"I'm sorry for your suffering," said Sara, fighting down the maelstrom of conflicting emotions that filled her when the topic of the war, and particularly the Jews, came up.

"That's kind of you," said Max, smiling again. "Perhaps I could tell you our story. Would you like that?"

"Yes, I would."

He glanced at his watch. "It's getting late for all of this. Have you eaten?"

Her heart skipped a beat. "I . . . no, I haven't."

"Would you like to get something with me?" She hesitated in her answer and he scrambled to explain. "I'm not proposing this as a date. Just some food, perhaps a little wine, and I can tell my tale."

"Yes," she found herself answering. "I'd like to hear your story."

"Excellent," he said. "Give me just a few moments to tidy up. I know a place just a short walk away. It's a little run-down. The war, you know. But the food is excellent and it's quiet inside."

She nodded and then waited while he shuffled about the store, pulling blinds and turning off lights. In ten minutes they left and made their way to the restaurant that was a few stores down. The space was small, just six worn tables hovering over a checkerboard-tiled floor. The chairs were wobbly and it was a little on the chilly side, but they found a nice seat by the window, and the waitress brought peppermint schnapps to warm them.

They ordered and then sat there for a little while in the low light of the restaurant, sipping their drinks and listening to the soft classical music in the background. They were the only customers. Max lit a cigarette and offered one to Sara, which she took gratefully. She felt anxious but she fought the feelings down. She had to be at her best now.

"Before I tell you my story, perhaps you would share your own?" he said.

She hadn't expected that. "There's not much to tell."

He leaned forward. "Please. I want to know more about you."

Sara felt a tide of uneasiness washing in, splashing at her soul. She didn't want to try to talk about her past. She forced a smile. "We came here for your story, not mine."

"Ah, I see," he said, chuckling. "We are in a fencing match. Well, I suppose we negotiated the terms of this meal ahead of time, and your story wasn't in the contract. So fair enough, I'll give you mine, and you can decide whether you wish today, or some other day, to share yours with me."

She nodded, relieved.

"Well, I hope I don't ruin your appetite with my tale, as it runs rather along the lines of a tragedy. Karl and I grew up in Munich. My father owned an antiques store there not far from the Marienplatz—a far grander affair than what you've seen here, with a showroom and a substantial warehouse. We lived just a few streets down in a flat. We were upper-middle class, although I didn't even know what that meant at the time."

"Did you grow up in the Jewish faith?" Sara asked.

Max shook his head. "We celebrated a holiday here and there with family, but the traditions meant more to us than the faith. I hardly thought of us as Jews, until Hitler took over. Even then, they left us alone for a couple of years. I was fifteen in 1935, when they started really restricting my family. Eventually we weren't even able to attend school anymore—let alone university, which my parents had saved and worked for. But things really grew nasty after the war started. First, they took our business away, then our apartment. We were forced to move in with my uncle and his family—twenty of us in two bedrooms. We had to sell our jewelry and furniture, piece by piece, just to buy a little bread."

The waitress appeared just then with their dinner. Sara had ordered *Maultaschen* and Max some *Schnitzel*. She placed the food on the table. Sara had been famished before but now she found she'd lost her appetite. She picked at the stuffed pasta, forcing a smile, while he continued.

"We thought we'd lived through the worst. Germany was winning the war everywhere. We assumed all this Jew-baiting and hatred would simmer down once the war was over, but we were wrong. It became dangerous in the streets. Karl was badly beaten up by some Hitler Youth one day when he was bringing some bread home for the family. He needed medical attention, but we couldn't even take him to the hospital. Fortunately, we had a family friend, another Jew, who was a doctor—or should I say a former doctor, since he was no longer able to practice. He still had his equipment and he was able to help Karl. My brother had a broken jaw, three broken ribs, and internal bleeding. He was in bed for a month."

"I'm so sorry," said Sara. "No wonder he hates us."

Max smiled at her, shaking his head slightly. "I wish I could say that was the worst of it, but I'm only beginning to tell you our troubles." He poured both of them a little wine and then took a sip. He closed his eyes for a few moments, as if steeling himself to go on, then he drew in a deep breath.

"It was only a little while after—that they came for us. The Gestapo broke down our door in the middle of the night. They shot my uncle straightaway. He'd been a minor government official in the old days, and I guess he was on some sort of list. They took the rest of us to a labor camp south of Munich. We managed to all stay in the same facility. For the first few weeks, we had nothing to do, although the SS that were guarding us kept us busy, running around in the mud, carrying bricks to one side of the camp, only to return them to the other side the next day. There was no food, no medicine, our barracks were unheated."

"How awful," said Sara, feeling a little guilty about her own wartime life.

"If only that was the worst of it. One day the whole camp was carted off in trucks to a cave system underneath Haiger-loch. They used us as slave labor to carve out a space and install electricity and facilities for a group of SS scientists. The lead of the group was a man in his midforties named Heinz Hoffman. He was a fellow Bavarian who was recruited to run this special operation. We didn't know at the time, but they were constructing a reactor made up of hanging uranium cubes."

"A nuclear facility?" asked Sara, amazed. "I had no idea the Germans even worked on an atomic bomb during the war."

Max nodded. "I don't think they were very far along. At least compared to the Americans, because as far as I know they never even attempted to put a bomb together. But they had the basics down and they were doing their best to advance their technology."

"Why did they use you?"

Max shrugged. "I think because we were available. Also, this was a top-secret project, obviously. Once we were done with construction, they didn't want the builders around to tell anyone what they'd been working on."

Sara took a gulp of wine, amazed by the story she was hearing. "What happened to you and your family?"

"Hoffman and his team were cold-blooded taskmasters. They worked us sixteen hours a day. We were starving and the rations from the labor camp were almost nothing. Some of the scientists felt sorry for us and tried to share their food with us—but Hoffman wouldn't allow it. One of the workers, a young man I'd met in the labor camp, passed out one day from hunger. An SS guard drew a pistol and executed him on the spot."

"How awful," Sara said. "Did Hoffman order him to do it?"

"I don't know," said Max. "But he must have known what happened."

"How did you survive?"

Max took another gulp of wine. She could see he was fighting back his emotions. "One day, late in the war, they evacuated the site. I heard some of the scientists arguing, suggesting that we be freed, but Hoffman would hear none of it. We were held under strict guard until trucks arrived for us, then we were sent to the Mauthausen concentration camp. My mother and father, and all of the rest of my family besides Karl, perished over the next few months from starvation and exposure."

"I'm so sorry, Max." Sara reached across the table and squeezed his hand. "I've heard these stories, of course, but most people I know just dismiss them as propaganda."

"They are all too real."

"How did you and Karl make it?"

"We were fortunate. We joined a labor group that installed and repaired electrical fixtures and wiring. We had experience from the caves. Our guards left us alone and we were able to scrounge up a little extra food. We still lost weight and were terribly weak by the end of the war, but we managed to hang on until the Americans liberated the camp."

Sara was stunned by his story. "I'm so sorry," she said at last.

"It's not your fault," he said, smiling. "At least I don't think it is. Your parents weren't Nazis, were they?"

She shook her head. "Definitely not. Although my brother was a soldier."

"Where is he now?" Max asked.

Tears filled Sara's eyes. "He's missing."

Max reached out and took her hands. "And your parents? Are they gone too?"

She hesitated for a moment, her eyes facing her plate, then nodded.

"Ah, then you're worse off than me. Sometimes I forget that Karl and I don't have a monopoly on misery. You suffered too."

"But of course, it's not the same," she responded, looking at him again. "I know that. My brother was a soldier. He had a rifle. He could fight back. But your people were murdered. They were innocent."

"In the end, they are all just as dead," he responded, a trace of sadness in his voice. He still held on to her hand. She thought about pulling back but she realized she didn't want to. She felt safe here with him. And not alone. For the first time in a long time, she wasn't by herself here.

They sat there in silence, sipping their wine, holding hands across the table.

"We want to go get him, you know," Max said at last.

The statement surprised her. "Go get who?"

"Hoffman."

"Surely he's in prison—or dead."

Max shook his head. "No. He was never arrested. We've heard stories, rumors mostly, that he's still in Bavaria. His family was well-known there. Minor nobility that had lost all their money, or some such thing."

"How could he have escaped without any justice?" she asked, her features morphing into surprise.

"Lots of Nazis did. Thousands maybe. There are former members of the SS running organizations right here in Berlin."

Her eyes widened. "They can't be doing it with the knowledge of the Allies."

"They're doing it not just with the knowledge of our American friends, but with their blessing." He gave her hand a little squeeze. "Don't kid yourself, Sara. The Americans have moved on. All they care about is the Russians now. Think about it. They need German help. Who are the most connected Germans? The most experienced?"

She shook her head, not answering.

"For twelve years, a generation almost, the Nazis were in control. The most important people in Germany were members of the party. Those same people are needed now to run the government agencies, the police, the businesses, factories, and hotels."

"I can't believe that's true," she said. "At least not for the truly evil ones."

"Trust me, it's the truth. But I can't do anything about all of them. Who am I?" he asked, smiling, his shoulders shrugging. "I'm nobody. A Jewish survivor with nothing—not even a store anymore—at least not more than half of one. I can't fix the system. But I can try to do something. I can attempt to hunt down Heinz Hoffman—well, that is my plan, at least."

"Why not go now?" she asked. "You and Karl?"

"The blockade," he said, waving his hand in a circle. "The Soviets have us boxed in. I can't get transportation or permits to leave West Berlin. So, we are stuck here," he said, with an ironic grin. "Stranded without much to do. I guess we'll try to rebuild our business plate by plate. I don't know how we will pay the rent though."

"Maybe there is something I can do," she said. "I might be able to secure passes for you and Karl to travel to Munich."

His eyes widened. "Is that possible?"

"I'm not sure," she said. "But I can ask. Mr. Varberg goes in and out all the time. And he's arranged for others to do so also, from time to time. I haven't tried to obtain a pass for myself, but I might be able to, and this is a worthy cause."

"When you say *you* . . .*"

"I want to go with you—with both of you."

"You can't be serious, you barely know me."

"Max, I'm a German woman. You've opened my eyes tonight about what's going on with the Nazis—with the Americans. If there is something I can do, some way to help—then I'd like to do it. With your permission, of course."

Max shook his head. "I couldn't allow it," he said. "It could be dangerous. There are secret organizations out there—protecting hidden Nazis. Have you ever heard of Odessa?"

She nodded. "I've read intelligence reports about them. They help sneak former SS members out of Germany, don't they?"

"Their operations are a little more widespread than that. They also help hide people within Germany itself. And they aren't opposed to using whatever means—including violence—

to protect their interests. We don't know exactly where Hoffman is. When we get there, if we get there, we are going to have to start asking questions. We may end up connected to the wrong people. We could be killed. I can't take you with us for that."

She smiled. "My life is my own. And you're not going to get anywhere without my help."

He laughed. "I see there is no dissuading you."

"Not if you want those passes."

"Very well, if you can secure the permits, we shall see. Although I'm going to have to convince Karl as well."

"He's in the same boat you are," said Sara. "If you want to travel to Bavaria, you're going to have to take me with you."

Max laughed. "I guess I'll have to talk him into it then."

Sara smiled. She lifted her glass. "To finding Hoffman," she said.

Chapter 3
The Future

Monday, October 4, 1948
5:40 p.m.
Bavaria, Germany

Hannah screamed. The little girl tore across the room, rushing for the door, a flash of white dress and blonde curls. Hands reached out from behind her, jerking her from the stone floor. She screamed again.

Heinz whipped his daughter around, spinning her, his arms stretched out. Hannah squealed with joy. "More, Vater, more!" He lifted her high over his head, tossing her into the air; she crashed back into his arms, throwing her hands around the back of his neck and laughing.

"Quiet, you two!" Elsie commanded. Heinz turned to his wife, who was frying some sausages over a tiny stove set in the corner of the room. She was frowning. "You can't be so loud," she said. "You know what time it is."

Heinz glanced at his watch. She was right. If they kept it up, they would be noticed. Questions might be asked. He couldn't afford to be careless. Not now.

He heard footsteps in the hallway, clattering along the tiled stones. Elsie's face grew ashen. She rushed to Hannah, lifting her up, her arms wrapped tightly around their little girl.

Heinz rushed to the rickety dresser near their bed and rustled in a drawer, withdrawing a pistol. He checked the safety and made sure there was a round in the chamber.

There was a loud banging. Heinz lunged toward the clatter, waving his wife behind him. He aimed his pistol chest high at the door. "Who is it?" he asked, his voice cracking.

"It's Brother Michael," said a voice, muffled through the thick wood.

Heinz relaxed. *Not this time.* He stepped to the door of their little apartment and pulled it open. Brother Michael was in front of him, a tall, lanky young man swimming in brown robes. The Franciscan bowed slightly.

"May I come in?"

"Of course, please," said Heinz. "Elsie is just making some supper for us. It's not much, but you're welcome to share some if you'd like."

The monk shook his head. "It's the holy hour. I can't stay long." He reached into his robes and pulled out a newspaper. Michael ran his bony fingers along the pages, flipping through a few until he found what he was looking for. "Here, take a look at this."

Heinz retrieved the paper and scanned the page Michael had selected. His eyes whipped along the words, his mood dampening.

"What is it?" asked Elsie.

"It's an article about so-called war criminals who have not been brought to justice."

"A travesty," said Brother Michael. "In the history of civilized war there has never been such a wholesale condemnation of the losing side."

Heinz nodded absently, his eyes still on the page.

"Are you named in the article?" Elsie asked.

"Almost at the top," he said, motioning to the paper. Elsie lowered Hannah to the ground. The little girl, thinking this was part of a new game, dashed off and hid behind the bed. But her mother was not paying attention. Elsie took the paper from Heinz, her eyes skimming through the article until she found her husband's name.

"Ridiculous," she said at last. "You were a scientist, working on a sanctioned government project. Are the Americans rounding up all of their own nuclear researchers?"

"Perhaps they should," said Heinz with a wink. "They actually managed to build some of those monstrosities, and then had the gall to use them."

"Thank Gott the war was over with us before the bombs were ready," said Elsie, giving the sign of the cross.

"Yes," said Michael, repeating the gesture. "Surely it was our Father who sheltered us."

"And who will protect us from the Americans?" Elsie asked.

"God again," said Michael. "Look around. Are you not secure here?"

"Yes," said Heinz. "And we appreciate it very much. But surely this is not a permanent solution?"

"No," agreed Michael. "It is not. I've spoken with our Odessa contact. They are ready to move you. Sunday night, we will drive you to the Swiss border. From there, it's on to Italy, then a ship to Argentina."

Heinz felt the relief wash over him. Finally! They'd waited for months. "You have the false papers then?"

Michael shifted, hesitating for a moment.

"What is it?" asked Heinz.

"Odessa has papers for you."

Realization crept over Heinz. "What do you mean? Are you saying *only* me?"

Michael nodded. "You have to understand how difficult it is to secure the documents—to arrange for the transportation. This is costing our monastery thousands of marks as it is."

"We appreciate everything you've done for us," said Heinz. "But please tell them respectfully, I will have to wait until we have paperwork for all of us."

"No!" said Elsie, her face flushed. "You have to go now!"

"We've been through this a dozen times," said Heinz. "I'm not going without you and Hannah."

"We can join you later," insisted Elsie. "Look at that article," she said. "Do you know what they will do if they catch you?"

Heinz shrugged. "It's difficult to say."

"No, it is not," said Elsie. "They'll have a rope around your neck before you can get out a few words in your defense. That's if they even bother to arrest you and they don't just shoot you out of hand."

"Bah," protested Heinz. "They aren't the Russians. I'd get a fair trial."

"And then what?" asked Elsie. "If we're lucky, you serve twenty-five years in prison? You get out when you're almost seventy? When Hannah is thirty and doesn't know you? And all those years, how do I keep us alive? What work would I do?"

"Odessa will take care of you," said Heinz.

"Would they? They have too much else on their plate. We're not the only people in hiding. I appreciate everything they do for us, but at the end of the day, I would be on my own."

"Your wife is right," said Michael. "You can't put all of your faith in our friends. Who knows what the future will bring? You should go while you can. Once you reach South America, you'll be able to obtain work. We have many contacts there. A man with your knowledge and skills will be in demand. Once you're set up there, you will be in control of your own destiny. You'll be able to bring Elsie and Hannah out on your own terms, and you won't be worried about jail sentences . . . or worse."

Heinz shook his head. "I won't do it."

Michael stepped forward and put his hands on Heinz's

shoulders. "Think about it," he said. "Elsie and Hannah can stay here. They will be safe. Nobody will be interested in them once you're gone. They can stay as long as they need to. We have a school here. Hannah can attend when she's old enough if need be. In a year or two, you will be with them again. Think on that, Heinz. A year or two. How can it be better than that if the Americans take you?"

"Find the resources for my family, and obtain the paperwork, or I won't go." Heinz shrugged Michael's hands off him.

Michael took a deep breath as if he had more to say, then he turned to Elsie. "Talk to him, will you? We have a very small window. Odessa will be here tomorrow night at about seven o'clock. You have until then to decide. They won't be pleased if this is a wasted trip." The monk bowed solemnly to them. "Now, I must go, I'm very late for our evening service."

"Thank you, Michael," said Elsie. "Thank you for everything."

The monk left, quietly closing the door behind him.

"Heinz," Elsie started.

"I don't want to talk about it," he said. Heinz stepped over to the solitary cupboard over the stove. He retrieved a bottle of schnapps, pouring himself a full glass. He took a deep drink, the fiery liquid burning his throat. Retrieving the newspaper, he sat down on a hard chair and reread the article, sipping away at the remainder of his drink. Elsie finished dinner and called him to the table, but he ignored her, lost in his thoughts. He rose a couple of times to refill his glass. Hours passed, and still he said nothing. Elsie moved around as if he didn't exist, taking care of Hannah and cleaning away the dishes. Finally, it was time for bed. Heinz lifted himself up from the chair, setting his empty glass on the table. He stumbled out of their apartment and down the hallway to the bathroom. Returning a few minutes later, he changed into his pajamas and lurched into bed.

"*Mein Liebling*," his wife whispered.

"I'll go," he said. "There's no honor in it, but I'll go."

Elsie moved close to him, wrapping her arms around him and kissing his cheek. "Oh, my dearest, of course it is honorable. You are taking care of your family with this decision. Don't you see that?"

"By leaving you?"

"It's no different than the war," she said. "Truly, it is better than that. So, we will be parted for a while. But we will be entirely safe while you're gone, and so will you. That's all that matters to me," she whispered, kissing his cheek again. "I couldn't live if something happened to you."

"That's precisely why I don't want to leave you and Hannah behind," he said, putting his arms around her.

"I know you would never leave us," she whispered, eyeing Hannah, who was asleep in her little bed a few feet away. "But you're not abandoning us. You are doing what's necessary for us to be together."

He kissed her and she kissed him back. She reached over and shut off the light. They held each other closely in the darkness, clinging to this last night together.

Chapter 4
Permission

Tuesday, October 5, 1948
6:30 a.m.
West Berlin, Germany

Sara awoke early. Her tiny flat was freezing cold. She desperately wanted to light her stove, but she knew if she did she wouldn't have enough coal for tonight. She stretched, shivering, trying to take in the morning. Then she smiled, remembering last night, the restaurant, the warmth of Max's hand on her. The plan.

She rose and hurried to the sink in her kitchen, sponging herself with freezing-cold water. She stomped her feet, trying to force a little warmth into her body. She dressed in a rush, moving quickly around the little space. After a few minutes, the shivering stopped and she felt she could face the morning. Her thoughts kept flittering back to last night's dinner. She shook her head, forcing her attention back to her routine. What was she, a schoolgirl? She felt like she was fourteen again and dreaming about a boy *in that way* for the very first time. This was unexpected and unwanted. She had to focus.

She finished dressing and ate a piece of toast. She hurriedly packed a little lunch. She wanted more but just like the coal, she had to be careful or she would run out of food for the week. Still, she cut an extra piece of cheese and put it into the tin container. She could afford it, she decided. After all, she'd had a free dinner last night.

The electric excitement coursed through her again. Usually, she dreaded going into the office. She certainly appreciated having work, but the day-to-day job so far was primarily typing an endless pile of letters. She also had to juggle Jeffrey, particularly when Mr. Varberg wasn't present. Today she didn't mind. She had a purpose, and she couldn't wait to hear Mr. Varberg's thoughts on her proposal.

She finished her scant breakfast and made her bed. She looked over her one-room flat, the tiny kitchen, the metal table with two rickety chairs. She didn't even have a sofa. Still, the small space was easy to heat with the cast-iron stove in the corner, and she wasn't forced to room with anyone else. Compared to most Berliners, she was living in luxury right now.

She left her flat, bounded down the three flights of stairs to the street level, and started the half-mile walk to the office. Dawn was just streaking across the sky. She adjusted her coat against the cold. The snow hadn't started yet here, but it couldn't be far off. There was a biting wind. She would have to remember tomorrow to throw on another layer of clothing and bring her gloves. Still, she hardly felt the discomfort today. She had a purpose.

She arrived at the office ten minutes later. The building was already warm, equipped as it was with electric heat, a rare and wondrous feature that came as a bonus with her position. She turned on all the lights, washed the dishes from the day before in the little kitchen sink, and brewed a pot of coffee for the day. She checked her watch; it was not quite seven thirty. She would have another half hour by herself before the men arrived.

She set to work on some typing from the past few days that

had been marked to complete "as time allowed." These were lower-priority messages, mostly update reports for Mr. Varberg's superiors in Washington, D.C. It seemed her boss was worried about the diminishing morale of the population within the American district of Berlin, and he was seeking more money and perhaps another staff member to assist him. In particular, he wanted more latitude in providing direct funds to needy families and struggling businesses. Sara thought of Max and Karl. If only they had those resources now. But then again, she wasn't sure they would give the money to the Portnoys even if they had it, for other political reasons that seemed terribly unfair to her.

The door rattled. She felt her excitement rising. Mr. Varberg always took a few minutes in the morning to chat with her before he started his day. She was sure he would listen to her idea. She looked up, her mouth half open, but she dropped her expression immediately. It was Jeffrey.

The American waltzed into his office and she could hear him shuffling around for a few minutes. "Sara," he said in his most imperious voice, "be a good girl and get me some coffee."

She ignored that comment but rose and returned to the kitchen, pouring him some coffee with a dash of cream and a spoonful of sugar, just the way he liked it. She thought about adding something extra, something unauthorized and full of phlegm, but she decided against it. She didn't want any trouble today and besides, she refused to let Jeffrey ruin her mood this morning. She brought the coffee into his office. Jeffrey was at his desk, scanning a newspaper, a cigarette dangling from his lips. She set the coffee down and started to leave.

"Just a moment," he said. "What are you in such a hurry about today?" His eyes moved up and down her figure. She felt uncomfortable and took a step back. "Well?" he asked again.

"Nothing, sir. I'm just working on some of the typing backlog. Do you know when Mr. Varberg will be here this morning?" she asked.

"He won't be."

"What do you mean?" she asked, her heart falling.

"He was called away yesterday."

"For what reason?"

Jeffrey looked up at her, his face turning into a frown. "That's little of your business. I'm in charge until he returns."

"How long will that be?" she asked.

"You don't fancy me at the head of the office?" he asked, his features morphing into a smirk.

"No, not at all," she lied. "I just had something to talk to him about."

"And what is that?" asked Jeffrey, leaning forward.

"Oh . . . it's nothing. Nothing that can't wait."

"I demand that you tell me immediately," he said.

Sara hesitated. She didn't want to reveal anything to Jeffrey, particularly something that had to do with Max. But now she didn't know what to do. She cursed herself for bringing it up.

"Spit it out," he demanded.

"It's really nothing," Sara sputtered. "When will Mr. Varberg return?"

"It could be a week," said Jeffrey. "And if you have something to share with him, you will share it with me. This moment. Or you will find yourself without a job."

Sara wasn't sure Jeffrey had the authority to fire her. Then again, he might. If Mr. Varberg was not returning for a week, it might be too late to help Max and Karl get to Munich. She realized she had no choice. Taking a deep breath, she explained her conversation with Max last night. She left out the details of their interaction and their dinner, trying to keep her emotions in check and her face neutral.

Jeffrey listened, taking out a piece of paper to write some notes. When she was finished, he reread his scribblings, then looked up at her, scrutinizing her closely. "Where were you with Max when you learned this information?"

Sara felt the heat fill her cheeks. She looked down. "I delivered the funds from Mr. Varberg to the store last night."

"You had this conversation at his store?"

"Max, I mean Mr. Portnoy, asked me to dinner."

"You had dinner with a Jew?" asked Jeffrey, whistling. He chuckled. "I didn't think you Germans went in for that sort of thing. Our friends who vandalized the store wouldn't like that much," he commented, lighting up another cigarette. "Well, I suppose your private life is your own. This is interesting information. Let me check out this Nazi scientist and get back to you. I'm not making any promises, but I'll see what I can do."

Sara was surprised. Jeffrey had never acted this way before. Just now he had treated her almost like a co-worker, like a human, instead of a piece of furniture or a slave to get his coffee and fetch his laundry. She left his office, smiling to herself, brimming with hope that her plan might work out after all.

She worked the rest of the day in good spirits. Jeffrey called her into his office several times to dictate messages. Again, his demeanor was polite. He treated her more like Mr. Varberg usually did. Had he seen something in her because of the initiative she had taken with Max? Something he'd neglected to realize before? She was shocked he was not angry about the dinner . . .

The day wore on and neared an ending. She decided to catch a cab right after work and visit the Portnoys' shop. She wanted to give them the news that Jeffrey was checking into things — and she wanted to see Max. Finally, the clock ticked to five o'clock, and she rose to collect her things.

"Sara, are you leaving for the day?" Jeffrey asked.

"Yes, sir," she responded.

"Come in, would you?" he asked.

She took a deep breath and stepped back into his office. He

was still sitting there like he had been all day, his desk an ocean of paperwork, a cigarette dangling lazily from his lips.

"You wanted to see me?"

"Good news," he said. "I talked to Washington. They are very interested in having me talk to Max and Karl. Heinz Hoffman is high up on the list of people they are seeking. Also, and this is fortuitous for us, they don't have any photographs of him. If your friends can truly identify him, that would be an incredible benefit to us."

"That is exciting news," she said. "I'll go see them and give them the information tonight."

"No need," said Jeffrey. "I rang them. They are coming in first thing in the morning."

"Wonderful," said Sara, a little disappointed. Still, there was nothing stopping her from visiting Max tonight. Even though the surprise was spoiled, she still could discuss everything with him. "I'll be off then," she said.

"Unfortunately, I need you to stay late," said Jeffrey. He motioned at the mountains of paperwork on his desk. "I'm doing two jobs now without Mr. Varberg. I'll need your help. Be a doll and brew another pot, will you? Then I've got a bunch of letters to dictate." He glanced up at her dress, and then the cardigan she wore over it. "Lose the sweater," he said. "It's too hot in here for it."

She froze, feeling the hot shame and anger bubbling up again. She forced it down. She was so close to getting what she wanted. For now, she would suffer Jeffrey. For now.

Sara arrived at the office the next morning and was surprised to find the lights were on. At first, she feared someone had broken in, but she saw that Jeffrey's door was closed and that light was peeking out under it. She tiptoed up and realized there were muffled voices inside. She thought she could recognize Max's voice. She checked her watch—it wasn't yet seven. Why hadn't Jeffrey told her that he was meeting with the Portnoys so early?

Feeling a little unsettled, she went about her regular morning routine, although she noted that Jeffrey had also made coffee. She was surprised; she didn't know he was capable of such a feat. Eventually she sat down at her desk and started in on her paperwork. She rolled a blank sheet of paper into her type-writer and began a letter, but the muffled voices kept drawing her attention. She strained to hear the words, but they just eluded her. She tried to focus on her work but she kept strain-ing her ears to hear what was being said. The meeting lasted most of the morning. She couldn't imagine what was going on, and time passed ever so slowly. Finally, near noon, the door opened and, amid laughter, the Portnoys stepped out into the waiting room.

She looked up and found Max smiling at her. "Good morn-ing, Miss Sturm," he said, his voice lilting a little.

"It's almost noon," she said.

Max checked his watch. "So it is. I didn't realize how long we'd been in there."

"Lots of details to work through," said Jeffrey, who was leaning against the doorjamb. "Thank you again for drawing this issue to my attention, Sara."

Max looked like he wanted to say more, but Jeffrey was ush-ering them out of the office. She glanced at Karl, who was scowling. The older brother walked directly to the front door and departed, without even saying goodbye. She wondered why he was so upset.

"You'll have to forgive my brother," said Max. "As I think I've said before, he doesn't trust government officials. But I am more open-minded. I appreciate this meeting very much, Jef-frey, and I hope we will hear back from you soon."

"You certainly will," said Jeffrey, extending a hand. Max shook it, and then with a final look toward Sara, he departed.

"What was decided?" she asked, as soon as the door was closed again.

"That's rather bold of you to ask, isn't it?" asked Jeffrey, frowning at her. "Still, since you brought the matter to my attention, I suppose you deserve an answer." He turned to her. "I've spent the morning poring over their story, and also confirming a number of details with Washington. It looks like they are telling the truth. This Hoffman did run some kind of nuclear program during the war. He was apparently also in charge of slave labor, including Jews."

"How did he escape justice?" asked Sara.

Jeffrey shrugged. "It was chaos in Germany when the war ended. At first, we were far more concerned about potential guerila redoubts. The last thing we wanted to do was fight a war against Nazi patriots hiding up in the Alps, for years to come. Fortunately, that never came to pass."

"Why wasn't he apprehended after that?" she asked.

Jeffrey shrugged. "He went into hiding with his family right away it looks like," he said, reaching into his coat pocket and retrieving a silver case. He removed a gold-trimmed cigarette and lit it, taking a deep breath before he continued. "Besides, we were looking for the leaders, for the butchers. Compared to Goering or Himmler, Hoffman is a nobody. He's not even in the same league as the concentration camp commanders or the other Gestapo. But that was then and this is now. We've caught most of the really nasty fellows," said Jeffrey. "At least those who haven't gotten away for good. Now we have time to dip into the next layer down. And within that group, Hoffman is near the top of the list."

"So, you'll send the Portnoys and me?" she asked. "Thank you, Jeffrey, I appreciate it very much."

"Hold on," said Jeffrey. "Don't get excited. All I've done so far is establish the truth of their story and that Hoffman is a target of interest. Do you have any idea how much paperwork is involved in getting someone out of Berlin right now? The Russians have everything blocked off. There is an absolute order of priority on goods and supplies coming in, by the limited number of planes we have available. The only people authorized to leave the city on those planes are senior military and government officials."

"But if we have a chance to capture a top Nazi—"

"Hoffman isn't a top Nazi," snapped Jeffrey. "I just told you that. And frankly, Sara, you must keep your priorities straight. We're not at war with Germany anymore. The Russians are our enemy. They are the ones choking off this city. They are the ones with thousands of troops set on our borders. Our first and foremost priority must be preparing for war against the Soviets. Everything else is far down the list."

"But you said he's an important target now."

"He is," said Jeffrey. "Important enough to investigate. But not essential. Now look, Sara, as a favor to you, and because this might have a marginal value overall, I've forwarded this information on to Washington. But you must understand that these things take time." He stepped over to her desk and sat on the corner, taking another puff. "Now don't you worry your pretty little head about things. I'll let you know as soon as I hear what the decision from Washington is. For now," he said, glancing at her completed work for the morning, "I need you to focus on your job. Let the men handle the big things."

"Here's to our journey," Max said over dinner, raising a glass of red wine.

Sara had rushed to the Portnoys' store as soon as her day was over. Fortunately, Jeffrey had not kept her late. She'd been impressed with the progress the brothers had made with the store. The mess was entirely cleaned up, the shelves and walls were repaired, and the glass removed from the storefront windows and replaced with plywood. Max had told her it would only be a few days until the replacement windows were available. Of course filling the store with antique china again was another thing altogether.

"To our journey?" Max said the words again and she realized she hadn't been listening to him.

"I'm sorry," she said, "I was thinking about the store. You've done so much, so fast."

He nodded. "It's Karl really. He's the real workhorse in the family."

"When will you start replacing the dishes and antiques?"

"Well, thanks to your organization, and a little money we had socked away, we can buy some now. It won't be more than a quarter of what we lost, but at least it's something."

"Will you reopen in the next week or so then?"

"We would," said Max, smiling at her over the candlelight, "but I think thanks to you we will be busy with other things for a few weeks."

She blushed. "It's not guaranteed," she said. "Jeffrey said they are only looking into it."

"They'll approve it," said Max. "I know they will."

"How can you be so sure?"

"An organization like yours being involved in a high profile arrest? Your young office assistant isn't going to miss that chance. Besides, it gets us out of Berlin for a few weeks, maybe longer than that."

"Why would they want that?"

Max stared at her. "You know why. Because we are Jews. Because it's awkward to have us around, given the past. Even worse now after the incident at our store. If we are gone doing something else, the people will forget about us, at least for a while. And with the blockade, with the Russians, they have enough worries, don't you think?"

"I don't know, I—"

"Well, that's the way your bosses will think about it, at least."

She was shocked he understood all of that.

"You have to realize, Sara," he said, as if reading her thoughts, "for years our lives depended on reading every event, every emotion." He reached out and took her hand again. "When you're an instant from death, you see the world for what it is, in bold print, not for what you wish it to be."

"You're right, of course," she said. "That's exactly how they feel. That's why they gave you less money. They want you to go somewhere else." She felt tears welling in her eyes. "I'm sorry I didn't tell you before."

"Don't feel bad," he said. "I expected as much. And truly, it was a great generosity for them to help as much as they did. If they grant our travel, if they let us track down Hoffman—why, I would be forever in their debt, and in yours."

"What does Karl think?"

"Karl doesn't want Jeffrey's help. Or yours. He thinks we should wait until the blockade is over, and then we can seek our revenge on our own—take care of things directly."

"Do you mean you would kill Hoffman yourself?"

Max nodded. "That's what Karl wants to do."

"But that's murder."

"I agree, but Karl doesn't care. He wants to avenge our family with his own hands. And he doesn't trust the government, German or American. He thinks you will betray us."

"But why would we help a Nazi?" she asked.

"Who is to know?" said Max, shrugging. "Look, Sara, I know Karl is wrong about you. I trust you completely. But I understand how he feels. We've been betrayed so many times, and it has cost us just about everything. But don't worry, Karl will come along with me if we get the chance. If we're allowed to travel, he won't give up the opportunity to go after Hoffman."

"What if we do catch him? Will he turn Hoffman over to the authorities? Like you've promised to do."

Max hesitated for a moment. He removed his hand and picked up his wine, taking a sip as if considering the question. "He will do what I tell him to do."

"Are you sure? You're his younger brother."

"He trusts me."

She looked at Max closely, a new fear rising in her. "What about you, Max? Will you turn Hoffman over? Knowing what you know about *governments*."

He didn't hesitate. "Absolutely, I will turn him over to a government. I will do what is right. And I also trust you."

She felt better after his answer. She had to know she could trust him. If she persuaded the US government to allow them to hunt down Hoffman, only for the brothers to kill him, it would be a catastrophe. They would be the ones arrested and put on trial, and she would be indicted right along with them.

They finished their meal, the subject turning to lighter subjects like their childhoods, life before the war, before the Nazis. When they were finished, he offered to accompany her to her flat, to assure she was safe. She resisted, but not too much. They held hands in the taxi, his thumb moving up and down the back of her hand. She felt her pulse rising, and a tingling up and down her arms.

They arrived at her building before she knew it. He stepped out and walked around the back of the car, opening her door for her. She stepped out and he drew her into his arms, holding her closely. She held on to him, his warmth, his musky smell. He turned his head and kissed her cheek softly.

"I could stay," he whispered.

Her heart raced. She wanted him to, but she was afraid too, this was all happening so fast.

"Never mind," he said, reading her emotions again. He kissed her on the forehead.

"I'm sorry," she said.

"You have nothing to be sorry for," said Max, smiling at her. "But how could I resist asking?"

He made her feel so alive. It had been so long, but she couldn't remember anyone making her feel like this. "Another time," she said at last.

He bowed slightly. "I hope to see you tomorrow. Do you think there will be news?"

"I hope so," she said, smiling at him again.

"Until then," he said, blowing her a kiss.

She stayed there for a little while until he had driven away, then she hurried up to her flat, her mind racing, her face flushed, full of happiness.

She hurried through her bedtime routine, excited for the morning, and all the promise it brought. That night she tossed and turned, unable to sleep. She daydreamed about Max, of their future journey together, of tracking down Hoffman. She would be promoted at work, she was sure of it. Her mind kept playing out impossible scenarios where she and Max spent their lives together. She knew these were all just fantasies, but something about him captivated her. She couldn't wait to see what tomorrow would bring.

Finally, the morning came. She rushed to the office and set up everything just right. She even took a trip to the local bakery and bought Jeffrey his favorite pastry. When he came in, he thanked her for it, and told her he should have an answer that day. Each time the phone rang, she held her breath. When a call came in from their Washington headquarters, she could barely contain her excitement.

"Sara, I need to see you," he called. She rose, rushing in, her face flushed. He looked at her, breaking into a crooked grin. "I take it you already know who I was talking to?"

"Yes," she said. "Is there any word?"

Jeffrey's smile widened. "The best kind. They've approved the travel."

"Oh, Jeffrey, that is such great news!"

"Yes it is," he said. "I can't wait to get started."

She felt her heart lurch. "You're coming with us?" she asked.

His smile widened. "No, my dear, I'm going with *them*.

You'll be staying here, to answer phone calls and mind the shop."

"But I brought this to you," she protested, her anger rising. "They want me to go!"

"They'll do what I tell them to do," said Jeffrey. "What kind of delusion were you operating under?" he asked. "Honestly, a woman on a sensitive mission like this. Now, be a good girl and fetch me some coffee, I've got planning to do."

Chapter 5
Frustration

Saturday, October 9, 1948
West Berlin, Germany

Sara woke Saturday morning to bright sunlight. The temperature was noticeably warmer and she could smell the crisp autumn air as she walked through the Tiergarten. Although it was only midmorning, the park was already full of Berliners out for a stroll, soaking up the sunshine and perhaps one of the last warm days of the year. But the weather did nothing for her. She was battling to keep her composure. Her eyes darted this way and that, searching the people. Finally, she spotted Max, sitting on a park bench, pipe in his mouth, reading a newspaper. She hadn't seen him since Wednesday night—before Jeffrey gave her the news that she wouldn't be going on the trip. She hadn't been able to face Max until now. He looked up and immediately rose, regarding her with an understanding look tinged with a little sadness.

"Sara, I'm so sorry," he said, reaching his hands out to her.

She stepped back from him. "I . . . I can't right now," she

said, turning away. She felt the tears welling up in her eyes. A moment later his hands were on her shoulders.

"This is not what I wanted," he said. "We never discussed Jeffrey coming with us, I promise you. I had no idea what he had in mind. He never said a thing to us that he was intending to go in your place."

"I believe you," she said.

"Let's walk," he said, taking her hand. She didn't want to go, didn't want to even be here, but she allowed herself to be led by him. They strolled that way for some time, not talking, under the warmth of the sun and the brilliant reds, yellows, and greens of the late fall leaves. Despite herself, the touch of his hand and the fresh air made her feel a little better.

"This used to be mostly forest," she said. "But the trees were cut down for firewood late in the war. My father used to come here to bring back fuel for us. It was all we had."

"I was here once before the war," he said. "My family took a vacation when I was just a boy. Before they took all our rights away—our ability to work and to travel. We visited the Brandenburg Gate and the zoo, and we walked all over the park. I remember the trees. But we're close to the government sector too," he said. "The center of the storm."

"That's all gone now," she said. "Gone with the National Socialist dream of a thousand-year German empire."

"A thousand-year nightmare, you mean. But it didn't last a thousand years, it barely made it twelve."

"The Nazis did a thousand years of damage though," she said.

"True enough," he said, taking her in his arms. She buried her face in his shoulder and held on to him, letting tears of frustration loose. He patted her back and held her. It felt good to let her sorrow go.

"It's not fair," she said at last.

"No, it's not," he said. "But what is? I lost most of my family in the war. Not because we were soldiers, not fighting an enemy. They died because of their religion, or race, or whatever it was the Nazis thought of us." He stopped and took a step back so he could look at her, still holding her hands. "And you. You lost your brother, your parents. You're right, Sara, the world is an unfair place. But look around us," he said, motioning to the park. "The sun is out. We are in one of the most beautiful city parks in the world. Despite all the bombing, the war, the death; nature comes back, life goes on." He kissed her lightly on the cheek and then they started to walk again.

"I just can't believe Jeffrey," she said. "He took my idea, took my place. He will get all of the credit for this operation. And all because I'm a woman."

Max stopped again. "I'll tell him we won't go without you. You're right, this was your idea. I don't want to deny you the chance to go with us. It would be selfish for me to do otherwise."

Sara appreciated his words, but how could she demand that, knowing what Jeffrey would say? That wasn't the answer to this. "No," she said. "This is everything to you—to Karl. I'm not going to ruin your chances just because I want to be part of things."

"Are you sure?" he asked.

She wasn't, but she knew this was everything to him. She nodded. She would have to figure something else out. For now, he needed this and she needed to let him have his moment. Otherwise, he might abandon the whole plan.

"Sara, I have so much to thank you for. I just don't know if I can do this without you."

"You have to," she said. "There won't be a second chance for this. Who knows how long the blockade will go on? And if the Soviets take over West Berlin—"

"Then I'll never be able to travel to West Germany," he finished for her. "I'll never have a chance to go to Munich, to hunt down Hoffman."

"That's right. It's almost impossible for anyone in the East to travel to the West. I don't think we'll lose Berlin, but who can know for sure." She took his hands in hers again. "You have to go now, Max, this may be the only opportunity you will ever have."

"If it wasn't for that idiot Jeffrey, you could go with me. Why isn't Varberg back yet? I'm sure he'd put an end to this nonsense."

"I don't know," she said. "I don't even know where he went. But the problem remains. Jeffrey is here, he's in charge, and he's arranged to go along with you, without me."

"Something will come up. These things have a way of working out. You'll see."

She nodded. If she had any say in it, things would certainly change, and soon. But there was nothing they could do today, and it was so beautiful out. She decided to push her thoughts out of her mind, to pretend she could have a day of peace, of happiness.

They spent the rest of the day together, walking through the Tiergarten. They had a picnic lunch and then napped, lying close, holding each other. They didn't talk very much, there was nothing they could say to comfort each other. They'd both lived lives wrought with tragedy, they knew it was part of life, even if they hated it.

They had planned to have dinner together as well, but Sara cut things short, feigning weariness. They rode in silence in a taxi to her apartment building. She opened the door to leave but he jumped out with her.

"I'm sorry, again, Sara," he said, putting his arms around her. She rested her head against his chest and they stayed that way for long moments, until the cab driver honked his horn.

"It's not your fault," she said.

"I cannot thank you enough for understanding." He kissed her on the cheek and then moved toward her lips, but she turned her head away. "Sara."

"Don't worry," she said, reaching up on her tiptoes to kiss him again on the cheek. "I'll be all right. And you have a trip to plan for."

He looked up at the building. "Still no invitation to come up?" he asked wryly.

She smiled back at him. "Not tonight," she said. "But you won't wait forever, I promise."

"Farewell then," he said.

"Farewell, Max." She turned and stepped into the building. It was only when she'd reached the inside that the tears of bitter frustration rolled down her face. She flew up the stairs to her flat and threw herself into her bed. She lay that way for long hours, her eyes wide-open, staring into the darkness, her mind racing, formulating a plan. She ran a number of ideas through her head, playing out the scenarios before she came up with something that she thought might work. Even after this, she couldn't sleep, and she spent the night staring at the ceiling.

Chapter 6
Papers

Sunday, October 10, 1948
Franciscan Monastery
Bavaria, Germany

Heinz woke Elsie gently the next morning. He held a tray of pastries, cold meats, and cheese, along with a pot of steaming tea. Hannah was already awake, playing in the corner with her favorite doll. His wife yawned and stretched, scanning the tray with surprise. "Breakfast in bed," she said, an eyebrow arching. "To what do I owe this honor?"

"I'm leaving you tonight, my dear. I want today to be special."

"As special as last night?" she asked, giggling. "That will be hard to surpass."

Heinz tried to ignore that comment. He handed her the tray, reaching out with both hands. His wife gave another laugh.

"Is my husband blushing?" she teased. "You're still the same shy schoolboy I spied in the cafeteria so many years ago, fumbling over those dirty plates."

"The dirty plates of the privileged," he said. "It's a wonder you noticed me at all."

She reached out and took his hand. "I didn't want one of them," she said. "I wanted you—my brilliant, hardworking husband."

Heinz grunted. "My family used to have wealth, used to have privilege, but the First World War did away with all that. Well, I guess we showed all of them in the end, didn't we?"

"That's right, my love. All those boys you went to school with, with all their connections and money, yet you rose above every last one of them."

He squeezed her hand. He remembered the taunts, the hours of extra work each day so he could earn his keep. He had made it through the elite school, and then university. He had surpassed them all, earning his doctorate in physics from the University of Munich. Then the SS, the hard training, and the years of mid-level positions until he'd fought his way to the top of the German nuclear program.

"Most of my old friends are dead," he said at last.

Her smile turned to sadness. "Through no fault of yours. They died for their fatherland, for their Führer."

"A lot of good it did them."

"We almost conquered the world," said Elsie, her eyes brimming. "We came so close."

"Until we went too far into Russia, and then they crushed us."

"Even that wouldn't have been the end," said Elsie, "if they would have funded you properly. With more resources and more scientists, you could have provided a nuclear bomb for our beloved Führer. Then it wouldn't have mattered how many men the Allies had. We would have crushed them."

He felt the old frustration. He'd battled for years to build his program. But nobody had taken him seriously. They all thought the atom bomb was a dream. Until it was too late, until the Americans dropped two of them on the Japanese. Germany could have ruled the world. They were so close, even after the tide turned, but his superiors would not listen to him. "Of course you're right, my dear," he said at last. "But what can that matter now. They ignored me and we lost the battle of tanks, and airplanes, and men. Now my nuclear program is just a dream within a dream."

"Germany will rise again," she said. "Our people haven't forgotten. A new generation of National Socialists will grow up. They will hear the stories of our heroes, of our great leader. They will throw out the Americans and the Russians, and we will rule Europe again."

He smiled. "No, my dear. Our enemies control our land. There is no way we can rebuild. And the Americans have the keys to ultimate power. They have that atom bomb that I was never allowed to build." He reached out and ran his fingers through her hair. "All we can do is honor the past. We can keep the spirit of our great country alive in our hearts. But Germany will never be free again. We had two chances at greatness, and we lost them both. The barbarians from east and west have stormed our borders, and we must make the best of what is left."

She reached up and kissed him. "We shall see, my love. Nobody knows what the future holds. But we must stay together, no matter what."

He left her to her breakfast and quickly dressed. He left their apartment and marched down the narrow halls of the monastery, leaving the guest building and passing through a courtyard into the administrative offices. He passed a number of monks along the way. They nodded to him, eyes down. Very few people knew who he was exactly, but all of the residents were aware that he was a person of some importance and that his residence here was a secret. In another few minutes he reached Michael's office. The monk was at a desk, writing a letter to someone, his handwriting neat and flowing. Heinz stood back for a moment, watching the man work. He was truly an artist. The scientist cleared his throat and Michael looked up, smiling at his friend.

"Ah, you're here," he said. "Pardon me, I was intent on this letter."

"What are you working on?" Heinz asked.

"A request for donations," said Michael. "Always donations. We live humbly here and we grow much of our own food, but there are expenses of course, and"—he looked at Heinz—"other projects that we assist with."

"Yes, of course. Should I come back?"

"Not at all," said the monk. "Please, have a seat."

Heinz took the chair across from Michael's desk. The monk reached down and opened a drawer, fumbling around for a few moments before he retrieved a large brown envelope.

"Here it is," said Michael. "This just arrived a few hours ago."

"My papers?" asked Heinz.

"*Ja.*" The monk reached into the envelope and pulled out an unfamiliar passport. He handed it to Heinz, who opened it and read the contents.

"This is in Spanish," he said. "I don't speak Spanish."

"Don't worry about that," said Michael. "You will soon enough."

"But Immigration—"

"Will be taken care of at every level. The only thing you need to remember is your new name."

Heinz looked down at the passport again. "Heinz Cavallero?"

"It means *knight.* I thought that was appropriate, given your former position in the SS."

"My current position," snapped Heinz. "The SS still lives."

"Of course," responded Michael hastily. "My apologies."

Heinz glared for a few moments, taking a few deep breaths. Michael had been good to him and he was leaving his family behind here. No reason to burn a bridge over a minor slight. During the war, things would have been different, but now . . . "Think nothing of it, my friend. How will all of this work?"

"An associate of ours from Odessa is meeting us here tonight," said Michael. "He will escort you to Switzerland and get you over the border. From there, you will stay a few days in one of our brother monasteries. Then you will travel to the Vatican, where we've arranged for a two-week stay for you while the rest of your visas are obtained. After that, it will be travel by ship to Buenos Aires."

"Who is meeting me there?"

"I don't know yet," said Michael. "But don't worry, everything will be taken care of." He reached into the envelope again and pulled out a thick stack of multicolored banknotes. "Here is currency for Germany, Switzerland, and Italy. There is more than enough for anything that might come up. If you would be so kind as to leave the remainder at the Vatican, we will be able to use it again for our next friend."

"Of course," said Heinz. "What about money for Argentina?"

"That will be provided to you when you reach Italy."

Heinz nodded. "Anything else?"

"Yes," said Michael, reaching into the envelope a final time. He withdrew a tiny pistol and handed it to Heinz.

"What is this? I have my own . . ."

"Your Luger is too bulky and cumbersome," said Michael. "Besides, we thought you should leave that with Elsie."

Heinz felt fear explode in his chest. "Why would she need a pistol? Is there some danger?"

"None that we can imagine," said Michael. "But best to be prepared for any eventuality."

Heinz calmed himself down, nodding. "Of course you are right again." He examined the pistol, which fit practically in the palm of his hand. It was a 6.35mm Mauser, a pocket pistol developed during the First World War. The pistol held a nine-round clip for .25 caliber ammunition. He checked the weapon and then carefully placed it in his pocket. "Thank you."

The two men talked for another hour or so about the logistics of the plan. After they had covered all the details to Heinz's satisfaction, he rose and shook Michael's hand. "Will I see you tonight?" he asked.

The monk shook his head. "None of the brothers can assist in the actual transfer," he said. "You know I would be there if I could be, but we must maintain the fiction that we are unaware of your presence here. As ludicrous as that is."

Heinz smiled. "I understand. Thank you so much for everything you have done for me, and what you will do for my family."

Michael extended his hand.

Heinz clicked his heels and shot his right arm into the air. "*Heil* Hitler," he said, granting the monk the highest possible honor.

The monk stood for a moment as if he didn't know how to respond, then he bowed to Heinz. "God be with you, my friend."

Heinz returned to his apartment, excited to fill Elsie in on the details. He was surprised when he opened the door to see a look of fear on her face.

"What's wrong?" he demanded.

"It's Hannah," she said.

"What about her?"

"She's taken ill."

"What do you mean?"

Elsie gestured to the bed where Hannah lay under their covers. She was sleeping and her face was flushed. Heinz stepped up to her and put his hand on her forehead. She was on fire.

"A fever," said Heinz, frowning. "But she was just fine an hour ago."

"She started complaining she was cold, a little after you left," said Elsie. "I put her to bed and she fell asleep almost immediately. Since then, her temperature has been higher each time I checked her."

"Have you called for a doctor?" Heinz asked.

Elsie shook her head. "She's not so bad right now. And it's Sunday. Who would we call? Hopefully this will be gone before you leave."

But as the hours passed, morning giving way to noon and then afternoon, Hannah grew hotter and hotter until even Heinz was worried sick. "I can't go tonight," he said at last, looking at his watch. It was four o'clock. The man from Odessa was supposed to pick him up out front in three hours.

Elsie's face grew alarmed. "You must go," she said. "Hannah will be fine—she just has a little fever."

Heinz checked her forehead again. "She's burning up," he said. "I can't leave her like this."

"I told you, she'll be fine."

"That may well be," said Heinz. "But I'm not going anywhere until I know for sure."

"Heinz, you can't mean it."

"I do."

She looked around, desperation in her eyes. "What if she's seen by a doctor?" Elsie asked. "If a physician says she'll be all right, is that enough for you?"

Heinz hesitated. How could he trust the word of a doctor? He was a scientist himself, and he knew that in the medical field nothing was certain. Still, if there was a level of confidence that the child would be all right . . . He shrugged. "It doesn't matter," he said. "There is no doctor here, and no time to find one."

"You leave that to me," said Elsie. She hurriedly changed her clothes and then darted from their apartment. Heinz stayed with Hannah, holding her hand. The child moaned, still asleep, her head turning this way and that as if she was in pain. He stayed that way, constantly checking his watch. Fifteen minutes passed, and then a half hour. They were running out of time.

The door tore open. Elsie was there, along with Brother Michael. "We've located a doctor," she said frantically. "But he's in town. I have to take her right now." Heinz reached down to pick Hannah up.

"Not you," his wife said. "There isn't enough time."

"I'm going with you," Heinz commanded.

"But, my dear . . ."

He stared her down. "I said I'm going with you." He reached down and picked his daughter up. Her nightgown was drenched. He wrapped her in a blanket and then followed Michael and Elsie out the door. A car was already waiting at the entrance, a rickety old thing, the sole vehicle owned by the monastery. Heinz jumped into the back with Hannah and Elsie, and Michael took to the wheel. In a few moments they were speeding down a narrow road, with thick dark trees enveloping each side of the corridor.

They arrived in town twenty minutes later. Michael sped through the streets, honking at vehicles to get out of their way.

"Be careful," warned Elsie. "The last thing we need right now is to alert the police."

Michael nodded and slowed the car down a fraction. He took a sharp right and then sped to a stop. They'd arrived at the doctor's office. Heinz tore the door open and pulled himself and Hannah out of the back seat. The front door was already open and the doctor was waiting, an elderly gentleman with white hair, a mustache, and a kind face. He motioned them in and then took Hannah out of Heinz's hands, gesturing for the small party to stay in the waiting room. The doctor and a nurse, who appeared at the doorway, hastened into another room, closing the door behind them.

Heinz checked his watch. It was 5:45. He turned to Michael. "You should call it off," he said, nodding to the time.

The monk shook his head. "There's still time."

The doctor returned a half hour later.

"What's wrong with her?" Elsie demanded.

The doctor smiled. "Nothing more than a common flu," he said. "All of her vitals are just fine. Her lungs and heart are strong. You have nothing to worry about. I do want her to take some medicine. I'll need a little time to prepare it."

"Hurry please, Doctor!" said Elsie. Heinz kept checking his watch; it was 6:40. They had to leave now or they would miss the contact. He didn't think they would wait around for him.

The doctor reappeared and handed them a brown paper bag. "Here is some medicine for her. Give this to her twice a day for the next ten days. If her symptoms grow any worse, give me a call and I'll have you bring her back in."

"But she will be all right?" asked Heinz. "There is no danger of . . ."

"No danger at all."

"Thank you so much," said Heinz. "What do we owe you?"

The doctor reached out his hand. "You owe me nothing," he said. He reached down to his lapel and turned the fabric over. Underneath, a tiny pin was hidden. It was a swastika.

Heinz took the hand and squeezed it. There were still friends in Germany. The nurse came out, carrying Hannah. The little girl was awake now, although she appeared exhausted. Elsie took her and she held tightly to her mother. Heinz checked his watch. There were fifteen minutes to go. "We're going to be late!" he said.

They piled back into the vehicle and Michael took off again into the night. The monk was more careful now. They were all aware that a traffic stop at this juncture could be catastrophic to their plan. Heinz sat in the back with Hannah and Elsie. He held his wife's hand. He realized in all of their worry about Hannah over the last few hours, they'd never really said good-bye. And now it was too late.

Elsie smiled at him. "We've missed our chance to say farewell," she said, obviously thinking about the same thing.

"We won't be parted long," he promised. "I'll work hard

and I won't stop until we are together again. It won't be two years, it won't be six months if I can help it."

She took his hand. "I know you will, my love. Besides, last night wasn't such a bad farewell."

He laughed, squeezing her hand. "No, it was not. Make sure you watch Hannah closely," he said. "Call the doctor even if you aren't sure she needs it. I couldn't go on if something happened to her—or to you."

"Don't worry about a thing," she said. "I'll take good care of her and of everything else until we are together again."

Heinz could make out the monastery entrance now. He could see the lights of a vehicle; the man from Odessa was right on time. He reached over and kissed her. "I love you," he said.

"I love you too, my darling."

They drove through the gates. Heinz reached out for Hannah. He heard Michael gasp and he knew something was wrong. He looked up and was shocked to see not one vehicle but many. There were men out there too, many men, and they were armed. He heard the shouts in English, the demand that Michael stop the car. The Americans were here.

Chapter 7
The Plan Ripens

Monday, October 11, 1948
West Berlin, Germany

On Monday morning she stormed into Jeffrey's office. "You have to change your mind," she demanded.

Jeffrey was at his desk, drinking coffee. Taking a deep pull on his cigarette, he turned his head to regard her. "Good morning to you as well, Miss Sturm. And as I've already explained, I'll be taking the Portnoys into Bavaria, and you will be staying here, to mind the shop while I'm gone."

"I want to talk to Mr. Varberg about this."

Jeffrey's face flashed scarlet. "I already told you, he's not available, and I'm in charge. Really, Sara, you are too bold. You've a long pile of dictation on your desk, I suggest you tend to it. I don't want another word about this."

"Another word about what?" said a voice from behind her. She turned to see Mr. Varberg, coat and umbrella still in hand, leaning against the doorjamb of Jeffrey's office.

"Nothing," said Jeffrey, stifling a look of surprise. "I was just discussing something with Miss Sturm. It's nothing that we need to bother you with, sir."

"There are no secrets in this office," said Varberg sternly. "What is it?"

Jeffrey glared at her, an unspoken threat in his eyes, but she ignored him. "Sir, I came to Jeffrey with some information about the Portnoys."

"I forbid you to discuss this with him," snapped Jeffrey.

Her boss stared at Jeffrey until he closed his mouth. "You're not in a position to forbid her, Mr. Scott. You're not even technically in charge of her. You're my assistant and she is my secretary."

"Surely I outrank her, a woman who does our typing and makes our coffee . . ." said Jeffrey.

"It's a debatable point that you outrank her. But for now, you will keep your mouth shut while I find out what has transpired from Miss Sturm," said Varberg. "Now, Sara, please tell me what's going on."

Sara explained the story that Max had told her, Jeffrey's investigation into the situation, and his decision to take her place. Jeffrey tried to interrupt several times but Mr. Varberg kept lifting his hand to silence him. When she was finished, he stood there for a few moments and then spoke to them.

"That is fascinating information about the Portnoys, Sara. I am going to need a little time to think about things. Jeffrey, you are to bring me all the information you have on this immediately, including the names and telephone numbers of everyone you've talked to."

"But, sir," protested Jeffrey. "The trip is already set up, the passes issued. There is no way it can be changed by tomorrow, and that's when I leave."

"You won't be leaving tomorrow, Jeffrey. I have no idea what possessed you to do any of this without waiting for me to return. But I'll discuss that with you in private. For the time

being, I need some coffee and I need those phone numbers."
He turned to Sara. "Miss Sturm, would you mind getting the
coffee for me, and if we don't have a full pot, if you could please
brew some more. It's going to be a long morning, I fear."

Sara turned and walked out of the office quickly, keeping her
eyes away from Jeffrey. She was elated. She didn't know what
was going to happen, but it didn't sound like things were going
to work out like Jeffrey had thought. She poured Mr. Varberg
some coffee, fixing it just how he liked, and brought it back to
his office. The door was closed, so she knocked and then entered the room where the two men were discussing the situation. The air was thick with tension. She stepped up to the desk,
keeping her eyes away from Jeffrey, and placed the coffee on
Mr. Varberg's desk, leaving as quickly as she could.

The day passed slowly. She could hear the muffled voices in
Mr. Varberg's office, sometimes rising to a shout. Finally, late
in the afternoon, the door tore open and Jeffrey rushed out,
heading for the office front door. He paused at the entrance,
turning to glare at Sara. "Don't think I'll forget this," he said,
his voice dripping venom. He stormed out, slamming the door
behind him.

"Sara, can you come in for a moment?" Mr. Varberg asked.

"Of course, sir," she said, grabbing her dictation notepad
and stepping into his office.

Varberg waved her in, a grim expression on his face. "Well,
that was interesting," he said. "I'm afraid you haven't made a
friend in our young Jeffrey, today."

"We've never been and we never were going to be friends,"
she said. "But don't worry, I can handle him."

"Yes, I know you can." Mr. Varberg rubbed his forehead for
a moment. "Well, in any event, I've managed to arrange everything so the departure can still occur tomorrow. I've called the
Portnoys and they are on board with proceeding."

"Proceeding?" she said. "But, Jeffrey — "

"Will not be going," he said. "But you will."

"Oh, Mr. Varberg," she said, excitement filling her. "I don't know how to thank you!"

"Don't thank me too much," he said. "You've made an enemy today, one who has some connections out there in the world. Besides that, you're heading into a dangerous situation. With the blockade going on, we are spread pretty thin on resources. I'm not going to be able to give you any other help. You're heading into uncertain waters. The Germans aren't exactly thrilled when we rub their noses in the past, and capturing prominent Nazis is pretty much first on their list of resentments. Don't forget Odessa. Hoffman is probably protected by powerful friends. I won't lie to you, Sara, you could be putting your life in danger with this trip."

"I understand, sir," she said. "And I thank you. I'll be all right, I know I will. If something comes up with Odessa, I think we'll be able to handle it."

He shook his head. "You're something else, Sara. I knew I made the right decision when I hired you. Just remember, you cannot let them kill him. He must be delivered, and he must be brought in alive. If he isn't, there are going to be questions about the decision I made today. Not everyone was thrilled with me pulling Jeffrey off the job and giving it to you."

"I won't let you down. I'm sure I can handle this."

"You're heading into a dangerous situation, Sara. You'll have to use your wits. Just remember, there are enemies among the Germans, but there are friends as well. Keep a lookout for those who might help you."

"Where should we start, sir? Do you have any idea? Max and Karl know what Hoffman looks like, but other than that, and the vague notion that he might still be in Bavaria somewhere, I'm not sure they know where to begin."

"I've got good news on that as well. I was able to get ahold of a friend of mine in army intelligence. There's a beer-hall owner in Munich named Adolf Alderbricht. He's former Waffen-SS, well connected. He is privy to all kinds of information at his establishment. There are groups of veterans there every night, and the beer flows freely. He picks up interesting tidbits now and then and he's seen fit to pass some things on to the US government—for a price, of course. I'd start by visiting him." Varberg passed Sara a piece of paper. "Here is the name and address of his establishment."

"Thank you so much, sir! I can't wait to tell Max . . . I mean the Portnoys!"

Varberg smiled at her. "You're doing well, Miss Sturm. Why don't you take off a little early and let them know. I'm sure *they'd* love to hear the news from you."

"Oh, thank you, Mr. Varberg! I will!" Sara hurried out of his office and collected her things. She grabbed a taxi and sat in the back seat, brimming with joy. She arrived at the Portnoys' store a few minutes later. There was a truck out front, and workers behind it were unloading giant plates of glass. Max and Karl were out front, watching the process. Sara bounded out of the taxi, rushing up to them.

"Sara," said Max, his face erupting in joy. "What a pleasant surprise. What are you doing here?" He checked his watch. "It's not half four."

"Mr. Varberg let me off early," she said.

"Ah, so Varberg's back. Did he—"

"Clear things up? He certainly did. He spent the day in the office with Jeffrey, chewing him out, I think. When it was over, Mr. Varberg told me Jeffrey's not going and he's letting me go in his place!"

"How delightful," said Max, taking her hands. "I cannot believe our luck!"

"Yes, how fortunate," said Karl. "I told you, we don't need any of them."

"Enough, Karl," warned Max. "We've been through this. Sara is the one—"

"The one who brought the idea to the Americans. Yes, I

know that, and I appreciate it. But we can handle things from here. We're going to be dragging your girlfriend all over Munich, and probably trying to pull her out of one disaster after another. We don't have time for that. She's a liability."

"I can take care of myself," said Sara sternly, glaring at Karl.

"Oh, I'm sure you can," said Karl. "A little German girl who spent the war in Berlin. What have you faced? What do you know of danger, of pain?"

"She knows plenty," said Max. "She lost her brother and her parents. We aren't the only ones who suffered. Just because she's not a Jew."

Karl spat on the pavement. "Fine enough. I appreciate the passes, but I'll not be her nursemaid. She'll have to keep up, and if something happens to her, it's on your soul, not mine." Karl turned and marched into the store, slamming the doors.

"Don't worry about him," said Max. "He'll settle into the idea. Are we still on for tomorrow morning then?" he asked.

"Yes. Will you be ready?"

"We're already packed," said Max. "We were waiting for the replacement windows but they're here now. We don't have to be present when they install them. I have someone who can come by and make sure everything is taken care of. How about you?" he asked. "Will you have time to prepare?"

"If I have to stay up all night," she said, the excitement coursing through her.

"Do you want us to swing by in a taxi to pick you up in the morning?" he asked, then a grin spread over his mouth. "Unless you just want to spend the night."

She laughed, blushing. "That's a conversation for another day, Mr. Portnoy. But for now, I will need to be at my flat to get my things together."

He sighed dramatically. "I suppose you are correct. So we'll reserve that for another day—or should I say another evening."

The door behind him opened up. Karl was back, scowling as

usual. Sara felt frustration—she wanted to be alone with Max. But Max didn't seem to mind at all. He turned to his brother. "What is it now?" he asked, his voice taking a jesting tone. "Are you still wanting to berate me for bringing a maiden on our journey?"

"Our journey is canceled," he said.

"What are you talking about?" asked Sara.

"Look at this," he said, pointing at a newspaper article. He handed the paper to Max, who read the column. His face paled.

"According to this, Hoffman is already in American custody. He was captured last night at a Franciscan monastery in Bavaria. It's over."

Chapter 8

Escape

Monday, October 11, 1948
10:25 p.m.
Franciscan Monastery
Bavaria, Germany

Heinz sat in the office, staring across at the American officer. He was a lieutenant and he was carefully reviewing his notes. They'd been harassing him for a day now. "Anything you want to add?" the American asked.

Heinz shook his head.

"Well, that's settled then," said the American, starting to rise.

"I could use some more coffee though, and another cigarette."

"Sure thing," said the lieutenant. He rose and stepped out of the room. He did not close the door behind him.

After the officer left the room, Heinz took a deep breath. His mind was reeling from what had transpired in the past day. He wanted to see his wife and child. He wondered if they would let him again before he'd . . .

"Dr. Hoffman."

Heinz was startled by the voice. He looked up. Michael was there, a terrified look on his face.

"Michael, thank God. Can I see my family?" His voice shook with the words.

The monk shook his head. "You have to come with me now."

"But—"

"There's no time." Michael turned and motioned for Heinz to follow.

He rose and followed. The corridor was empty and Michael moved quickly, leading him a dozen yards or so down the hallway before turning to his left. He reached out with a key and unlocked the door, leading Heinz into another office. He closed the door behind them and turned on the light. Michael moved to the other side of the room, and Heinz saw there was a back door to the office. The monk unlocked it. "Go," he said to the scientist.

"I can't," he said. "I've got to see them again."

"You have to go now."

Heinz didn't want to listen, didn't want to obey, but he knew that Michael was right. He stepped up to the monk and took his hand. "Thank you for everything," he said. "Take care of my family—if there's anything you can do for them."

"I don't think it will be in my control, but if I can get anything to them, or communicate with them, I will."

"Where I'm going, I won't be able to . . ."

"I know, my friend. Your contact is waiting for you in the cottage through the woods. Do you remember where it is?"

Heinz nodded.

"Good. Get there as quickly as you can. It's freezing out. And here," he said, handing him a small bag.

"What's this?" asked Heinz.

"A flashlight and a loaf of bread. God go with you."

"Thank you." Heinz took his hand again and then Michael moved over to the door and unlocked it, opening into the darkness.

Heinz poked his head out. They were in the back part of the monastery. He couldn't see well on this cloudy night, but he thought he could make out the line of trees marking the start of the forest, a bare fifty yards away. He took a step out and then another, his boots crunching noisily in the snow. He winced a bit at the noise, but it couldn't be helped. Heinz moved out into an open field, picking up speed as his eyes adjusted to the dim light. In a few minutes, he reached the trees.

Heinz moved through the forest in the darkness. Branches clawed at his face. He was freezing, but he had to keep moving. After an hour, he felt he was far enough away that he could hazard some light. He took the small flashlight that Michael had given him. The monastery was miles back now. He thought of Elsie, of Hannah. His fear and anger tore at him, but what could he do? He had no choice in the matter. He knew the Americans would treat them well. There was no question of their safety. Still, to be torn away from them for years, perhaps forever. Wasn't there something he could do?

He checked his watch and then his compass. He was still going the right way. He would reach the cabin in the next hour. Someone was supposed to be waiting for him there with food and a change of clothes. He kept moving, trying not to think about his family, about his future. All of his plans had gone awry. It was one thing for his family to stay at the monastery until he could arrange for their travel. But now, with the Americans involved—everything had changed.

He kept stomping through the darkness. He couldn't feel his hands. His feet ached from the cold. Why hadn't he just stayed behind? He should have stood up to them and waited for his trial. But he kept hearing his wife's words. *A lifetime in prison away from her and Hannah.* No, no matter how difficult this was, it was the right decision. He would take his chances and see what the future might hold. So, he had fled into the woods with the knowledge that this contact would be waiting for him not far away.

Ahead in the distance he thought he could make out a thinning of the trees. He kept moving in that direction and now he could see it, a pinprick of light in the distance. He reached the edge of the trees and found the cabin, just like Michael had described it to him. The structure was less than a hundred yards away. Lights filled the windows. Smoke billowed out of the chimney.

What if I don't go to the cottage? he thought to himself. The contact was going to assist him, he knew that, but what if he simply struck out on his own? He had some money. The Austrian border wasn't far and the Swiss border not that much farther. If he could get across to Switzerland, he might settle down there, find some work, and wait for six months or so before contacting his wife again. Switzerland was so much closer than where he was destined to go . . .

He shook his head. He couldn't do that. Without assistance, he probably would never make it across the border. Worse yet, the Americans would likely move his family out of reach. No, he had to stick to the plan, even though he hated it.

Heinz steeled himself and made his way across the meadow. His legs would barely move now, he was half frozen, but he kept shambling forward until he reached the cabin. Stumbling up the snow-filled steps, he collapsed against the door and beat on the wood. Nobody answered. He tried again, more insistent this time. The door ripped open and he fell inside, crashing against the floor. An iron hand gripped his throat and he felt a hard object against the back of his head.

"*Wie heissen Sie?*" a harsh voice demanded.

"Heinz Hoffman."

"Show me your papers!" the man demanded.

"I don't have any," said Hoffman. "I had to leave them behind."

Heinz was pulled into the cabin and thrown violently on his back. He was facing a monster. The man was massive, with hulking muscles and a mottled, angry face that was carved from granite. A scar ran down the left side of his forehead, through the eyebrow and down his cheek. That eye was covered with a black leather eye patch. His head was shaved and his sneer revealed a mouth full of silver teeth. The man put the pistol to Heinz's eye.

"Why don't you have your papers?"

"We were betrayed," said Heinz. He explained their trip to the doctor, the return to the monastery and the waiting Americans. The man lowered his pistol.

"I was there," he said. "I was not far from the monastery, pulled over on the side of the road, waiting for the time to pick you up, when a convoy of cars flew by me. I got out of the car and snuck up on foot to see what was going on. When I saw the Americans milling around, I snuck into the monastery through the back and talked to the monks. I told them where you could find me, if they could spirit you away."

"Who are you?" Hoffman asked.

"Otto Berg."

Heinz's eyes widened. "I know you," he said. "You're the—"

"*Ja*," said Otto. "I'm *Der Dämon*."

Heinz couldn't believe it. The Demon. The most famous member of Colonel Skorzeny's SS commando unit. He'd been drummed out of the elite group for executing American prisoners during the Battle of the Bulge. Heinz had heard rumors that Berg was associated with Odessa, but he was wanted by the Allies and nobody he knew had seen the man for years.

"It . . . it is a pleasure to meet you, Herr Berg."

Otto grunted. He reached down and took Heinz's hand, jerking him to his feet. He pulled him over to a chair and shoved him down. "There's hot coffee in that container," he said. "And a little bread. Stay here and don't do anything stupid."

"Where are you going?" Heinz asked.

"I'm going to make sure you weren't followed." The soldier stomped over to the door and drew on a heavy jacket. Checking his pistol, he opened the door and marched out into the darkness.

Heinz settled into a chair by the fire, peeling off his frozen clothes and warming himself. *Der Dämon.* He didn't know what to think. The man was by all reports a cold-blooded killer— but also possibly out of his mind. Instead of feeling relieved at finding his contact, Heinz felt more afraid. This unhinged demon could ruin everything. He needed a smart, smooth operation, not a dangerous and unpredictable lunatic.

Heinz slept restlessly that night. American soldiers moved in and out of his dreams, chasing his family through the hallways of the monastery. They caught him over and over, his wife screaming, the GIs roughly handling their daughter. But each time The Demon appeared, wielding a dagger and his pistol, mowing down a score of soldiers to free him. The commando always reached him, always freed him, but when the smoke cleared, Elsie and Hannah lay among the dead.

He gasped and sat up. He was lying in the solitary bedroom of the cabin, blankets piled over him. The door was partially open and he could see Otto in the other room, moving rapidly about on some task or another. The air was freezing. Reeling from his dreams, Heinz wanted to burrow himself in the covers and stay here forever.

The door flung open. Otto was staring down at him. "Are you going to sleep away the day?" he asked, his voice gruff and

sarcastic. "There's no breakfast in bed for you today, Dr. Hoffman. We've got to get going."

"To where?" he asked.

"Munich."

"We can't go there," said Heinz in surprise. "There are
dozens of people who might recognize me. And now that the
Americans have my family and my possessions, they may have
circulated pictures."

Otto scoffed. "With all respect, I doubt they printed posters
overnight and tacked them up. You're hardly the biggest Nazi
they are looking for. Besides, you overrate our American
guests. They're nothing if not scattered and lazy. It will be
some time before they organize a real search for you."

"But why Munich?" Heinz asked.

"We've got to get you new papers. I have a connection
there."

"Can't I just stay here?"

Otto shook his head. "We'll need a new photo. And we must
coordinate the information for your passport and visas. Where
you are going, there may be multiple stops. You'll need to
know your information inside and out. The more we can tailor
it to something you connect with, the better you'll do with
your story."

Heinz nodded. "I guess that makes sense. Is there some way
we can check on my family?"

"*Nein.* That's too risky. But don't you worry. The Americans are easy on prisoners. If the Russians had them for an interrogation, they'd already be at our front door and there'd be
little left of your wife—or your child, for that matter."

"Aren't you in danger?" Heinz asked, the thought suddenly
occurring to him.

Otto grinned. "You figured that out, did you? Yes, my little
friend, some American departments want me rather desper-

ately, far more than their interest in you, but they'll never catch me. After all, I'm invisible."

"What do you mean?" Heinz asked. The six-foot-three Berg, with a massive build and a prominent scar and eye patch, would stick out anywhere he went.

"You'll see," was all he said.

"When are we going?"

"Now, if you're done sleeping away the day?"

"Is there breakfast first?"

Otto snorted. He reached into his jacket and pulled out a tin of sardines. He tossed it roughly to Heinz. "You can eat these on the way."

Heinz, taking the meager breakfast and throwing on a down jacket the commando had brought for him, followed Berg out of the cabin and into the blazing morning sun. The day was frigid but the sky was an azure blue without a cloud in sight. On the other side of the cabin, a Mercedes was warming up, the tail pipe belching charcoal smoke into the crisp morning air. They piled in and were soon sliding and skidding down the snowy back-country roads.

"Who is the contact we are going to meet?" Heinz asked.

"Someone I know."

"Could you be more specific?"

Otto glanced at him sideways as he steered the vehicle. "Someone I know from the war."

"I see this is going to be a long trip today," said Heinz. He waited for a response but there was none. He would try a different tack. "Perhaps you'd like to hear some stories of my nuclear experiments during the war. I know the Americans built the atomic bomb, but we—"

"No."

"But I thought you might—"

"No."

Heinz took a deep breath. "All right then. How about if you tell me some of your adventures? I've heard about your experiences during the Battle of the B—"

"No."

"Well, I'm not just going to sit here with nothing to do," said Heinz.

Otto slammed the vehicle's brakes. Heinz crashed into the dashboard as the car slid this way and that, eventually coming to a thudding stop. The commando turned his head to face him.

"Listen. I'm in charge of getting you where you need to go. And keeping you alive. That's it. You're not a comrade. We didn't serve in the same unit. I'm not going to be your friend. If you need me to tear the arms off a GI, I'll do it. But I'm not going to chitchat."

Heinz nodded. "I understand. Although I don't know what I'm going to do for the next hour."

Otto reached over and tore the sardines out of Heinz's hands. "Sardines. Open. Eat."

Heinz opened the container and started to eat the oily fish. The smell filled the car, almost making him gag. He started to unroll the passenger window but Otto snapped at him.

"Too cold," the commando said.

After a few more minutes of driving, Otto reached a main highway and turned right. The road here was groomed and they were able to speed up somewhat, although the car still slipped here and there on the snowy pavement. Another hour passed and Heinz could see the spires of Munich in the distance.

He felt a surge of excitement. "I haven't been to the city in over a year," he said. "We've been hidden away in that monastery for so long, I've almost forgotten what the real world looks like."

Otto grunted. "The city is the same as every other place. Full of live people. Some are targets, some are not." He reached over and grabbed the lever to Heinz's seat, jerking it violently back until Heinz was facing the roof of the car.

"What the hell was that about!"

"Keep down," Otto ordered. "You can't be seen."

"I thought you said the Americans were lazy and wouldn't be looking for me."

"*Ja.* But I'm alive because I'm prepared, even when I think something isn't going to happen."

The car rumbled and jerked, and Heinz began to see the tops of buildings on each side of them as they drove into the city. He yearned to look out of the window and see the community where he'd grown up, where he'd risen to prominence, but he knew Otto would only shove him back down again, so he tried to spot landmarks he recognized from his position.

The vehicle pulled into a side street and then came to a stop. Otto turned the car off.

"Where are we going now?" asked Heinz, starting to sit up. Otto reached over and shoved him back into the seat.

"We aren't going anywhere," he said. "I've got some things I must do. You'll stay here for a while. Don't sit up, don't get out. Don't do anything."

"What do you have to do?" Heinz asked. "You've got to be joking. You're supposed to be protecting me. I demand that you stay here with me."

Otto ignored him. He opened the door and exited the vehicle. Almost as an afterthought it seemed, he reached into his coat pocket and retrieved another tin of sardines. He threw them at Heinz, who fumbled to catch them. "Here's lunch."

"This is it?" protested Heinz. "What am I supposed to do in here? I'm going to freeze. There's nothing to drink."

Otto sighed. He reached into the back seat of the car and retrieved a blanket and a cup. He tossed the blanket at Heinz and then moved around the front of the vehicle, his boots crunching heavily in the ice. He opened the passenger door and shoved a tin cup at Heinz. It was full of snow. "There you are," he said. "Food, water, shelter. All needs are met." He pointed a finger at Heinz. "Don't move."

The boots crunched away again, fading in the distance until he couldn't hear anything. Heinz stared up at the ceiling again. What in the hell was he supposed to do all day? He had nothing to occupy his mind, nothing to read. How long was this monster going to be gone and what did he need to do that required them to separate? He stared at the tin of sardines. He hated the things. He thought about throwing them out but what else was he going to eat?

As he sat there, trying to stay out of sight inside the freezing car, Heinz thought back to their tiny apartment in the Franciscan monastery. He'd complained at the time about how cramped the space was. He was used to the villa he'd been allocated by the SS during the war. Back then, they'd lived in luxury. He'd had servants, and he and his wife had lived like royalty—well, at least like aristocrats. The house was in the countryside, near the secret cave holding his precious uranium reactor. They'd escaped the bombing. His special status afforded him and Elsie the best food. He'd been supplied with real Virginia tobacco cigarettes and a monthly allocation of coffee. At times, it had seemed the war wasn't even going on.

Then the damned Americans had ruined everything—and at the worst possible time, with his wife already pregnant and ill from morning sickness. They'd been forced to flee to the countryside, where a sympathetic farmer had taken them in. They'd hidden there for several months while the war ended and the American occupation settled in. The SS, officially disbanded, reorganized along with other Nazis into small cells of mutual assistance. Heinz and his family were moved from location to location throughout southern Bavaria, always a step ahead of the Americans, until a year ago when they settled into the monastery.

They'd been lucky. All their moves had been by vehicle. And they'd had warm locations to hide, with comfortable beds and enough food to get them by. The past twenty-four hours were the worst that Heinz had experienced. Tromping alone through the snow, he'd nearly frozen to death in the darkness. Now this. Lying back, unable to move, with these intolerable fish as his only lunch. And the car was already freezing up. He was going to have to have a word with Otto about things going forward. He was an SS officer after all, and a scientist. He deserved better treatment. He thought again about his family, and then about his future. He wondered if where he was going, his life would be even worse. How couldn't it be? Well, there was nothing he could do about it, he had chosen his course and he would have to stick with it.

Hours dragged by. The car was getting colder by the minute. His breath bellowed out in wispy white clouds. He opened up his tin of sardines, wincing at the smell, and gagged down the contents. He was terribly thirsty, but the snow Otto had given him wouldn't melt, and he was forced to take bites of the freezing, powdery stuff. He also noted there was dirt in the stuff. Otto hadn't even bothered to go the extra few feet to collect fresh snow. He'd scooped it out of the gutter, or very close nearby. The bastard.

Time ticked by. He tried his hardest to think about other things, and to not glance at his watch very often, but every time he did he was shocked by how little time had passed. He tried to doze off but his teeth were chattering from the cold, and he was apprehensive about being spotted by somebody. The afternoon passed, then the early evening. The darkness was already starting to fall when the door abruptly opened on the driver's side and there was Otto, his hands full of packages, pulling the seat forward so he could load the bags into the back.

"What is all of that?" asked Heinz. "Supplies for where we are going next? Ammunition? A radio?"

"Gifts," said Otto.

"What?" demanded Heinz incredulously.

"For my wife. I don't get a chance to get into the city very often."

"Wait. Are you telling me that you haven't done anything today related to our mission? That you've been out getting presents for your wife all day!"

"Keep it down," said Otto, starting up the car. He rubbed his hands together. "It's cold in here," he commented, cranking the heater.

"You're damned right it's cold!"

"I told you to be quiet," said Otto. "We don't want to bring attention to ourselves. And yes, that's what I was doing. We can't visit our contact until dinnertime," Otto explained. "So I ran some errands."

"You could have left me at the cabin," said Heinz, incredulous. "I didn't have to sit here and freeze all damned day!"

Otto shook his head. "Too much petrol," he said. "Besides, I had to shop. I wasn't going to make another trip."

"Do you know how cold I was!"

Otto looked over at Heinz. "One time, during the Bulge, I lay in the snow for forty-eight hours without moving a muscle. I pissed in my pants and let the urine freeze to my legs. I didn't eat, I survived on snow. All of that so I could take a shot at an American colonel. Those whole two days, he never showed his head at the window of his headquarters. It was a little cabin, just like where we stayed last night. Forty-eight hours and he never gave me a shot." Otto pulled his seat back a little and closed his eyes. "That's cold."

Heinz was about to respond when he heard a snort. He glared at Otto, only to realize the commando had abruptly fallen asleep, his snores filling the car. He wanted to say something, to wake the man up, but he was terrified of what would happen if he did. Besides, what could he say? How could he complain after what the commando had just shared with him? And how long were they going to sit there now? Well, at least the heater was running now. Heinz settled back into his seat, the warmth starting to envelop him. Before he knew it, he had drifted off to sleep as well.

"Wake up!" ordered Otto, shaking him roughly.

"What is it?" asked Heinz, blinking his eyes, the adrenaline coursing through his body. His eyes darted to the windows, expecting the car to be surrounded by police, or worse. But there was nothing. He checked his watch—he'd been asleep no more than twenty minutes.

"It's time to go," said Otto.

"Did you have to wake me up like that?" demanded Heinz, trying to calm himself down. "I thought we were in real trouble."

"*Nein*," said Otto. "But we must get started." He shut off the car and opened his door, slamming it behind him.

Heinz was trying to force himself awake when he realized the commando was already marching rapidly away down the sidewalk. He scrambled to get his door open and race after Otto, slipping and sliding in the snow as he went. He was a full block away from the car before he caught up. "You can't do that," said Heinz, fighting for his breath.

"Did you lock the door?" asked Otto, still striding forward with a rapid gait.

"The door? I . . . I don't know."

"Go back and check," he ordered. "The gifts . . ."

Heinz couldn't believe this man. What was wrong with him? He turned and moved back to the automobile. When he got to the door he tried it and sure enough, the door opened. He pushed the button down on the door and closed it, turning back to Otto.

"Test it!" shouted the commando, his powerful voice reverberating down the street.

Heinz tried the door again; it was locked. He stomped back

toward Otto, who at least had the courtesy to wait for him now. "It's locked," he said when he arrived back. "And what happened to being quiet? You just rattled the whole neighborhood."

The commando shook his head. "I told you," said Otto. "I'm invisible." The towering man turned and strode off again, at the same rapid pace.

Heinz followed after as quickly as he could, taking two steps for every one of his protector's. Heinz wasn't sure where they were at first, but soon he started to recognize the streets. Ettstrasse gave way to Kaufingerstrasse and finally to Marienplatz. The traffic increased here, both on the street and the sidewalk. Heinz felt terribly exposed. "What if somebody spots me?" he said.

Otto gave him a withering look.

"I know, I know," said Heinz. "You're invisible."

"Correct."

They moved into the Marienplatz central square, the center of Munich. The beautiful Neues Rathaus and Frauenkirche dominated the square to the north. The Mariensäule, a huge column, stood in the center. There were various stands set up on the edges of the square. The foot traffic here was significant, but it was already dark now and Heinz kept a step behind Otto, trying not to look anyone in the eyes. They crossed the square and turned left on the Burgstrasse. A couple of blocks later, they arrived at a massive structure on the corner of Burgstrasse and Altenhofstrasse. Heinz realized the building, which took the entire corner of the block and a good distance in both directions, was a beer hall.

"You're not suggesting we go in there?" he demanded.

"We have to," he said. "My contact owns it."

"But there could be a thousand people in there," protested Heinz. "It's madness to enter." He was starting to think that was just the right word for Otto, this monster of a man who fancied himself impossible to see.

"Follow me, little scientist."

Otto tore open the door and stomped inside, with Heinz trotting close behind him. Heinz hadn't been inside a beer hall since the war. The inside was filled with dark beams extending across the structure. Row after row of tables were filled to the brim with people talking loudly over the accordion music that rained down on them from a small stage. Most of the patrons held liter-sized glass mugs of beer that they were in the process of sloshing about with the beat of the music or tipping back for a deep drink. Some of them were singing loudly and often off-key to the music.

Heinz felt like all eyes were on them as they entered the hall, but Otto ignored all of this, striding right through the middle of the tables. Heinz thought about turning around and fleeing before he was identified, but what could he do? Where would he go? He was sure that if he didn't obey Otto's orders, the commando would desert him in the dark snowy streets of Munich without so much as a second thought. His heart was throbbing and he felt dizzy, but he took a deep breath and plunged into the middle of the chaos, half running to catch up with the former commando.

Otto waded through the tables like a stone golem; waitresses flittered out of his way, stopping to stare, frozen with surprise in what seemed to be a mixture of admiring attraction and horror. Nearing the back, he took the arm of one of the servers and whispered into her ear. She glanced up at him for a moment and then nodded, setting a tray of dirty mugs down and darting into the back. Otto followed her until he'd passed the last group of tables, and then leaned against the wall, as if waiting casually for a train.

Heinz finally caught up to him. "Are you insane?" he whispered. "You marched right through the middle of the beer hall! We've been spotted for sure."

"Look around," said Otto, not bothering to do so himself. "Tell me what you see."

Heinz scanned the tables but he wasn't sure what Otto was getting at.

"These sheep are in the field grazing. They are here with family and friends, drinking their pilsners and stouts. They don't care a damn about you or me. We waltzed through the middle of them like we were taking a walk in the park. The eye doesn't catch the mundane, my little scientist. That's your first lesson in secret operations."

Heinz was surprised to see that Otto was right. Nobody was looking their way. Everyone out there was going about their business, as if two highly wanted men had not just strolled through the middle of them. Still, how could Otto be sure of that? It only took one person to call them out. "Otto," he started to argue.

"Let me guess. You want to tell me that surely one of them must have seen us, seen something."

"Well—"

"It didn't happen."

"How can you—"

"Shh. Quiet now, *mein kleiner Doktor*, here comes the chief."

A fat middle-aged man was ambling up to them. He was wearing lederhosen, complete with a feathered cap. Greasy tufts of blonde hair jutted out in every direction from underneath his hat. He had a large bulbous nose and his face was ruddy and splotched with scarlet. He was huffing and puffing, but he wore a jester's grin as he took Otto's hand in both of his.

"Otto!" he shouted. "It's been so long! And who do we have here?"

"A friend," said the commando.

The man spied Heinz with an appraising eye. "No names, aye? I understand!" He rubbed his hands together. "Well, it doesn't hurt to give you mine. I'm Adolf Alderbricht. I'm the owner of this establishment, one of the Führer's favorite places—in case you didn't know."

"Yes, I know," said Heinz. "I've been here a few times before."

Adolf eyed him again shrewdly. "I thought you looked familiar to me," he said, rubbing the sweaty folds of flesh in his neck with his thumb. "It seems I should remember who you are."

"Now's not the time for remembering," said Otto. "Better to leave it forgotten, *nicht wahr?*"

Adolf's eyes widened. "Perhaps so," he said.

The commando leaned in. "I need to speak with you for a few minutes, alone," said Otto.

"Of course," said Adolf, still smiling but not with his eyes. He peered at Heinz again for a moment. "Why don't you step into my office." He turned and snapped his fat fingers at one of the servers. "Bring my new friend here a liter of ale," he commanded, gesturing at Heinz.

"I want to come with you," Heinz said to Otto.

The commando grunted. "Best to drink your beer," he said, starting to follow Adolf, who was tottering off in the other direction.

"But, Otto—"

The former soldier whipped around and gave Heinz a stare that froze his blood. "Stay put, little man."

Heinz nodded, not trusting himself to say anything else. The waitress approached and handed Heinz a liter of beer. "On the house," she said, smiling and giving him a wink. "You must be a special guest indeed. Adolf doesn't give away anything."

Heinz took the beer absently, ignoring the waitress, who stood there for a second, obviously expecting a tip. When none was forthcoming, she stomped off in the other direction. Heinz stared at his watch, wondering how long this would take. Despite Otto's assurances, he felt terribly exposed here. He looked this way and that. There were a few eyes on him, perhaps drawn there by the appearance and departure of Adolf. His particular attention was drawn across the hall to the end table where a group of American officers in uniform were sitting. One of the men caught Heinz's eye, then his head darted down, as if the man was intentionally avoiding his stare. Heinz could see an American talking frantically to a soldier across from him. This second GI turned and glanced at Heinz as well, and then rose and hurried out of the hall. The scientist could feel sweat trickling down his forehead. He was sure he'd been spotted and that something horrible was about to happen. He looked at his watch again; it had only been a couple of minutes since Otto left with Adolf.

What was he to do? He thought about setting the beer down and running for it. Even if he was on his own, at least he'd be free of the danger that he felt closing in on him. But he couldn't bring himself to run. Foolishly or not, he kept his faith in Otto, hoping the man's reputation was well-founded.

Heinz glanced back at the table across the hall. The soldier was back and it looked like he'd brought three MPs. All of the men were staring right at him. He had to go. He started to turn when he was caught by fingers wrapping around his arm like an iron vise. "What are you doing?" Otto asked.

"Look across the way," Heinz whispered, keeping his eyes averted. "The military police are here. I think they know who I am."

Otto glanced their way for a second then returned to Heinz. "I met with Adolf," he said.

Heinz glanced back toward the MPs. They were fanning out and starting to head in their direction. "Otto," he whispered, "we've got to get out of here."

"Don't you want to hear what Adolf had to say?"

Heinz hazarded another look. The MPs were halfway across the hall. "They're coming for both of us."

Otto stifled a yawn. "Adolf said he can get you new papers, but it will be about a week."

"Otto, we've got to run for it!" said Heinz.

Otto glanced over at the MPs again, grunting. "We'll need to find a different hideout than the cabin. Too many people know about it. We can only trust those monks so far. We can stay one more night, then we have to leave."

"Otto!" Heinz was panicked. The MPs were almost there.

"Are you ready to go?" he asked.

"Yes! Is there a back way out?" Heinz demanded.

Otto turned and started walking directly at the MPs. Heinz was frozen, not knowing what to do. Was his protector going to kill these Americans here, in the middle of the hall? The man truly was insane. Otto stepped directly in front of one of the MPs and Heinz winced, waiting for the attack. But nothing happened. Otto just moved around the soldier and kept walking. The MP, ignoring the commando, stepped up to one of the tables near Heinz. He tapped on the shoulder of one of the men there, a German, and seized the man by the shoulders. The other MPs rushed in and, ignoring the voices of protest at the table, they pulled the man out of his seat and handcuffed him. Otto had nearly reached the other side of the hall. He turned, as if expecting that Heinz had not followed, and waved impatiently for the scientist to hurry along. Heinz, barely able to breathe, moved around to his right, giving the MPs a wide berth, and hastened to catch up with Otto. He finally caught up with the commando near the entrance to the hall.

They heard a stomping behind them and Heinz turned to see Adolf running up to them, sweat pouring down his face. He had two huge bottles of beer with him. "I almost forgot!" he yelled, drawing unwanted attention to all of them. "For the road!" he said.

Otto stepped forward and took the bottles. "*Danke*," he said.

"You're welcome," said Adolf. He turned to Heinz, a sly smile creasing his fat features. "And *auf Wiedersehen* to you, Dr. Hoffman."

Chapter 9
A Flight to Munich

Tuesday, October 12, 1948
8:15 a.m.
In the air over Germany

Sara was more uncomfortable than she'd been in her entire life. Her stomach was twisting and turning. She held on to the paper bag the pilot had given her before takeoff. She thought he was jesting when he'd said they were in for a rough ride, but now she knew he was merely prophetic. Her teeth were clenched and she fought back the vomit as the plane pitched and bobbed in the air. She was sitting on the side of the plane, wedged between some sacks and boxes and holding on to a strap. Still, as uncomfortable as she was, she couldn't help but praise their good luck. She held in her hand the telegram from the US military to Mr. Varberg after his inquiry, explaining that Heinz had escaped their custody. The Portnoys would still have their chance to track him down, and so would she.

They were flying in a Douglas C-54 Skymaster transport plane, a four-rotary-engine aircraft based on the DC-3. Sara,

Max, and Karl were huddled together, sitting directly on the floor, surrounded by pallets of garbage. The plane was hauling out refuse and the smell was almost unbearable. The interior had no windows and was dimly lit. The Skymaster was the only transport that Mr. Varberg had been able to arrange for them— all of the regular passenger flights being full of VIP passengers. The plane was fighting through a thunderstorm apparently, and the engines were laboring, sputtering now and again. Sara was terrified the pile of bolts might go down. Only thirty minutes into the flight, her stomach wrenched and turned, and she fought to hold back her nausea.

Karl had already given up. He was hunched over a few feet from her, his back spasming as he vomited profusely into and all around his bag. Sara glanced his way and then gagged, holding up her bag again and fighting back the bile. She turned her head toward Max, who was sitting on the other side of her, his teeth clenched and his face a horrible shade of green.

"Nice accommodations, huh?" he managed to say, a forced grin setting in on his features.

"I guess we can't complain," she said. "At least we are here."

"As always, you are wise beyond your years," he said. He started to say something else, but midsentence he shoved his face into the bag, beginning to throw up violently.

Sara closed her eyes, blotting out the sight, if not the smell. She wondered how long the flight was going to be. She hadn't thought to ask, but now she was desperate to know. She almost wished the plane would be struck by lightning or crash into a mountain and release her from her misery. She tried to relax, to think about the mission she was on. This was beyond anything she could have hoped for, she knew that, but still, at this moment, she wished she was at her desk, typing some mundane dictation. She almost could have stood up for a session of Jeffrey's barbs and wandering hands. Almost.

At some point, by the grace of God, she drifted away to

sleep. She woke later to the feeling that the plane was descending. She checked her watch—she'd been out more than an hour. She looked over at Karl—he was passed out as well, his head against a bag of refuse he'd fashioned into a rude pillow.

"Up at last, I see," said Max. "I don't know how you managed to sleep, but I'm thankful . . . at least for you."

She turned back to him. He was propped against a couple of boxes. His face was still in a grimace, but it had lost most of the verdigris and he was managing a real grin now. "The bumpy bumps fell off about an hour ago," he said. "I wasn't sure if we were going to go down with the ship, but it looks like we're going to make it—assuming we don't crash on landing."

As he said this the plane lurched and jarred as it made contact with the runway. The pilot hit the brakes and the piles of garbage tumbled and slid toward the front of the plane, dragging the three of them with it. Sara was afraid she was going to be crushed in the jumble, but after a few seconds things slowed down and the pressure dissipated. The plane kept rumbling along for a few minutes until it lurched to a final stop. A moment later the side hatch was opened and a man dressed in overalls stuck his head in, peering around until he saw them. When he spotted the small group, he waved his hand one time in their direction, then turned and left the space without speaking a word.

"We're getting the VIP treatment it seems," said Max wryly. "And after such a pleasant flight." Max reached out to help Sara up from the mess surrounding her.

"I don't want to hear a word out of you until we're out of this death trap," grumbled Karl. "I'm never going to forgive you for this."

"Oh, come on now, brother, we've seen far worse, haven't we?"

"Those days are long over," said Karl, refusing to look at Sara as he stumbled by. "And I wasn't interested in repeating them."

"You'll feel much better when we've tracked down Hoffman," said Max, placing a hand on his brother's shoulder as they all stretched and twisted, trying to work out the knots and nerves from the horrid journey.

"When we track him down? Don't you mean *if*? There are a lot of *ifs* on this trip. *If* we find Hoffman. *If* the Americans haven't sent us on a wild-goose chase. *If* we aren't mowed down by Odessa at the first opportunity."

The door to the cockpit opened and the pilot gestured toward the hatch for them to depart. Karl lurched toward the exit, pushing his way past Max.

"My brother, always the optimist."

"I guess I can't blame him," said Sara. "I'm so sorry about this."

"Don't you apologize for a second," said Max, taking her hands. "You got us here. Karl will forget his discomfort within the hour, you watch. We're on Hoffman's trail now, and that's all that matters."

"I hope you're right," she said. She followed Max out of the airplane hatch and down a set of aluminum stairs to the tarmac. They grabbed their luggage and entered a glass door into the terminal. They had gone only a few steps when they reached a checkpoint manned by West German officers. A police officer waved them over and looked over their papers, staring at each of them as he did so.

"What is your business in Munich?" the man asked.

Sara wasn't sure how to respond. She hadn't expected this.

"We're antiques merchants," said Max, stepping smoothly to the front and addressing the officer. "We had an attack on our store, and we're here to look at some new merchandise."

"An attack, aye?" asked the officer. "What sort of an attack?"

"An anti-Semitic one," explained Max. "We're Jews, you see. Well, not the lady, but my brother and I."

The officer flinched almost imperceptibly and took a step

back. He looked at the two brothers, then at Sara. "Give me a moment," he said, and he stepped away.

"Isn't it a mistake to tell him you're Jews?" asked Sara. "Particularly after what happened to you in Berlin?"

Max shook his head. "It's a slight risk, but there are two kinds of Germans now—the small minority that still want to stick it to the Jews, and then the rest. Many Germans are guilty, and nervous to do anything that might be considered anti-Jewish. Most of the time these days, our status gets us better treatment—particularly with government officials."

The officer hurried back with another uniformed gentleman who was obviously his superior. The new man, in his forties, looked nervous. He stepped up with an enormous grin on his face. "I'm sorry for any inconvenience," he said. "And I also apologize on behalf of Germany for what you went through in Berlin." He offered them back their papers. "Please, please, take these and be on your way. We hope you enjoy your stay in Munich."

Max gathered their documents and then motioned for them to move on. They walked through the checkpoint and into the regular terminal. In a few minutes, they had collected their luggage and were outside the airport at the curb. "See what I mean?" said Max. "That's what usually happens."

"And what if you'd been wrong?" asked Sara. "What if it was the other type?"

"We would have been strip-searched and questioned. I don't know, maybe shot?"

"Shot!" said Sara, her eyes wide.

"I'm joking with you, Sara. They would have hassled us, perhaps detained us for a few hours, but that would have been the extent of it. We would have loudly protested. Eventually somebody would have caught wind of what was going on, and then we would have received a big apology and been on our way. It's not the official Germans you have to worry about, Sara. Remember that. It's the ones that have gone underground. They are the ones still perpetuating the Nazi lie. The Germans we need to fear will come at us out of the darkness—not the light."

Sara felt a pinprick of fear. That's what Mr. Varberg had warned her about. About Odessa. She was sure they were protecting Hoffman. How long would it take that secret organization to find out they were looking for him? How long before they came after them?

They took a taxi to the center of Munich, which deposited them at the Hotel Blauer Bock, an iconic Munich establishment and former public house that was turned into a hotel in 1914 when the Schreiber family purchased the property. Sara paid for two hotel rooms with funds that were provided by the agency for the trip. She hadn't settled into her room long when there was a knock outside. She opened the door and Max was there. "May I come in?" he asked.

Sara's heart skipped a few beats. "Aren't we supposed to be going down for dinner?"

Max checked his watch and gave her a wry smile. "That can wait for a few minutes, don't you think?"

Sara blushed. She turned and gestured for him to come in. Closing the door behind her, she felt the excitement and fear racing through her. She hadn't been alone with a man in a long time. Longer than she cared to think about. She'd focused everything on securing this job, the training, and on her work since she started. There hadn't been time for romance. Max looked about her room. She'd put everything away already. She couldn't stand anything to be out of order. His eyes widened as he scanned the room.

"I didn't think we'd been here long enough for you to do all of that," he said, making an overexaggerated whistle. "Did you scrub down the whole space too before you put your things away?"

He was mocking her now, for the first time, and she didn't like it. "We should go," she said abruptly, heading toward the door. "We're going to be late." She felt a hand on her shoulder.

"Wait, Sara. I was only joking. I like that you wish to be organized. I do too."

She turned. He was close, a few inches away. His eyes weren't mocking now, they were kind. He reached out and took her chin in his hand. His fingers were rough, warm. He drew her to him and kissed her gently on the lips. She arched her back, enjoying the touch. He pulled her closer. She didn't resist.

A violent knock on the door jerked her out of the moment. She felt a little afraid. "Who is it?" she asked at last.

"You know damned well who it is," grumbled Karl through the thick wood. "Quit fumbling around in there. We need to get something to eat before our appointment."

"Ah, my brother," whispered Max. "Always with impeccable timing." He drew her to him again and kissed her forehead. "We will take this up again later. After our meeting. If that's all right with you."

She hesitated. She wasn't sure she should say yes. Finally, she nodded, not looking up at him.

"Excellent," he said. "I'll look forward to it."

"So will I."

They left the hotel by taxi and rumbled through the streets of Munich. It was dark now, although the sidewalks still crawled with crowds carrying groceries for their evening meal and even a few well-dressed souls with shopping bags. Sara looked at them with envy—oh, to be able to buy something new for herself.

"So much wealth," said Sara absently.

"Yes," said Max, "we forget what it's like to have plenty. The blockade has put an end to that—not that Berlin has been much of a cornucopia since the war."

"Germany's had things better than it deserved," said Karl. "If I had my way, you would have all rotted."

Sara could see the cab driver bristle in the front seat. "Perhaps another subject," she said. "Tell me where we are going tonight."

"We are on our way to a beer hall," said Max. "It's not the one where Hitler started his 1923 revolt, but rumor has it he liked the place."

Sara remembered reading about the 1923 Beer Hall Putsch, Hitler's first, unsuccessful attempt at an insurrection. Bavarian Nazis had tried to overthrow the local government, but they were crushed by the police and army. Hitler was arrested at the time, tried and sentenced to jail, but he came out of the whole process more popular than ever, and in prison he wrote his manifesto: *Mein Kampf*—which telegraphed all of his plans for the future to anyone that cared to read it. Sara was surprised they were headed to a Munich beer hall, given her present company. These establishments were still reportedly hotbeds of postwar Nazi intrigue. "Are you sure that is wise?" she asked.

"Why?" asked Max, then he laughed. "Oh, you mean the obvious reason. Well, that's where we must go if we are going to find anything out. We don't have a choice. But don't worry, we'll blend in just fine."

They arrived in front of the enormous building a few minutes later. Karl stepped from the front seat and Max helped Sara out. They sloshed through a little slushy snow to the entrance, where two enormous wooden doors greeted them. Max opened one and held it for Sara. As she stepped in she hazarded a glance back at the taxi. The driver was talking to another man and gesturing toward the beer hall. Sara felt a flicker of fear. She wondered if she should say something to Max, but Karl was engaging him in conversation and she decided against it. With a deep breath, she entered the establishment.

Sara's senses were overwhelmed and she took a deep breath. Max led them through the hustle and bustle of the hall. Sara felt like all eyes were on them, although she realized that was unlikely because there was nothing unusual about them at all. She did notice the number of long tables filled with men singing raucously and slamming their steins together. There were so many of them and they were just the right age to be veterans of the German army, or worse.

They found a table about three-quarters of the way across the room and they wedged in at the end. Max ordered them each a liter of beer. Sara looked at him in surprise. "I can't drink all of that," she whispered.

He glanced at her slim figure. "Don't worry, it's only for appearances. Just bang and slosh it around like everyone else, and pretty soon there'll be no more than a mouthful left in the bottom."

"What are we doing next?" she asked.

"Well, right now, I need to have one of our lovely servers fetch Herr Alderbricht for us." Max motioned for the woman who had taken their order. He whispered in her ear for a moment and then handed her a bank note. The server eyed the three of them, then nodded.

"Well, that's settled," said Max. "She should be back in a bit and we can settle our business and be on our way."

Their beer arrived and they each took a sip. Max made an effort at joviality, but Karl wore his usual scowl and was glaring at a group of men at the next table. Sara was sure the three of them didn't fit in at all. As she was looking around in discomfort, she spied a huge monster of a man with an eye patch, lumbering woodenly through the tables, a slim middle-aged man hurrying to keep up with him. She wasn't sure she'd ever seen anyone who exuded more power. He was bald, with a terrible scar running down his right cheek beneath the patch. What was worse, he seemed to be heading right for them.

"Do you see that man?" asked Sara.

Max glanced over his shoulder at the mountain as he marched past. "Scary," he said. "But he doesn't seem interested in us, so I'm not going to worry about it. Let's keep our eyes forward and concentrate on looking jolly. I don't want anyone to grow suspicious."

The server returned a few minutes later and whispered into Max's ear. "Our host is detained for a spell, but should be able to meet with us shortly," Max explained. He tipped his beer stein back and took a deep drink. "I guess I might as well partake in a bit of this. When in Rome, as they say."

Minutes passed slowly. Sara felt her anxiety increasing. Every moment they spent in this place felt like a risk. She thought back to what she'd seen right before they entered the beer hall. "I wanted to tell you something," she said to Max and Karl as quietly as she could. "When we were going inside, I glanced at the taxi. The driver was talking to some man and it felt like he was motioning toward us. I can't be sure but—"

"Why didn't you tell us immediately?" snapped Karl. "Fool of a girl, you're going to get us killed." He started to rise, looking around.

"Watch your tongue," said Max. "There's nothing to worry about."

"Indeed, what is that then?" asked Karl, nodding toward the door.

Sara looked up to see a group of American soldiers entering the hall. They wore black armbands with white *MP* lettering, identifying themselves as military police. Her heart raced with fear.

"That's nothing that concerns us, I'm sure," said Max. "Let's just keep our heads down and our minds on business. We'll be out of here soon."

The huge man stomped back past them, with the scurrying little man in tow. They walked directly behind their table and Sara was relieved to see they were leaving. She wondered if the police were here for them, but the officers walked right past. "The soldiers are heading this way," she whispered.

Max glanced their way and forced a smile. He didn't seem to have his usual confidence. "We won't worry about this until we know there is a reason."

The officers kept marching their way. To Sara's horror, they stopped directly behind Max and Karl. "*Entschuldigung*," said one of the men, tapping Max on the shoulder. He was looking at a card. "Are you Herr Max Portnoy and Herr Karl Portnoy?"

Max turned, not getting out of his seat. "*Ja*," he said. "What is this about?"

"We were looking for you at your hotel," the soldier said. "The bellman said you asked for a taxi to this location. You'll need to come with us."

"But what is this about?" Max asked.

"I'm not authorized to tell you." The officer glanced over at Sara. "The lady too, I'm afraid."

"We're not going anywhere with you," said Karl. "We've had enough of police."

The officer reached for a club he wore strapped to his belt, but Max put a gentle hand on the man's wrist. "That won't be necessary," he said. "We will come along peacefully."

Karl, on the other hand, was having none of it. One of the officers reached for him and he shrugged the hand off him. The officer seized Karl and pulled him out of his chair, holding him while another officer handcuffed him.

"Let's go," said the lead officer. "You're wanted at head-quarters."

The officers led them out of the beer hall, past a thousand staring eyes, and into a dark and ominous armored truck. Two officers jumped into the back with them, then the heavy steel doors were slammed shut and the vehicle rumbled off into the night.

Chapter 10
Delayed

Tuesday, October 12, 1948
10:35 p.m.
Munich, Germany

"Where are you taking us?" Karl asked one of the military police officers in English.

"You were already told this," he said. "To headquarters."

"But why?"

The officer ignored him. Removing a square package from his jacket, he retrieved a cigarette and lit it, staring ahead as if they didn't exist.

Sara wanted to talk to the brothers but there was nothing they could do right now. At least until they got away from prying ears. She hadn't the least idea what this could be about. She hoped it was merely related to their paperwork at the airport, or maybe some harmless harassment brought on by the disclosure that the Portnoys were Jewish. But her mind strayed to another possibility, that these officers might be in false uniforms—might in fact be tied in some way to Odessa. If so, they might not be headed to police headquarters at all, but perhaps out of the city to some secret location. She glanced at her watch—they'd already been driving for a half hour. That certainly seemed odd. Wouldn't the military have their station in the downtown district of Munich? If so, they should have been there long ago. She felt her fear rising. What if it was Odessa after all? That could change everything—the entire plan. The truck continued to rattle along. The trip was growing bumpier, and her anxiety increased.

"Shouldn't we be there by now?" she asked.

The officer smoking merely grunted, refusing to answer the question directly. "Be quiet," he ordered. "You'll know what is going on soon enough."

The brakes squealed and they lurched forward, slamming against the front wall of the truck. The vehicle took a sharp turn and continued rumbling along, much slower now, and they jarred up and down violently, as if they were hitting deep potholes in the road. Finally, they screeched to a stop. A few moments later the doors were ripped open, and the lead officer was there, shouting for them to get out.

Sara leapt down to the ground. They were on a dirt road in the woods. She scanned this way and that, looking for a place to run, but she was surrounded by more MPs. To her left, in a field, the bright lights of a car blazed at them, forcing her to squint. She felt a hand on her arm. She turned to see Max looking down at her, wearing a sad smile.

"What's going on?" she asked.

"I don't know," he said, "but I fear the worst."

An officer pulled Karl out of the back and then prodded them toward the lights of the waiting car. As they grew closer, she could make out an open-air vehicle, like a Jeep. There were several men standing nearby holding rifles. Another figure loomed in the back seat. It was a man, but she couldn't make out his features. The officers pushed them forward until they passed the headlights. She blinked, trying to make out who was there, what was happening to them.

The figure in the back seat of the Jeep lit a pipe, the flame illuminating his features. It was Jeffrey Scott. "Ah, Miss Sturm, how nice to see you," he said.

Sara's fear turned to anger. "What the hell are you doing, dragging us out here?" she demanded. "And what are you even doing here? Mr. Varberg sent me, not you."

"Temper, temper," said Jeffrey. "Now that won't do at all, coming from my secretary's lips."

"What are you doing here, Scott?" asked Max. His voice sounded as angry as Sara had ever heard it.

"Mr. Varberg decided to send me to command," said Jeffrey. He smiled. "Well, that's not the full story. After his ridiculous decision to send Sara instead of me, I placed a few telephone calls to Washington. Then we received some calls back. Then, Mr. Varberg sent me. He was a tad miffed, I have to say—something about going over his head. But really, sending a woman to do a man's job. And a typist at that. The man really must learn his place."

"He's your boss and mine," said Sara. "You had no right to go around him."

"I keep forgetting you're German," said Jeffrey. "You don't understand how things work in America. In my country, some families count for more. Mine happens to be one of them. In any event, I'm here, I'm in charge, and I'm ready to be briefed on the plan."

"The hell you are in charge," said Karl. "I might not want this woman here, but I'll follow her before I listen to you. You can turn around and go right back to Berlin. Sara told us how you cut off our funding—and what you said about us. I won't be taking orders from you."

"Even better," said Jeffrey. "I was told if you won't cooperate, to just bring all of you back right now." He took a deep puff from his pipe. "What shall it be? Do we venture forth or are we heading back to the airport?"

"I want to talk to Varberg myself," said Max. "I want to hear it from him directly."

"So sorry, but we don't have time for any of that. Frankly, after the calls I made, I'm not sure he's even employed with our agency anymore. But nevertheless, the issue remains the same. Are we going or are we returning home? Feel free to talk among yourselves, but don't tarry long. When I'm done with this pipe, I'll need an answer."

Jeffrey stepped out of the Jeep and ambled off toward the truck, where he slapped one of the soldiers on the back. The GI shrugged his hand off of his shoulder and marched away without speaking to Jeffrey.

"What do you think?" asked Sara.

"I say we go back to Berlin," said Karl. "I'm not going to take orders from that bastard. We can see Mr. Varberg when we get back and plan this trip again for later."

Sara felt a flash of fear. That wouldn't work at all. "They'll never send us back again," she said. "Besides, you forget that Hoffman is on the run. He won't be here a few weeks from now, by all accounts. No, if we are going to do this, we are going to have to go now, and we will have to put up with Jeffrey, whether we like it or not."

They both looked at Max. The younger brother was stroking the stubble on his cheek. He stared at the ground for long moments before he spoke. "I don't like it," he said. "I don't trust him and I don't like how he treats you, Sara."

"But, Max, if we—"

"You didn't let me finish. I don't like it, but I agree with you. We'll never have another chance at this. If we want to get Hoffman, we've got to do it now. I don't see any way around it."

"I agree," said Sara.

"I don't," said Karl. "I won't work with him. I'd rather go back home and put our store back together. To hell with him."

"Then we let our torturer go free," said Max. "Is that what you want?"

"Damn it!" said Karl. He spat on the ground. "Fine. I'll go along with this. But keep that bastard away from me. Otherwise, Hoffman won't be the only person I murder on this trip."

"Karl, we've been through this," said Max. "We can't kill Hoffman. We must turn him over to the authorities."

"We'll do our best," said Karl, scoffing and looking away. "But these are tricky matters, and accidents can happen. To captives, and to leaders."

Sara was surprised by Karl's words. He'd said something vaguely about this before, but she thought he was just spouting off. This was another thing to worry about. If Hoffman was killed during this operation, it would ruin everything—including her career. She couldn't let that happen.

"Well, folks," said Jeffrey, striding up to them. "Have we had a good chat?" He showed them his pipe, which was now empty. "My little smoke is done, so it's decision time. What shall it be? A heroic jaunt to catch the Nazi who murdered your family, or shall we fly back to Berlin in time for breakfast?"

"They've decided to continue," said Sara, her teeth clenched.

"And what about you, my dear?" said Jeffrey. He leaned toward her, looking her up and down. "Are you prepared to do what I say? Everything I say?"

She nodded, unable to speak. She knew if she said something defiant now, he would likely send her back by herself. She couldn't have that. This was far too important.

"Say it," he insisted.

"I'll follow your orders."

"All of them?"

"Yes, all of them."

"Good," he said, clapping his hands together. "As our British friends say, jolly good." He looked at his watch. "Well, it's getting late, we'd best get back to town. We don't want to miss out on our little meeting before the beer hall shuts down. I know you were interrupted, but the man has important information for us, and now that the proper leader is in charge, we can continue with our journey." They stepped back to the Jeep. Jeffrey jumped into the back. He snapped his fingers at Sara. "Be a good girl and drive us. I want Max here in the back with me. I've got a few questions for him about the mission."

Sara took the driver's seat. She hadn't driven in over a year. She fumbled with the stick, grinding the gears with the clutch until she finally got the vehicle to jerk into movement. Jeffrey, in the back, periodically shouted directions at her as they drove through the freezing night. "Why a Jeep?" she asked.

"I was told by the major at the base that this was the only thing they had available for us," he said. "This trip is low on the food chain in priority. You should be thankful I'm along now. At least you have your own transportation."

They drove that way back into Munich. Jeffrey was in the back, chatting away with Max as if they were old friends. Karl sat in the front, stone-faced, refusing to participate in the conversation or to even look at Sara. The woods gave way to farms and then the glistening lights of the city. In a few more minutes, they were back where they had begun this bizarre adventure, at the doors of the beer hall.

"Where should I park?" asked Sara.

"No need to do that," said Jeffrey. "You can just wait out here."

"But—"

"We don't all need to go in. Max and I will be quite sufficient. You can stay out here and enjoy Karl's charming company."

She wanted to protest but she knew there was no point. Max and Jeffrey walked through the front door, leaving her and Karl alone.

They sat that way in silence for a long time. Sara kept checking her watch nervously, wondering what was going on.

"His arrival is the end of this venture," said Karl suddenly.

She turned to him. "What do you mean?"

"He doesn't want us to succeed. That much is clear."

"Maybe it's best if we can't find him," Sara said.

"What the hell does that mean?"

She turned around to face him head on. "You can't kill him, Karl. No matter what, you can't."

He started to answer but was interrupted by the return of Max and Jeffrey. Sara could see immediately that something was wrong. Max's face was pale and drawn. Worse yet, Jeffrey wore a sly smile.

"What is it?" she asked when they climbed back into the Jeep.

"It's the end," said Max, mirroring Karl's words.

"Why?" she asked.

"I'll tell you why," said Jeffrey. "Our friend in there is going to be no help at all."

"He doesn't know anything?"

"Oh, he knows exactly where Hoffman is. He'll tell us where to find him too, but he wants one hundred thousand dollars in return."

"*Mein Gott,*" said Sara. "Is that possible?"

"For Hoffman," said Jeffrey, shaking his head. "Forget it." He lit up his pipe. "Take me back to the hotel, I want to get a good night's sleep before we go back to Berlin."

"But, Jeffrey."

"This is a waste of time, Sturm. Nothing to do now but go back to work." He leaned forward. "Frankly, I'm shocked you didn't think of calling ahead of time. You could have saved your boyfriend here and his brother a lot of their time, not to mention my own. Washington isn't going to be happy about this," he said. "I'll bet your job is going the same way as Varberg's. Too bad, you were a serviceable secretary, if a little mouthy." He spun his fingers around. "Turn around and drive, Sturm, I want my eight hours."

Stunned, Sara tried to say something to Max, but he wouldn't look at her. Not sure what else to do, her hopes crushed, Sara pulled out into the frozen darkness. They drove through the streets of Munich, Jeffrey bellowing out directions to their hotel, even though Sara already knew the way. She couldn't believe that their journey would end this way—without a hope or even a chance to catch Hoffman. They arrived at the hotel a few minutes later. The Portnoys hurried into the building without another word to either of them.

Realizing she was alone with Jeffrey, Sara stepped out of the Jeep and moved toward the front door, trying to avoid him, but he caught her arm before she could get inside. She froze, cringing at his touch.

"Well, they've had a bit of a shock," he said, snorting. He let go and stifled a yawn. Propping an eye open, he checked his watch. "It's not that late, fancy a drink before you go up?"

"That's very kind of you, Jeffrey," she said. Not feeling the words in the least. "But I'm exhausted and if we are leaving early tomorrow, I need to get my eight hours, as you said."

She started to step away from him but he grabbed her arm again, harder this time. "Really? Even now, with your job going up in smoke, you won't have a drink with me when there's a chance to save your future?" His grip was an iron vise.

"You're hurting me, Jeffrey."

He didn't loosen his grasp. "Think about it, Sara. This may be your last chance." He shook his head. "I don't know why I even bother with you. But think carefully now before you answer. Think about your future. Do you want to get a drink with me?"

She tore her arm away, her eyes flashing. "I said no before. I'm saying no now. If my job is on the line, then so be it. Go get some sleep, Jeffrey. And we'll talk no further about this. Ever again." She stormed past him and into the hotel. She made her way back to her room, fumbling for her key. She thought about

Max for a moment. She wanted to talk to him, to find out what he was feeling. Just to see him for a moment, but she knew now wasn't the time. As she struggled to open the door, she realized her phone was ringing within. She rushed in and answered it.

"Hello?" But the caller had hung up. Who had it been? Varberg? She wanted to talk to him too, but it was probably too late for him to call, and she wasn't sure she should try to reach him. Could it have been Max? She remembered what he'd said earlier, blushing a little—a flicker that turned to confusion and guilt. He wouldn't have called. And if he had, she didn't want to face him tonight. Not after what had just happened. She sat by the phone for some time, hoping whoever it was would call back, but a half hour passed and there was nothing. Eventually she lay back on the bed and shut off the light. Only there, in the darkness, did she let the tears come. She felt the anger, the frustration, but it didn't last long. She was exhausted, more tired than she'd ever felt, and before she knew it, she had collapsed into sleep.

Chapter 11

A Cottage in the Woods

Wednesday, October 13, 1948
2:45 a.m.
Munich, Germany

Sara's exhaustion could not hold her. She woke up two hours later, the fears racing through the dark passages of the night. The hotel room was stiflingly hot and the stench of ancient wallpaper and dusty upholstery filled the room. She felt like she couldn't breathe. She finally gave up on sleep and stared at the ceiling, her mind racing.

How could things have come to this? She'd been so confident when Mr. Varberg had returned and squashed Jeffrey's scheme to lead the trip in her place. The trip out of Berlin was uneventful if uncomfortable, and they'd made it to their contact with no issues. She'd even had a moment with Max—an encounter that promised an evening so different from what had finally happened. Now, in the space of a few hours, Jeffrey had appeared, and the contact had proved useless. She was heading back to Berlin in failure—and she knew what that meant for her future. She was losing everything she'd worked for and she would never have another chance with the Portnoys—or with her future.

She tried to go back to sleep but she couldn't do it. She lay there in the darkness as terrors weaved and darted around her. Finally, the sky outside her window began to lighten and she prepared for the day that would end this adventure and likely her career.

The phone rang, jolting her out of her mood. She stretched across the bed and answered.

"Hello?"

"Sara, is that you?" It was Mr. Varberg.

"Yes, sir," she said, fighting back tears as an overwhelming relief swept over her. Somehow, he would make it better.

"Tell me everything that has happened."

She did, and he listened for a long time, not interrupting her. "How could you have let *him* come here?" she asked at last. "He's going to ruin everything."

"The story he told you is true," said Mr. Varberg. "As far as he understands it. He did make some calls and stirred up enough influence to get himself invited on this trip."

"But he's not—"

"I know, Sara, I know, but for now you'll have to deal with him. Just think of this as an added obstacle. You've upped the level of difficulty on your routine. That's what they say in the Olympics, isn't it?"

"I guess it doesn't matter," she said. "Unless you're prepared to tell me you can raise that money."

Varberg laughed. "Hardly. Our Bavarian friend must think Hoffman is worth a mint to us. No, I'm afraid I couldn't manage half of that. I could call around and see if I could get some help, but I doubt it—and certainly not in time."

"Then we're coming home," she said, almost to herself.

"Unless you can pull off a miracle, Sara. Think. You're resourceful. That's why I hired you in the first place. I have confidence in you, Sara. If there's any way to make this happen, I think you can do it."

They ended the call and she took a shower to clear her head. The water felt delightful after her tortured sleep. She stayed there a long time, mulling the problem over. Wasn't there something they could do? She finished getting ready and packed up her things. She needed to be prepared for the worst. She checked the clock. It was only half past six. She made her way out of her room and down to the hotel restaurant. She was surprised to see Max and Karl already seated, sipping tea. She stepped over to the table. Karl still wouldn't look at her, but Max gave her a sad sort of smile and gestured for her to join them.

"I'm so sorry," she said as soon as she sat down.

"Sorry for what?" said Karl, not looking up. "That you sent us on this fool's errand or that you were fool enough to believe we would get somewhere?"

"Come on, Karl, that's enough."

"He's right though," she said, her eyes on her plate. "I should have found out ahead of time what this contact would want. I would have saved us a trip out here."

"I doubt he would have told you anything on the phone," said Max. "That's not how the underground world works. He would have told you to come out and you'd still be sitting here with us, sipping tea, waiting for Jeffrey to come collect us."

"The bastard," said Karl. "At least if he wasn't about, we could take a breath and think about things. He's the only one putting a timeline on our stay." He checked his watch. "At least he sleeps in. It gives me a chance to have some food while I can still stomach it."

"That's it!" said Max.

"What?" asked Sara.

"Time. We do have a little time. If we act quickly."

"What do you mean?" she asked.

"Do you still have the keys to the Jeep?"

She nodded.

"Well then," he said, starting to rise. "Let's get the hell out of here before Jeffrey finds us."

"What do you have in mind?" she asked.

"I don't know, but if there's any chance of doing something, we need to do it now."

"The keys are in my room."

"Well, hurry upstairs and get them before Jeffrey pokes his head out," snapped Karl.

They fled from the table, Max sprinkling some Deutsch-marks to pay the bill. Sara sprinted up to her room, taking the stairs two at a time. She was afraid that Jeffrey would already be in the hallway, and would catch her in the act, but the corridor was vacant and she was able to get in and out of her room without incident. Less than a minute later she was back downstairs. Karl and Max were waiting for her. Max had a folded map and what looked like a torn sheet of paper in his hands. It looked like a page out of the phone book. "Did Jeffrey see you?" he asked.

"No."

"Good, then let's get out of here while we have a chance."

"What are we going to do?" asked Sara.

Max nodded at the torn paper. "We're going to try to track down our beloved contact."

They left the hotel and jumped into their open-air Jeep. "What kind of an idiot takes this car around town?" asked Karl. "We're going to freeze to death before we ever get there."

"It can't be helped," said Sara. "We take this and we go now, or we go home."

"Well, we might all end up in the hospital before the day is through," said Max, laughing. "But by all means, my dear, drive on."

Sara started the Jeep and lurched off into the morning. The streets were practically empty at this hour. Max fumbled with his map, the wind blowing it around so he had great difficulty reading it. He gave her directions and she whipped this way and that through the frigid morning. She couldn't feel her fingers and she started to wonder if Karl was right, that they'd all come down with a case of frostbite or worse. Finally, when she wasn't sure she could take much more of it, they arrived at a townhome a few miles from downtown. The house was set in the Lehel neighborhood and the homes were upper-middle-class or better.

They pulled up in front of the house. Now that they were there, Sara felt a prick of fear. What did the Portnoys intend here? She checked her watch. It was nearly eight now and the neighborhood was starting to stir. There was a person outside here or there, sweeping the snow out of their walkway or strolling with their dog. She turned toward Max and Karl. "What now?" she asked.

"We knock on the front door," said Karl. "And that bastard gives us what we want."

"Or what?" she asked.

"Let's go," said Karl. He patted the inside of his coat and Sara was sure he had his pistol with him. Her anxiety increased. This could get out of control quickly, and if that happened, more would be at stake than just the success of this mission. She labored out of the Jeep, her legs and arms stiff from the cold. Her ankles were near frozen and she envied the men their trousers. Why were women required to wear these ridiculous dresses in the winter? She shook her head; that was a thought for another day. Right now, she needed all of her senses for what was about to happen.

They strolled up a few steps and along the narrow walkway to the door. The townhome rose five stories and it appeared that Adolf and his family occupied all of them. The beer master had done well for himself, perhaps too well.

They hesitated at the doorway. Taking a deep breath, Sara reached out and rang the bell. A few minutes went by and then the door opened. A woman was there, dressed in a uniform, obviously some kind of maid or housekeeper. She looked the three of them over and her forehead creased in a frown. "May I help you?" she asked.

"We'd like to see Herr Alderbricht," said Karl.

"What is this about?" the maid asked, the suspicion clear on her features.

"We've business with him from last night," said Karl. "It's a matter of significant importance and he'll want to see us. Tell him the Portnoy brothers are here."

"I'll tell him," she said, "but Herr Alderbricht doesn't conduct business at home." She started to close the door, but Karl shoved his foot in the jamb, preventing her from doing so. The maid jerked in surprise, her eyes widening a bit, and then she scurried off.

"Well, that got her attention," said Max.

Karl opened the door a little farther, and they stood there for some time, peering into the entryway. The room was narrow but elaborately furnished. A huge oil painting of a ship of the line adorned the wall. A handwoven rug rested over a walnut hardwood floor. Sara had never seen anyplace so finely furnished. Adolf had done very well for himself indeed. After a few minutes the maid returned, her face white as a sheet.

"Did you announce us?" asked Karl.

"I . . . I did, sir. But . . . as I explained, Herr Alderbricht does not conduct business at home. He thanked you for your visit and indicated he would be delighted to receive you again this evening at his establishment, assuming you are bringing the requested payment. Otherwise, he wishes you farewell. Now," she said, looking down at Karl's foot, "if you could please excuse me." She started to close the door again.

Karl shoved the door open, knocking the maid back. The woman hit the ground hard.

"Karl!" shouted Sara. But the older Portnoy ignored her. He stomped into the entranceway and started shouting. "Herr Alderbricht, you'll come down this instant!"

Sara rushed to the maid. "Are you all right?" she asked. The woman was stunned but otherwise seemed to be unhurt. "I'm so sorry for this," said Sara. The maid pulled herself to her feet, pulled her arm away from Sara, and fled the room.

A figure appeared at the top of the stairs. It was Herr Alderbricht. He was still in his pajamas and his face was an angry, mottled red. "Who in the hell do you think you are?" he demanded. "My wife and children are asleep upstairs. I'm sure you were informed, I do not conduct my business here. If you want anything more out of me, you'll do well to come back tonight to the beer hall, and you better bring my damned money. Now goodbye!" He turned and started to leave.

"Get your ass down here this moment!" demanded Karl. He reached inside his coat and drew a pistol.

"Karl, what are you doing? Where did you get that?" Sara demanded. She turned to Max but he was looking up the stairs, apparently waiting to see what would happen.

"What the hell do you think you're about?" asked Adolf. "Do you think a gun is going to intimidate me? Do you know how many times I've been shot at? And I haven't been hit yet."

"If you want to keep that record, I suggest you come down and talk to us," said Karl. He held the weapon level, and his hand was firm—the pistol seemed an extension of his body, like he'd trained with them for years.

Alderbricht stared down at them, his mouth opening and closing as if he wanted to say something. Finally, he stepped down the stairs, his eyes never leaving Karl. He reached the landing. "You're going to regret this," he said. "You have no idea the contacts I have."

"I know exactly who you associate with," said Karl, pushing him into an adjoining study. "That's why we are here."

"I'm talking to a dead man," said Adolf, as he settled himself into a chair. He still appeared entirely unfazed by what was happening to him. "Now, what is so important that you couldn't wait to talk to me until tonight?"

"We need to know where Hoffman is and we need to know it now," said Karl.

"And I told you I would let you know, when you paid my fee. How stupid are you?" he asked. "I'm not going to repeat myself again. Now, if you will excuse me." He started to rise.

Karl stepped forward and placed the barrel of the gun against Adolf's head. Despite the man's bravado, he winced when the cold metal came to rest against his temple. "We are renegotiating the terms of our agreement," said Karl. "We aren't going to pay you any money, but if you tell us right now, and if you don't lie to us, you'll get to keep your life."

Adolf turned his head to look at Karl. "I will give you one chance to leave here. One chance to walk away with your own life. Think. You announced yourself to my maid. If you kill me, eventually my friends will know. They will track you down, and they won't only kill you, they'll kill your family."

"Too late for that," said Karl, pressing the gun harder against his head. "Your *friends* already murdered my family. In the concentration camps."

"You are Jews," said Adolf in surprise. His face curled into a snarl. "Then you'll get nothing from me, at any price."

Karl lifted his thumb and pulled back the hammer of his pistol. "So be it," he whispered. "And your maid won't live out the morning to tell anyone about us, or your wife and children for that matter."

"Karl, please," said Sara, taking a step forward. "You can't kill him."

"Try to stop me," he said through gritted teeth. "If I can't have Hoffman, at least I'll put this fat Nazi out of his misery." His finger moved to the trigger.

"Fine, fine! I'll tell you," said Adolf. "He's hiding in a cottage in the forest."

"You'll have to do better than that," said Karl.

"I can show you," said Adolf.

"Mark it on here," said Max, stepping forward with his open map and a pen. The German took the pen. His hands were shaking now. He glanced at the paper for a few moments, then traced a finger from Munich south, following a highway. He traced a line down, finding a side road; at the end of that road, he marked an *x*. "He's there."

"And who is with him?" asked Karl.

"I don't know," said Adolf, "perhaps he's by himself."

"Don't lie to me," said Karl, shoving the barrel against his head again.

"All right, all right! He may have someone with him from Odessa," said Adolf.

"Who?"

"Have you heard of Otto Berg?" asked Adolf. "He's a commando, an assassin. Very dangerous."

"What does he look like?" asked Max.

"He's a giant, a monster, almost two meters tall and built like the side of a hill. He has a rugged scar on his forehead and cheek, and he wears a leather eye patch. You couldn't miss him in a crowd if you tried."

"*Mein Gott*," said Sara. "We saw him."

"What are you talking about?" asked Max, looking to her in amazement.

"Remember, he walked right past us that first time we were at the beer hall. He's a monster." Her eyes widened. "He was trailed by a slight, middle-aged man. That must have been—"

"Hoffman," confirmed Adolf. "That was Hoffman, all right." The German laughed. "You had your chance at him and you didn't even have the wits to know it."

"Don't you worry," said Karl. "He'll be dead by the end of the day."

"Karl, I told you we—" said Sara.

"Not now, Fräulein," said Karl. "Anything else you can tell us, Alderbricht?"

The German shook his head.

"All right, that's it then," said Karl, pressing the gun up to his head again. "Then we will say *auf Wiedersehen*."

"You can't kill him!" shouted Sara, rushing forward.

"Try to stop me," said Karl.

A hand reached out and grasped Karl's wrist with an iron grip. It was Max. "We aren't going to do that, Karl," said Max.

His brother looked up in anger. "Getting sentimental on me, are you?" he asked.

"Not sentimental, sensible. We aren't going to do it, brother. If we kill him now, the police will be combing Bavaria looking for us. Not only that, but if we're caught, we'll spend the rest of our lives in a West German prison cell. Think, brother. Think about what we are doing. Where we come from. Think about the future."

Karl took a couple of deep breaths. It looked like he might ignore his brother and kill the German regardless, but instead he shouted and raised his pistol. He struck Adolf hard in the head with the weapon. Alderbricht crumpled over on his side, his body spasmed one time, and then he lay still.

"Did you kill him?" Sara said, gasping.

Max kneeled down and checked the man's pulse, shaking his head. "He's alive." He turned to his brother. "Why did you do that?" he demanded.

"You're joking, correct? The moment we leave here, our Nazi friend is going to pick up the phone and tip off Hoffman. We would arrive to find an empty nest for certain. Worse yet, we might find a dozen members of Odessa, armed to the teeth.

I'm not interested in a shootout in your OK Corral, as Sara's American friends would call it."

"Perhaps you're right," said Max. "He'll likely be out for hours and likely disoriented when he wakes up. We have a little time, but not much." He checked his watch. "We'd better get going."

"Perhaps we should go back and get Jeffrey," said Sara. She couldn't stand the fellow, but she was growing alarmed about Karl. The elder Portnoy was growing more erratic by the minute, and threatened to ruin everything. She wasn't sure she could handle him on her own.

"You can't be serious," said Karl. "I won't have that little shit spoiling our fun."

"But what about *Der Dämon*?" she asked.

"I'm sure we can deal with him," said Karl. "They won't be expecting us. Not yet anyway."

Sara turned to Max. "I hate the idea of involving Jeffrey," she said. "But what do you think?"

"We can't risk him," said Max. "This time I have to agree with Karl. He'd probably have us arrested for what happened here, and even if he didn't do that, I doubt he'd let us continue. He wants us to fail."

Sara didn't believe that. She thought she knew exactly what Jeffrey wanted. But she didn't know what else she could say. The die was cast. "All right," she said, "where do we have to go?"

Max studied the map. "It's a fair piece from here," he said. "An hour, maybe two. We'd best get on our way." He looked toward the entranceway. "Besides, that maid will have woken up the wife. It won't be long now before our friends in the police will arrive. The good news: they won't be able to track us until Adolf wakes up."

They stepped out of the study. Sara glanced up the stairs. The maid was there, a look of hatred in her eyes. They fled the Alderbricht house and rushed back into the frozen morning.

* * *

Max navigated them through the streets of Munich and finally back out onto the highway, shouting directions to Sara as she maneuvered the Jeep. She felt herself calming down after the tension in the townhouse. Her mind raced, trying to figure out some solution to her problem. She hadn't expected Karl to act so erratically. She knew she was finished if he killed Hoffman. Particularly now that they'd left Jeffrey behind. She would lose her position and perhaps more. She might be abandoned by the agency and left in a West German prison. She had to do something to make sure he didn't act out on his threats. She needed more time to think. She wondered how she could slow things down a little. Finally, she came up with an idea.

"I'm hungry," she said out loud.

"How can you think about food at a time like this?" asked Karl.

"Now, now," said Max. "Sara didn't get breakfast, nor dinner for that matter. We should find something to eat. Besides, we will need petrol soon enough as well, I think. Before we get too far out of the city." Just as he said this, a gasoline station appeared on the right-hand side as they bent around a curve, as if it was summoned out of the forest at Max's command. "Pull over there," he said.

Sara turned in and an attendant stepped out to assist them with the fuel. The young man looked them over in surprise, staring at the Jeep and at the three of them. Sara realized how ludicrous they all looked in the open-air Jeep, and none of them were in uniform. Fortunately, the man didn't ask any questions. There was a restaurant attached to the structure and Max excused himself, heading inside. He came back a few minutes later with a basket. Inside was warm bread and a little cheese. "I talked them out of this," he said. "Sorry it's not more. They wanted us to come in and buy a proper meal, but I told them we didn't have the time. They charged me a lot for this, maybe twice what we would have paid if we had sat down for lunch, but then again, they parted with the basket." He handed Sara some of the bread and a chunk of strong-smelling cheese.

"It's perfect," she said, taking a bite out of the bread. It tasted better than anything she'd had in a long time. She realized she was actually hungry. She was grateful for the few minutes of extra time she'd had sitting here as well. She'd had time to formulate a plan. She was sure now what she would do if necessary.

"Between you ordering food out of line and this damned Jeep, there won't be any folks that forget our coming through," growled Karl. "Let's get out of here before they phone us in."

"For someone who just about shot our guest an hour ago," observed Max, "you're worried about the niceties now."

Karl grunted. "That's different."

"No, it's not," said Max. He turned in his seat as they pulled away, looking earnestly at his brother. "And I will reiterate to you, that under no circumstances are you to kill Hoffman. We are not going to ruin our lives over this fellow. He's done enough to us already. We will turn him in to the authorities."

"And what about this *Dämon*?" said Karl. "What are we to do with him?"

"They won't be suspecting us," said Max. "With any luck, we can surprise and disarm him before he causes any trouble."

"What if we can't?"

"Then we will do what is necessary to catch our prey."

Another thing to worry about. Sara was certain that any fatalities would be a disaster. Still, she had done what Mr. Varberg charged her with. She had found a way to continue the mission. If she hadn't, she was sure they would all have been on a military airplane right now headed back for Berlin. Jeffrey would be taunting them the entire way.

Jeffrey. She could only imagine how angry he must be. He probably had the army out looking for them already. That was all right, they'd be searching in the city—unless they managed to track Adolf to his home, and even then, they would have to wait for him to regain consciousness. There was nothing she had to fear for a while. With any luck, they would apprehend Hoffman within the hour. After that, when everything was played out, she would face the consequences with Jeffrey—and she doubted at that point there was anything he could do to her.

"The turn is coming, up ahead," said Max, interrupting her thoughts. "At least it should be."

Sara scanned the trees on the left side of the road, and sure enough, a half mile ahead she could see what looked like a narrow opening. She slowed down and took the turn onto an unplowed roadway. She was thankful now that they had the Jeep, which was made for handling rough and slippery surfaces. The vehicle had no problem plowing its way through the foot-deep snow. "How far along this road do we have to go?" she asked.

Max scanned the map. "It's difficult to say. I'm not sure Adolf even knew what he was doing when he marked the spot. I'd guess a half hour or so at this speed."

"What if he lied to us?" asked Sara.

"Then we'll go back and deal with him," said Karl. "For now, keep your eyes on what's ahead. We need to stop before we reach the cabin."

"Quite right," added Max. "It would be no good to just drive up to the front door. We will have to keep a sharp eye out and stop beforehand if we can."

Sara wasn't sure how they would manage that. The road was narrow and the trees on both sides crept right up to the edges, their dark evergreen limbs extending over them until they nearly blotted out the sky. She slowed down instinctively, sure that they would turn the corner and the cottage would be in front of them, with *Der Dämon* on the front porch, rifle in hand. Even as she thought this, she saw a clearing in the trees up ahead and she spotted something above the trees. She slammed on the brakes.

"What is it?" asked Max.

"There's smoke up ahead," she said, pointing to the sky on the horizon. "And the trees are thinning out. That's got to be the cottage."

"Well done, Sara," said Max, reaching over to give her arm a squeeze. "You've been so brave through all of this." He started out of the Jeep. "Keep the car running. We'll be back, with any luck, in just a few minutes."

"I'm not staying here," said Sara in surprise. "I'm going with you."

"You have to stay," said Max. "You heard Adolf. There may be a Nazi commando out there. It's too risky."

"You didn't stop me from coming into Adolf's house," Sara protested.

Max turned to her. "That was very different. You have to see that, Sara. Don't worry, we won't be gone but a minute."

"I'm coming with you," she insisted, turning off the Jeep and stepping out of the vehicle.

"Oh, for God's sake, let the little tart come with us if she wants," groused Karl. "We don't have time for the two of you to flirt and fiddle. We've a monster to bring to justice."

Max looked like he still wanted to protest further, but he nodded without saying another word. Sara stepped into the snow that was still ankle deep here. Her shoes quickly filled with the frozen stuff and her stockings soaked it up. She was terribly dressed for what they were doing, but she didn't even feel the cold. They were about to apprehend Hoffman! She felt an electric surge of adrenaline. She'd never done anything like this before in real life, and she could taste the excitement and fear tearing through her.

Karl took the lead. He had drawn his pistol, their only weapon. He pressed his finger to his lips, an order of silence, and he started down the road, moving as quietly as he could through the snow.

Seconds passed like minutes. The road curved to the left, and as they trudged on through the snow, Sara craned her neck, willing the cottage to come into view. The gray smoke was close now, just over the trees. A few steps farther and the cottage materialized. The structure was small and ramshackle. The chimney tilted to the left. The roof sagged at the front, looming over the porch as if the entire edifice was poised to consume any visitors. They stood there for long moments, frozen, watching for any movement in the windows. There was none. But a car was parked on the side of the cabin. Somebody was home.

Doubt filled her mind again. What if Adolf had lied to them? They might be advancing on some innocent strangers—some poor relatives of the beer hall owner perhaps, fighting to scratch out an existence in this miserable hovel. "What if this isn't Hoffman at all?" she whispered, voicing her thoughts.

"We'll know soon enough," responded Max. "But just the same, Karl, make sure of things before you take any action."

The elder Portnoy grunted and motioned again for them to be silent. Karl started tiptoeing forward again, his pistol clenched firmly in his hand. Sara's heart raced. It was madness to approach like this—in broad daylight with one pistol. They should wait until darkness fell, when the inhabitants would be blinded by the fire and the dancing reflections on the glass. But she knew they could not. Who knew how long Adolf would be out, and she had no doubt of what he would do once he awoke. No, they must act now, if they had any chance of catching Hoffman. This was it.

They were less than fifty yards away now. They were moving forward single file, with Karl in the front and Sara coming up last. She moved her head around Max's shoulders now and again to get a view of the cabin, but still there was no movement inside. They closed the remaining distance. Sara was sure something would happen, a scream, or worse yet, shots coming from the building, but there was nothing.

"Are we going straight in?" she asked, surprised by the approach. Karl raised his hand, gesturing for her to remain silent.

They reached the porch. Even Karl looked tense now. He pulled the hammer back on the pistol and climbed the steps as quietly as he could, motioning Max and Sara to the other side of the door. Sara stepped up and pressed herself against the worn wood siding. She was shaking now and her heart raced up into her throat, threatening to choke her. Her mind reeled. This was the moment.

Karl reached down and grasped the door handle. He twisted it, and to Sara's surprise, the door yielded. Karl ripped it open and sprinted inside, his weapon raised. Max and Sara rushed in right after. Sara's eyes darted around the room. A dying fire filled the hearth. A pot gurgled and spat on a stovetop, oatmeal vomiting down the side. Clothes were scattered on the floor. There was a back room and Karl dashed to it.

"There's nobody here," he said.

"How can that be?" said Sara. "Look at the stove. They were just here. And there's no back door." Then she saw it—in the back bedroom, there was an open window just over the bed. "They must have escaped that way," she said, pointing to the opening.

Karl hurried to the window, his head darting this way and that as he stared out toward the woods. "Damn it," said Karl. "They've bolted."

"Do you think it was Hoffman?" asked Max.

"If it was, there'd be no way to know."

"Were they warned?" asked Sara.

"I don't see how they could have been," said Karl, looking around. "There's no telephone in here, no wires connected to the roof. Even if Adolf has woken up, he couldn't have warned them. No. I'd say they saw us somehow and bugged out."

Sara could feel the disappointment washing over all of them. They'd failed. If it was Hoffman, they'd missed their one chance to catch him. Now they would have to return to Jeffrey's wrath—not to mention Adolf's. They would certainly face charges for Karl's assault. It was all over.

"Why didn't you circle through the woods?" she asked Karl, frustration boiling over. "You may as well have announced our presence, coming right up the road, bold as brass."

"And I am supposed to believe you'd have tromped through the woods for an hour in your stockings?" he said sarcastically, glancing down at her soaked shoes. "You'd have lost your feet if I'd led you through there. Not only that, but we didn't have the time. Hoffman could have had friends arriving any minute. And we didn't know if he had a telephone. We had to take the chance."

"What are we going to do now?" asked Sara.

"We're going to drop you off at the hotel with the Jeep," said Karl. "And then we'll continue the hunt."

"What do you mean?" she asked, stunned by his response. "You can't do that."

"Why not?" said Karl. "We're not going to give up the chase. Not while there's still a chance. But your Jeffrey isn't going to allow that to happen. So we either all go back, or you go back."

"I can't believe you'd say that to me," said Sara. "We are all in this together. I agree we must go back now, but we'll figure something else out." She turned to Max, who wasn't looking at her.

"I'm afraid my brother is right this time," he said, turning toward her with a deep sadness on his face. "I'm sorry, my dear, but I don't see what else we can do." He stepped over and tried to take her hands, but she pulled away from him. "Don't worry. When this is all over, we will go back to Berlin. I want you in my life, Sara, but you must understand how important this is to us. This is everything."

She knew the lie in his words. They weren't planning on going back. She shook her head. Feeling a rising panic. They couldn't proceed without her! "Forget Jeffrey," she said. "We will keep up the search. We'll dodge the police, find a new contact on our own. We'll figure something out."

He smiled again. "You have to realize that's not realistic," he said. "Besides, if we drop you off, you can blame us for everything. That way you'll be protected, and you'll have returned the Jeep. No assault, no stolen property."

"You don't understand," she said. "I'll have lost everything."

"What?" said Karl. "Your job as a secretary? You'll find something else. Sara, you must understand. We're talking about revenge on someone who destroyed our lives. What's your clerical position compared to that?"

"Quiet, Karl!" shouted Max, angry now. "You've said enough." He turned back to Sara. "I understand your position means much to you. But we don't know you'll lose it. Even if you do, there are other jobs. And if you can't find anything else, you can come and work for us."

She knew that would never happen. "Max, I know—"

"Enough," said Karl. "Minutes are wasting. We need to get going now—back to Munich, if we're going to have any chance to catch him while the trail is still warm."

"Why not just follow them into the woods?" said Sara.

Karl scoffed. "We don't have the boots for it. Nor the food. And I'm not following a commando onto his home ground—if he is there. No, we need to drop you off and start fresh. We're not without friends in the area."

Sara's mind reeled. She could not leave them. Still, there was nothing she could do right now. They were more than an hour away from the hotel. She wasn't worried about Hoffman. She was sure they could pick up his trail again if they were given the chance. She just had to keep them all together. The big problem would be Jeffrey—but one thing at a time. She let the ground shift beneath her. "Karl is right," she said at last. "We aren't doing anything here. We've got to get back while we can." She looked out the window at the sky. "It will be dark in a few hours. We better get a move on it."

"Are you sure?" said Max.

She nodded, not looking at him. She stepped to the door and opened it, heading back into the snow toward the Jeep. She could hear Max and Karl arguing behind her. Perhaps Max would make things easier by insisting that she come. They would reach the Jeep in a minute. Her mind was already working on another plan—an argument in favor of them sticking together. She thought it through as she waited for the brothers to catch up. She was sure it would work. She turned to the brothers, who were rushing up to her. "We don't have to separate," she said, "all we need to do is—"

Karl's head exploded before her eyes. She stared in disbelief, as the thunderous retort of a rifle echoed in her ears. The elder Portnoy brother spun from the impact and collapsed into the snow, scarlet liquid frothing out of a gaping wound near his temple.

Chapter 12
The Sniper

Wednesday, October 13, 1948
4:14 p.m.
Bavaria, Germany

Otto lowered his Mauser Karabiner 98 kurz sniper rifle. The barrel smoked in the frozen air. Heinz stared in awe at the commando, whose expression looked like he'd just ordered a cup of tea.

"We'd best get going," said Otto. "No telling how they'll react now."

"Did you?"

"I killed him, yes," said Otto. "It was clean and fast, right through the skull. He was alive one breath, dead the next."

"But you fired two shots," said Heinz. "Did you miss with the first one?"

"Did I miss?" asked Otto, raising an eyebrow. "I don't miss. The second shot went through the engine of their car, of course."

"What are we going to do now?" said Heinz.

"We make our escape." Otto shouldered his rifle, picked up a large pack he'd brought from the cabin, and set out in the opposite direction.

"Wait a moment," said Heinz. "You can't mean we're walking out of here in the snow? Your car is back at the cabin."

"And we've just killed a man in that direction." Otto shook his head. "We won't be going that way. Too many problems. Killing someone tends to get the survivors a little worked up. No, we'll head back out to the road."

"And then what?"

Otto shrugged. "Something will come up. Something always does."

"What about this," said Heinz, motioning to the heavy backpack he was carrying. "Can't I leave this behind?"

"Not a chance," said Otto.

"But you're making me carry the damned presents for your kids and wife. Surely you can get some more when this is all over."

"No reason to," said Otto. "I've already got them. Now let's get moving."

"I won't carry all of this!" protested Heinz.

"Fine," said Otto. "If you don't want to help me, then go back to the cottage and wait for your friends out there to collect you. I'm sure they're in a very good mood just now."

Heinz stared in exasperation as Otto stomped off through the trees. He looked around, wondering if there was anything he could do. Finally, he heaved the heavy pack onto his shoulders and stumbled off after the commando.

They marched that way for some time, with Otto leading the way through the forest and Heinz struggling to keep up. His back ached and his legs were frozen, but he willed himself to continue, wondering whether his protector had any idea where he was going. Finally, they reached what looked like a break in the trees. Heinz hurried and caught up with Otto. They were

on a slight ledge that slanted down sharply about ten feet toward a road. It looked like the main highway.

"How did you get us here?" asked Heinz.

Otto raised a hand to reveal a German army compass. "You
just find north, then go the way you want."

"I know how a compass works."

"Good for you, little scientist."

"What do we do now?" asked Heinz, ignoring the comment.

"We catch a ride," said Otto. That said, the former soldier
leapt down the ledge, landing at the bottom, his knees bending
deep to absorb the blow. He turned back to Heinz. "Now your
turn."

"I can't do that," said Heinz. He took a tentative step down
the ledge. His foot found a rock and he put his weight on it.
The rock broke loose of the hill and Heinz tumbled forward,
slamming against the side of the hill and sliding to the bottom,
where he crashed against snow and ice. He landed hard and his
backpack tore loose, smashing against his head before it sailed
into a ditch.

"My way is better," said Otto, reaching down to pick up the
pack. "You also dropped the presents for my family. You must
do better."

Heinz struggled to his feet. He was covered in snow and
mud and his entire body ached. He could taste blood in his
mouth. "You bastard!" he shouted, anger ripping through him.
"You're supposed to be protecting me."

"I killed for you today. What more do you want?" He
dropped Heinz's pack on the ground. "Bring the presents."

Heinz had no choice but to obey, as much as he wanted to
lash out at the man. During the war, he would have outranked
Otto. Even then, he doubted the man would have followed orders from him. He was unused to being treated this way. Even
after the war, he was respected by those around him—both in
Munich and then at the monastery. But this dolt didn't seem to

understand the rules—and what was more, didn't seem to care. When he arrived at his ultimate location, *if he arrived*, he was going to complain mightily about his treatment—but that was a long time, and a long way off it seemed. For now, he had to do what he was told.

They walked along the highway, heading back in the direction of the road that led to the cottage. Heinz was afraid a police vehicle might apprehend them, but there were few cars on the road and they traveled the half hour or so back to the side road without incident. Otto carried his sniper rifle in his right hand, taking no precautions to hide it as vehicles drove by. He wanted to ask Otto why but he already knew the answer. *He's invisible*, thought Heinz. What an *idiot*!

As they approached the road Heinz worried that they might run into the rest of the group that had approached the cottage. Would they have stayed cowering near the vehicle or perhaps returned to the main road, looking for him? Surely, they would be hell-bent on violence if they managed to find Otto and him again. He peered down the road, trying to see if there were any figures coming along in the snow, or along the line of trees, but it was twilight now and visibility was low. He could make nothing out that way and would have to trust to luck that they weren't going to be confronted.

"What do we do now?" asked Heinz.

"We wait for help," said Otto. "Ah, it is here already."

A flash of light caught Heinz's attention. A pair of headlight beams walked along the trees on the other side of the highway, flashing past them and then farther down the road. A vehicle was approaching. As it drew nearer, Heinz realized it wasn't one car, but three.

"Here they are," said Otto, marching out into the middle of the road.

"Who is here?" asked Heinz, but the commando ignored him. Throwing his arms up in despair, he followed the former soldier toward the blazing brightness that was already slowing to a stop. Otto stepped out into the highway and walked up to the first vehicle, leaning in to talk to the driver. Heinz strained his eyes to see who might be at the wheel, but the headlights from the other two cars were flashing in his eyes. He took a few more steps forward and was surprised to see Adolf Alderbricht at the wheel of the first car. Heinz peered in and saw three other men with him. Adolf was talking quickly to Otto. Heinz noticed a large bandage on the man's head that was stained with blood.

"Ah, Hoffman, you're still alive, I see," said Adolf.

"What are you doing here?" Heinz asked.

"I'm coming with some friends to take care of the bastards that stormed my house today."

"Who was that?" he asked in surprise.

"Two Jews and some woman," he said. "They were looking for you. They held a gun to my head and threatened to kill my family if I didn't tell them your whereabouts." It seemed to Heinz that Adolf might have felt he had said too much. He glanced at Otto. "I'm sorry, my friend," he said. "I didn't have a choice."

Otto grunted and looked at Adolf as if he was a worm or a gnat. "You are a coward, so why worry? Besides, you flushed out the prey."

"So you saw them?"

"They motored right up the road and then approached the house as if they were Sunday visitors. I made off when they shut the engine off, dragging Hoffman here with me. Like fools they marched right up to the door. Bad tactics. I waited for them to leave, then I took the head off one of them."

"Which one?" asked Adolf, staring hard at Otto.

"The right one. The other two dove for cover."

"What if they followed you?" said Adolf, looking around in alarm.

"No chance, I'm—"

"I know, I know, you're invisible," finished Adolf, sparing an exasperated look at Heinz. "Are they still out there?"

Otto glanced at the side road. "*Ja*. Only one set of tracks going in, none coming out. I put a bullet through the ridiculous Jeep they brought. They didn't come out that way."

"What if they escaped on foot?"

"The woman wasn't dressed for it," said Otto. "I'll wager they went back in the cottage, trying to stay warm and grieving for their dead friend."

"What are you going to do now?" asked Adolf.

"I'm going to take my guest and leave. I have a spot to hide him."

"How are you going to get there?"

"I'm taking your car."

Adolf sputtered. "What do you mean? You can't have my car."

"Not have. Borrow." Otto looked down the line. "Look at you, beer master, you have three cars. I only need one." He reached for the handle.

"The hell you are!" shouted Adolf. He fumbled for something near his belt.

Otto reached out lightning fast and thumped Adolf hard on his head, right over the bandage. Adolf didn't even make a sound. His head rocked back and he slumped over. The other men inside gasped and one of them raised a pistol. Heinz thought they were going to be killed for sure, but Otto didn't even flinch. The commando just stared hard at the men inside, and then at the other cars. The man inside lowered his weapon, dropping it and then raising his arms in the air. Heinz could see the terror in the man's eyes.

"Get out," Otto said at last. He didn't shout, he nearly whispered. The men inside hesitated for a moment and then scrambled for the handles, throwing the doors open. They were out in seconds and moving toward the other two cars.

"You forgot something," said Otto, gesturing toward Adolf. Two of the men returned to drag the unconscious man back toward the cars. "What will you do next?" the commando asked as they were getting loaded into one of the other cars.

One of the men looked up. "We're going after the Jews."

"You should have no problem finding them," said Otto, a scowl of disgust on his face. "They're amateurs."

Chapter 13

Despair

Wednesday, October 13, 1948
4:14 p.m.
Bavaria, Germany

Sara stood in the snow, watching the life run out of Karl. Max rushed to his brother's side. He clutched Karl's head and emitted an animalistic howl of sorrow. Another shot rang out, this one hitting the engine of the Jeep. The vehicle snarled and hissed, and steam drifted out of the hole made by the bullet. Sara rushed behind the Jeep, crouching down and clutching the doors. Her heart was tearing out of her chest and she could barely breathe. She looked over at Max, who was still at his brother's side, his shoulders rapidly rising and lowering as he sobbed in grief.

"Max!" she shouted. "You have to find cover!"

He ignored her for a moment. She held her breath, waiting for the shot that would end his life. A second passed and then another. "Max!" she repeated urgently.

He raised his head, looking toward her. His eyes were red

and swollen. Max glanced at the Jeep and then into the woods where the shots had come from. He took a deep breath as if he was going to stay there, then, with a lurch, he stumbled to his feet and launched himself toward the Jeep, crashing down next to her.

"Thank God you're safe," she said. He didn't respond and she put her arms around him, pulling him close. He started shaking, burying his head in her arms. She held him that way, trying to comfort him while the fear still coursed through her body. She was sure they could not remain here. The Jeep was no real protection. At least the sniper couldn't see them right now. So long as there was only one of them . . .

"We have to go," she said.

Max didn't respond. He was still trembling, clearly in shock and unable to speak. After long moments he seemed to collect himself and he looked up at her, shaking his head. "Our best bet is to sit tight for now. If we try to move, whoever is out there will shoot us for sure."

"Are you all right?" she asked.

"I'm a long way from all right," he said, his voice shaking. "But right now, we've got to focus on staying alive."

She glanced at the woods, less than ten yards away. "Couldn't we make it to the trees?" she asked. "We could stay ducked down. The Jeep would shield us."

He nodded. "At some point yes, but let's wait a bit. If the shooter or shooters are still out there, they may lose patience and take another shot. Besides," he said, glancing at his brother's body, "I can't leave Karl—not yet."

"Max, he's—"

"I know he's gone. But he's all I have left. I just . . . I just need a little while."

They sat that way for some time. The sky darkened. Sara shivered in the cold. Her legs ached from crouching behind the Jeep. Thankfully, and perhaps by some miracle, there were no further shots. Finally, she felt they had to do something. "Max," she said, but he didn't respond. She squeezed his shoulder. "Max, we've got to go, we have to try something."

He looked, with eyes dark and red. He stared at her for long moments and then nodded his head slightly. "You're right, of course," he said. "We've got to try." He looked up at the sky and then glanced at the Jeep. "How long have we been here?"

"An hour at least, I think," she said. "Perhaps two."

"And there haven't been any more shots in that time." He sat with his head against the Jeep, his eyes closed. "It doesn't mean anything, of course," he said at last. "The bastard could still be out there, just waiting for us to poke our heads up."

"He might be, but he doesn't need to do anything and we're dead," said Sara. "We'll freeze out here eventually. My feet are already numb and I'm worried about frostbite if we stay out here much longer."

"What shall we do then?" he asked. "Can we try the Jeep?"

"It's shot through."

"The woods then?"

"I think we've been out here too long," she said, shivering in the freezing cold. She nodded toward the clearing. "We've got to get back into the cottage. It will be warm in there—at least warmer—and we may find more clothes and some food."

"And if he's still out there?" asked Max.

"Does it matter at this point?"

"You're right. But let me get up first. I'll start toward the cottage. If nothing happens, you can follow."

She shook her head. "We'll go together."

Max started to protest but perhaps realizing that his delay had caused their current predicament, and that Sara was not going to change her mind, he reached a hand up to the hood of the Jeep and started to scramble up. "Let's go then," he said.

He reached his feet and she rose up at the same time. She couldn't feel her feet and she was unstable. Her head was dizzy but she willed herself to continue. They tried to stay hunched over and they stumbled out, heading back toward the cottage. Max made a wide berth around Karl's body but Sara moved toward it, leaning down and groping in the snow. She winced as she searched, expecting any moment the bullet that would end her life.

"What are you doing?" he demanded.

"The pistol." Her hands, burning in the icy cold of the snow, kept slushing through it until she gripped something hard and metal. "I've found it."

"Let's go," he said, breaking into an awkward, shambling trot. She followed, moving as quickly as she was able, her frozen legs and feet refusing to propel her at anything like a normal speed.

The cottage re-emerged as they shambled along the path. Sara felt her elation rising as the moments passed without any gunshots. She was hopeful now that the shooter, or shooters, had left the scene, and they could safely return to the cottage. She glanced at the chimney. The fire was out, but no matter, the inside would still be far warmer and they could get another one going if they dared. The distance to the structure seemed to take an eternity to close. She was breathing heavily now, her breath coming in gasps. She was exhausted and frightened. Finally, they reached the porch. Max pulled himself up the steps and then turned to help Sara.

They threw open the door and stumbled inside. The cottage was dark, except for the last few embers of the fire. The temperature inside must have dropped significantly with the dying of the fire, but the inside of the cabin felt like a sauna to her. "Thank God," she whispered, stamping her feet and rubbing her hands together.

"I'll rekindle the fire," said Max, stumbling over toward the hearth. There was a small stack of wood nearby and he drew out a log, using the end to stir up the embers before placing it on the coals. In a few moments, flames began to lick up the wood. He added other pieces, crisscrossing them, and soon he had a roaring fire.

They both huddled by the hearth, oblivious to further danger. They warmed themselves, removing their shoes and stockings. Sara was relieved to see that her feet and toes had not darkened, and that feeling gradually returned to them.

"We've been lucky," Max said, his voice flickering for a moment with the old familiar joy before it lapsed into a wooden, metallic sound. "Unlike Karl."

She put her arms around him and held him, tears falling down her face this time. They held each other for a long time there in the darkness, near the warmth of the fire. Sara felt all of the emotion of the day overwhelming her, and she took comfort in his arms. At first he didn't respond, but then he put his arms around her as well and held her tight. After a long time she spoke. "I should see if there is something for us to eat."

"I don't want anything," he said.

"Nonsense. We haven't had anything since noon. We both need our strength." She rose, ignoring his protestations, and fumbled around in the semidarkness. She located some matches and a lamp. Lighting it, she searched around until she found the kitchen counter. Sweeping the light along it, she located what she was looking for. "There's a loaf of bread here and some cheese," she said. "Also, a half bottle of wine. And oddly, stacks of sardine tins. Somebody must have really liked them."

"Bring it over by the fire," he said.

She brought the food and wine over and then sat back down by him. They spread a nearby blanket down and laid the food and wine on it.

"There," she said, "a proper picnic."

He forced a smile but he picked up a piece of bread and broke off a chunk of the cheese. He took a bite, closing his eyes while he chewed. He took a deep breath. "You're right, Sara, I was hungry." He drew the wine bottle to his lips and drank deeply. "This helps a little as well."

"Nothing will make it better. Not for a long time," she said. "But we've got to go on."

"What does that mean now?" he asked, looking at her in the flickering light.

"I guess that's up to you," she said.

He took another few bites, not answering, as if considering the question. Sara watched him, letting him take his time. "We've probably missed our chance," he said at last. "If Hoffman was here, he knew we were coming. He's probably long gone now."

She nodded.

"Still," he said, "if there's any chance to find him, I would like to try. That's what my family would have wanted. That's what Karl would want."

"And I'll go with you," she said, taking his hand.

"What about Jeffrey? You must be in a lot of trouble by now."

"I'll deal with that when I have to," she said. "For now, let's see what tomorrow brings."

"Do you have any ideas what we might do?" he asked.

She shook her head. "I'm too tired right now. I think we should sleep here tonight. Tomorrow we can walk out to the highway. Somebody will stop and give us a ride back to Munich. From there, you said you have friends. Maybe we could go to them for help."

"Of course," he said, smiling genuinely now. "Yes, I have friends that might help us. At least they could point us in the right direction."

Sara moved the food aside. Wrapping the blanket around her, she laid her head down in his lap, facing the fire. His hands moved to her head and he ran his fingers through her hair.

Now that the excitement was over, she was exhausted. "Everything will be a little better tomorrow," she said, her eyes growing heavy.

There was a crashing sound and Sara bolted upright, gasping. She craned her neck. The door had been torn open. There were men there, guns drawn. Flashlights blazed in her eyes, obscuring her view. They were caught.

Chapter 14

Home

Wednesday, October 13, 1948
6:53 p.m.
Bavaria, Germany

Otto drove the car down the highway. The clouds gathered as darkness fell and snowflakes began descending on the vehicle, first a few at a time and then a veritable flurry.

The vehicle began to slip and slide as the snow on the pavement increased. At the rise of a particularly steep hill the wheels spun. Otto shifted down to a lower gear and just managed to maneuver the car over the crest of the hill before it completely stalled.

"What are we going to do?" asked Heinz. "I don't see how we can go on now. Look at that snowfall," said the scientist, pointing to the windshield. "We won't make the next hill."

Otto grunted but did not answer. The commando continued to drive for another few minutes before he spoke. "You're right, of course," he said. "But I'm not going to sit out in this damned stuff all night. You're lousy company."

"How kind of you," retorted Heinz. "What do you propose we do instead?"

"Well, you've been lugging my wife and children's gifts around for the better part of a day," said Otto. "We might as well deliver them."

"Are we close to your house?" asked Heinz. Otto had mentioned nothing about where he lived or that they were getting close to it.

"It's not so far from here," said Otto. "Less than ten miles. The turn is coming up here in just a few minutes. And there isn't any more significant incline. We might have a hard time stopping at the end though."

"What do you mean?" asked Heinz, his heart skipping a beat. He wondered what the unpredictable Otto might consider troubling about the end.

"You'll see," said Otto. "It's just like a ride at a fair. And look, here's our turn. It snuck up on me." Otto slowed the vehicle and took a left, the tire sliding so that the commando had to spin the wheel to keep the vehicle from crashing into the ditch.

"Was that necessary!" demanded Heinz. "You could have slowed down and taken that corner much more carefully."

Otto grunted. "What fun is that, my little doctor?"

"You can play games on your own time," said Heinz. "Right now you have to protect me."

"Says who?" asked Otto. "I'm paid to deliver you, nobody said in what shape."

Heinz was stunned by the statement from Otto. He was hoping the commando was kidding, but Otto gave no indication that his words were in jest. Heinz remembered again just how dangerous this man was and for the next few minutes he was quiet. He spent the time thinking about his wife and child. He hoped they were okay and that the Americans were treating them decently. He cursed the Franciscans for their carelessness.

If they'd only acted more quickly and if they'd ensured his entire family had proper paperwork, they would already be in Italy or Portugal awaiting a ship to South America. Instead, his family was in American custody and he was bumbling along on this journey to nowhere with Otto. He felt like a piece of bait on a hook—waiting for an American fish to strike him. Was Otto the line, the hook, or the fisherman? he wondered.

"Almost there," said Otto. The snow was several inches deep on the road now, but fortunately they were heading straight, and at a modest incline. "Hold on," he said, "we reach the fun part."

Heinz was horrified to see the road plunge suddenly down into a deep valley. The snow and the darkness obscured his vision.

"How long is this hill?" he asked, gripping the door handle with both hands.

"Not far," said Otto. "A mile at most."

"A mile! *Gut Gott!*"

"I told you stopping could be a little problem."

The vehicle was picking up speed. Heinz watched the speedometer pass fifty and then sixty. Fence posts were ripping by them on both sides, mere inches from the narrow road.

Heinz felt his heart in his throat as the vehicle picked up yet more speed. Worse yet, among the swirling snow and the darkness, he perceived that the road came to an abrupt stop at the end of the hill where lights flickered in the distance from what looked like a number of houses.

"What in the hell is that?" demanded Heinz.

"That's my home," said Otto, his voice casual as if they were not hurling through the ice and snow at eighty miles an hour. "You would love this neighborhood, Heinz," he continued. "Every house is occupied by one of my former mates in Skorzeny's unit. It's a wonderful place to raise a family."

Heinz was not certain at all that he would like living among a bunch of former commandos—particularly if they were anything like Otto—but he didn't say so out loud.

The car was sliding down the road uncontrollably now, and Otto was whipping the steering wheel this way and that, barely keeping it between the fences on either side. Heinz gripped the dashboard. He glanced at the speedometer, which had almost reached a hundred. They were within two hundred yards of the end of the road now and he could clearly see the huge fence lying perpendicular to the road. They were heading right for it. "What are we going to do!" he shouted.

"I told you this last part might be a bit tricky," said Otto as if he was ordering a meal that he wasn't sure was on the menu.

Heinz shouted in terror.

The commando abruptly slammed the vehicle into a lower gear. The scientist lurched forward, slamming into the dash. Otto ripped the wheel back and forth, somehow keeping the car on the road. They were within fifty yards of the fence now and still going impossibly fast. Heinz braced himself to be badly injured or perhaps killed. He would never see his family again after all.

They were almost to the fence when Otto slammed the car into a lower gear again and at the same time spun the wheel to the left, sliding the vehicle a few yards in that direction. He spun the wheel to the right, straightening the car out as it slid through a narrow gap between the fence lines Heinz had not seen before. They passed through safely and onto a long driveway. They were in the flat now but the car was still moving too fast and a house emerged out of the darkness. They were spinning and sputtering toward it. Heinz kept shouting, grasping for something to give him balance.

Otto slammed on the brakes a final time and spun the wheel again, the car whipped around 180 degrees, and they slid backward. Heinz closed his eyes, waiting for the crash, but the car was shuddering and sputtering as it slowed. Somehow, by a miracle, the vehicle rumbled to a stop. Heinz took a deep breath and opened his eyes. The car was no more than a yard from the house. Otto turned the engine off.

"We're here," he said jovially, as if they'd just driven to the market on a hot summer day and returned home for dinner. Otto stepped out the driver's door and closed it, moving around to the trunk, where he retrieved the bags of gifts for his wife and children. He trudged toward the door when he stopped, seeming to realize that Heinz was not with him. He set down the packages and returned to the passenger seat, knocking on the window and peering inside. "Little scientist, are you coming in?" he asked.

Heinz was still inside the car. He didn't feel like he could let go of the dashboard. His whole body was shaking. He was amazed that they had somehow survived, although now that they were stopped a new realization started to creep on him. Heinz perceived that Otto knew exactly what he was doing and had set this scenario up to toy with the former scientist. *Damned bastard*, he whispered to himself.

"What was that?" asked Otto, knocking again on the window with his meaty paws.

"Nothing," said Heinz.

"*Gut*," said Otto, opening the door and dragging Heinz out with one hand like he was a rag doll. "Let's go inside, unless you're planning to spend the night out here." There was a wry grin on the commando's face and he lurched away toward the door, not looking back. Heinz had no choice but to follow him, slipping and sliding through the snow as he trailed his massive protector.

Otto opened the door and they stepped inside to a nicely furnished and cozy little home. There was a nice fire roaring in the hearth, surrounded by a comfortable sofa and chairs and a small sitting room near the entranceway. On the other side of the house a dining room table and chairs filled the front room, which opened up through an archway into the kitchen.

Otto led Heinz that way and they stepped into the kitchen. There was a young woman, no more than thirty, there. She was short, no more than five feet three inches, and she wore a white floral dress that swam on her lithe frame. She was standing over a boiling pot of some kind of soup. She turned around and her face filled with surprise and delight as she rose on tiptoes to kiss her husband on both cheeks. "I didn't know you would be coming home today," she said. She turned, noticing Heinz for the first time. "And who do we have here?" she asked.

"Best not to know his name, *mein Liebling*," said Otto, reaching forward to kiss her on the lips. He turned toward Heinz. "This is my beautiful Aafke," he said, smiling. He looked around. "I found her in Eindhoven during the foolish American parachute attack. I convinced her to come back to Germany with me."

Aafke was smiling up at him. She had sandy blonde hair, straight and parted in the middle. Otto stood a foot taller than her.

"And where are my glorious *kinder*?" he asked.

"Over here, Papa!" shouted a young boy no more than four, who came storming out of the bedroom nearby. He was followed by a toddling girl of no more than two. Otto stepped over and picked both of the children up, twirling them around before he stopped again in front of Heinz. "This is Otto the second and little Greta," he said, smiling. "Little Otto is the man of the house when I'm not around and Greta already helps her mother. Don't you, my little girl?"

Heinz was surprised to see how proud and excited Otto was. The commando didn't see Heinz's expression; instead he was totally focused on his children, twirling them around the room while Aafke watched with a happy smile on her face.

"Have you brought us anything, Papa?" asked the boy.

"You mustn't expect a present every time I've been away now," said Otto with mock sternness.

"But, Papa," little Otto protested, "you didn't bring us anything last time either."

"Well, I suppose you're right," said Otto, running his hand over his cheek as if considering the matter. "It has been some time since I brought you anything. Very well, I suppose there might be something here for you." Otto retrieved the bag and took it over to the counter. He set it down and unzipped it, shuffling through the contents. He eventually retrieved a toy soldier wearing French revolutionary garb and handed it to his delighted son. Little Otto hugged the toy as if it were a doll, hopping up and down in excitement. Greta glared at the soldier, frowning and then looking up at her father expectantly.

"Don't worry, my little girl," he said, reaching back into the bag. Otto pulled out a porcelain doll nearly as tall as Greta was and handed it to her. She squealed in delight and took the doll in both arms, almost falling over from the weight of it. Both of the children were soon absorbed in their new presents and Otto reached into the bag again, unloading flour, sugar, and some spices and setting them on the counter.

"Dry goods, huh?" said Aafke, with an arched eyebrow. "The children get presents and you bring me something to make you meals with?"

"*Ach, eine Minute,*" he said, digging back into the bag. "I suppose there might be something else in here somewhere. Ah, here it is." He retrieved a white cloth blouse that was embroidered with beautiful sunflowers. He held it up and inspected it carefully. "I suppose you can have this," he said.

Aafke picked up the shirt and inspected it closely. "Yes," she said after a moment. "This will do quite nicely." She stepped forward again and kissed him. "But don't you have any presents for our guest?"

"His life," said Otto. "I got him his life as a present."

Aafke laughed. "I suppose that's fair enough."

Otto stepped over to the soup, sniffing a couple of times. "What is this?" he asked. "Is there enough left over for a couple of travelers?"

Aafke laughed. "There's plenty," she said, "and fresh bread too. I always make enough because I never know when you'll come home." She looked admiringly at Otto. "My husband the adventurer," she said at last, patting his arm.

Heinz watched this interaction in amusement, wondering to himself if Aafke had any idea just what Otto did when he was "adventuring." He also wondered whether she knew about his past.

As Aafke finished the soup and Otto sat on the floor playing with the children, Heinz had an opportunity to look around the room. He realized there was an entire wall of photographs of Otto in uniform, with various soldiers. There was even a picture of the commando standing with a group of soldiers along with Adolf Hitler.

Heinz was shocked; he hadn't realized how important Otto might be after all. He himself had certainly never been anywhere near the Führer. He wondered if Otto had just been lucky, perhaps when their leader visited the front. But Heinz noticed several other high-ranking Nazis in photographs with him, including one with Heinrich Himmler, the head of the SS—just the two of them. There was also a framed display on red velvet of Otto's decorations from the war, including the Iron Cross—Second Class and First Class—and also a Knight's Cross, one of the highest military decorations awarded by the Nazis during the war. Heinz whistled appreciatively.

"How did you win this?" asked Heinz, pointing at the medal.

"I'm not allowed to say," said Otto, looking up briefly.

Heinz laughed. "But certainly at this point—"

"I'm not allowed to say."

Aafke rushed in as if to prevent the awkwardness of the exchange. "The soup and bread are ready," she said. "You must both be starving."

They stepped to the table and sat down. Heinz had not realized until that moment just how hungry he was, but he was famished. The soup was a creamy potato and cabbage. It was fantastic, the best he'd ever had. There was also a delicious loaf of black bread and some cooked vegetables, and they washed it down with large steins of beer. Otto drank three of them during the meal and seemed no worse for the wear.

Throughout the dinner Aafke and Otto joked and flirted as if they had just met. The commando was obviously deeply in love with his wife and she just as clearly felt the same for him. Heinz was reminded painfully of Elsie, and sitting here eating this meal made him remember how much he missed his family and also about the lonely and dangerous road ahead for him.

He felt suddenly desperate, almost panicked. Was there no alternative? If Odessa could spirit him away was there no way to free his family from the Americans before he had to execute this ridiculous journey? But he knew there was nothing that could be done. Odessa would never sanction an attack on an American facility, even if his wife and child could be located, which seemed well-nigh impossible. No, Odessa would refuse. Spiriting ex-Nazis into foreign countries was one thing, but poking the Americans quite another. No, he was on his own and he had to travel the path that was set before him, even if he had little hope of seeing his family again.

After dinner Aafke settled Heinz on the sofa with a glass of peppermint schnapps while Otto stepped into the other room to use the phone. An hour later the commando returned and sat in a chair across from him. "I've got bad news," he said.

The former Nazi scientist felt cold terror creep through him, fearing it had to do with his family. "What is it?" he asked at last.

"I contacted all my sources," he said. "There's no way I can get you any new false papers in time. It would be at least two weeks and with people on your tail, we cannot wait that long. If we are going to get you on a train to Switzerland, we will have to do it using your real name."

"But surely I'm on the watch list," protested Heinz. "I'll be arrested immediately."

"Not necessarily," said Otto, a little grin creeping across his features. "There are many Nazis still wanted, and respectfully, my friend, you're hardly at the top. Besides, I may be able to sneak you on the train."

"How on earth could you do that?" asked Heinz.

Aafke looked up from the dishes. "He's invisible," she said.

She's as mad as he is. "I suppose there's not much of a choice," said Heinz. And it didn't matter. *If they've tracked me they may know who is protecting me, and that would lead them here.* "If you think there's some way you can sneak me into Switzerland, then we'll simply have to go and see what happens."

"Indeed," said Otto. "I've already called ahead and reserved our tickets."

"You called ahead?" said Heinz. "Why would you do that? That gives them more time to check my name against any list they have."

Otto shook his head. "The easiest way through any problem is to act natural. Only a lunatic would reserve tickets in advance if he was a fugitive of justice. Why look at reserved tickets carefully? It's the people coming in to buy them at the last minute that might be trying to sneak through. Besides, your name is relatively common. There's no reason we should suppose anyone would take you for who you really are."

"Listen to Otto," said Aafke, nodding her head and smiling up at her husband. "He knows everything."

Heinz was certain about two things. One, Otto did not know everything. Two, he would assuredly be caught at the train station. But what other choice did he have? He just wondered how everything would come together. His journey into darkness was about to begin. "When do we leave?" he asked at last.

"I got tickets for tomorrow afternoon."

"Why not tonight?" asked Heinz. "If we are taking a risk, why not take it now?"

"And make me lose the chance to spend the night with my children and my beautiful Aafke?" said Otto. "I think not, little scientist." He pointed at a door. "There's a bedroom for you."

"But I'm not tired," said Heinz.

"It's family time. The little doctor must sleep."

Aafke looked at him, nodding her head. "Go to bed now, tiny man," she said.

Heinz stood up, a rejoinder on his lips. But he'd seen and done too much today. He stumbled into the bedroom, closing the door behind him. He got into bed and turned off the lights, staring at the ceiling, listening to the laughter in the next room. But sleep wouldn't come.

Chapter 15

A Royal Welcome

Wednesday, October 13, 1948
8:18 p.m.
Bavaria, Germany

The men rushed forward, pistols at the ready. Sara reached reflexively for her pistol, but she'd left it on the kitchen counter and it was out of reach. "Max!" she shouted in vain, for there was nothing he could do. She was seized with iron hands and a hood was thrown roughly over her head. She heard Max shouting and trying to resist. There was a sound of something hard thudding against flesh and bone, and all was quiet.

Hands grabbed her arms and she was violently jerked to her feet. She was half walked, half dragged out of the cottage. Her bare feet stung as they pulled her through the snow. She was tossed into the seat of some sort of vehicle and then shoved into position. Men moved into seats on both sides of her, wedging her tightly in. She heard an engine fire up and then the car lurched into motion. Her body shook. She called out for Max again, but a harsh voice warned her into silence.

The car rumbled along for a long time, then stopped. When it started again the ride was smooth. She realized they must be on the highway. She wondered where they were being taken and why they hadn't simply shot them in the cottage. She thought about torture, something she was not sure she could endure. Odessa must have many former Nazi interrogators, and she knew full well what she might endure at their hands. As for Max, she had to pray they did not know he was a Jew. If they did, she couldn't imagine what they might do to him.

Calm. She couldn't think about these things. She strained her ears, listening for any snippet of conversation—or just any clue that the car might make as it moved along. But there was nothing. The men weren't talking and the car movement simply confirmed what she already knew, that they'd returned to the highway. If Max was in the car with her, she had no indication. She wondered if they'd killed him in the cottage, and she was the only survivor of their little group. If so, the pressure to obtain information from her would be immense . . .

The car ride seemed to take hours. Of course, there was no way to gauge the time. She was trying to steel herself, preparing for what would come. How could this organization operate like this, inside of a democratic nation? But she knew the answer only too well. There were plenty of Germans who resented the new government and the occupation by the Americans. They were ready, in secret, to give money, lodging, and more, to Odessa—a group they saw as freedom fighters.

The vehicle slowed and turned onto what sounded like a gravel road. It was bumpier again and the car proceeded slowly. She felt like they were proceeding up an incline, and she swayed to the left and right as the road curved. The vehicle lurched to a stop but the engine continued to idle. Long minutes passed, perhaps another half hour. She heard harsh voices, and hands grabbed her, tearing her from the car and setting her on her feet. She was led along a crunching pathway, which must have been gravel, for a while and then down a long set of stairs—

probably into a basement, she realized. A door opened and then slammed shut behind her.

They continued along what must have been a long corridor. The ground was hard and cold on her feet, like concrete. She heard a door open to her left and she was led that way and then pushed down onto a hard chair. Her hands reached out and gripped the sides. It was made of wood. The hood was ripped from her head. Her eyes squinted in the brilliant light she suddenly found herself facing. She looked around. Max was sitting next to her, his eyes blinking as he tried to grasp his surroundings. There was a bruise on his right temple—likely the thudding sound she'd heard in the cottage. He looked over at her, a grim smile on his face. She was surprised to feel relief. Whatever they were about to endure, at least they would be together.

The door opened behind them and they heard footsteps. A middle-aged man with short-cropped graying hair limped across the room and sat down across from them. He was wearing civilian clothes but he had the bearing of a military man. He reached inside his brown suit coat and retrieved a package of cigarettes. The man drew a cigarette out and lit it, inhaling deeply. He didn't offer them one or speak—he merely stared at the two of them across the way.

"Talk," he said finally, taking another puff.

"Who are you?" asked Sara, knowing the futility of the question.

"Talk."

"I work for the US government," she said, hoping that would mean something to this man. "For the Office of Public Affairs. I'm here in Bavaria assisting Mr. Portnoy here to try to reunite with some of his family."

"Well, you told a half-truth at least," the man said at last. "You work for the US government—but you're not here visiting family. You're trying to catch Heinz Hoffman—and you've bungled the job. Isn't that correct?"

"How can you know that?" asked Max.

"We know everything," said the man. "You were fools to come here. And you've paid the price for it."

"That's enough of that," said a new voice behind them. "You're scaring our guests, Jacob—and with no good reason."

A figure stepped around the table. He looked to be in his late seventies. He had gray hair and a closely cropped moustache. He was thin but looked strong, even for his age. "I must apologize to you," the man said. "You are among friends here. I am Crown Prince Rupprecht of the royal House of Wittelsbach," he said, his eyes showing kindness.

Sara was shocked. "Your Majesty," she said, not sure if that was the correct title for him. Max bowed his head.

"Don't worry about all of that," said Rupprecht, waving his hand. "You've been through enough already tonight. Jacob, why on earth did you bring them down here? And look at their feet! What were you thinking?" The prince turned back to them. "You must forgive Jacob," he said. "He's very protective of me and we've learned not to trust anyone. Please, go with him and he'll make sure you can have a bath and a change of clothes. When you're done, I'll meet you in the dining room. I'll have the kitchen throw something together. It's rather late and I'm afraid they won't be in much of a mood for cooking, but we'll get something together for you."

"But we've so many questions," said Sara.

"I know, my dear, and I'll have answers for you. But for now, please make yourself more comfortable. When you're ready, we'll have a long talk."

Sara and Max were led out of the room by Jacob. The man still would not look at them and he seemed less than pleased that they were being led into the comfortable part of wherever it was they were. As they climbed out of the basement, they entered what looked to be the servants' facilities. A huge kitchen gave way to smaller rooms and offices. A few bleary-eyed women were scurrying about, taking down food from a pantry and from a huge built-in refrigerator.

"This way," said Jacob, ignoring the commotion around them. They took another flight of stairs with a door at the top. When Jacob opened this door, Sara gave out a gasp. They entered the most beautiful room she'd ever seen. The ceilings must have been thirty feet high. The space was enormous, with marble floors. The walls were filled with works of original art, bordered by gilded frames. Jacob continued on, stopping once to glare at Sara and Max, who had paused at the door. He gave a firm jerk of his head to indicate they should continue following him. They made their way through the room and out into what looked like an entryway. To their right, a huge staircase, twenty feet wide with red carpet, led to the next level. Jacob led them up the stairs. At the top, a man and woman waited. Jacob gestured for Max to follow the man, and pointed at Sara to follow the woman, who was dressed in a maid's outfit.

The maid led Sara in the opposite direction, down a long corridor of cherrywood paneling. At the end of the hallway, the maid opened a door to her left, leading Sara into a large bedroom with a four-poster bed. There were fresh cut flowers and a table with a large mirror. At the other end of the room a door led into a bathroom from which steam was wafting. Although she was traumatized from the day, and was still uncertain if they were in danger, the thought of immersing herself in hot water was irresistible. She hurried forward, realizing in that moment as fear began to ebb just how cold and sore she was. The maid looked around, assuring that Sara had everything, then politely excused herself and closed the door.

Sara took off her tattered, dirty dress. Her legs were cut and bruised. She lowered herself into the tub; the water was so hot she almost couldn't take it, but she sank inch by inch, letting her body adjust until she was finally resting against the bottom. Steam was filling the room. She took a deep breath, leaning back until her head was resting against the back of the porcelain tub. She closed her eyes, taking a deep breath. Images flashed before her eyes. She saw again Karl's head explode in a misty cloud of scarlet as his body slowly toppled to the snow. She felt the frozen snow on her legs as she cradled Max. She fought those images down, giving in to the bath. The hot water soothed and relaxed her. She took some soap and washed herself thoroughly. After a time, there was a knock at the door. The maid came in with a towel and a new dress and stockings that were more or less her size. She left again and Sara let the water out of the tub. Drying herself with the towel, she dressed and did her best to fix her hair. Twenty minutes later, the maid arrived again to bring her to dinner.

Sara was led downstairs and through several rooms. Again, she was awestruck by the ornate decorations, the tapestries and portraits. Finally, they arrived at a dining room. The table must have measured a hundred feet in length. Dozens of mahogany chairs lined each side. At the far end, Max was already seated. The table was set for three. Max was dressed in a new suit and looked as handsome as ever. He rose when she appeared and he hazarded a smile, although she couldn't miss the deep sorrow in his eyes. She walked down the long table and took the seat opposite him. They seemed to be alone.

"Are we safe here?" she whispered, looking around.

He reached across the table, taking her hands. "There's no way to know for certain, my dear. But when we were captured, I thought we were dead, or worse. I don't know if they'd bathe and feed us before the torturing began. Still, Prince Rupprecht has a reputation for—"

"I trust you're feeling better," said the prince, stepping into the room from a door near where they were sitting. They both rose and Sara attempted a curtsey, which she feared she performed terribly. "Enough of that," said Rupprecht, waving them away. "We're long past all of that here."

Several servants entered, bringing trays of food. They were served cold pheasant with potatoes, a hot soup, and some bread. Sara wanted to ask questions, but she was famished and

Max seemed to feel the same. She dug into her dish. She had no idea how to eat properly before a prince, but she at least tried to control herself and forced herself to take small bites, chewing each one subtly before she moved to the next. Rupprecht sat and watched them closely, sipping away at some red wine. He kept encouraging them to eat more until Sara was positively stuffed. She finally waved the plate away and the servants cleared the table, filling up their wineglasses before they departed.

"Is there anything else I can get you?" the crown prince inquired. They both shook their heads. "Well then, I would love to hear your story."

Max spoke up, telling about their shop and explaining that it was vandalized, although he did not reveal the anti-Jewish details. He told about Sara and her department's assistance, and the offer to fly him and his brother to Munich to assist them in finding friends who might provide them financial assistance to get back on their feet.

Rupprecht listened carefully, not interrupting until Max had finished. Then he looked at the two of them and smiled kindly. "I apologize," he said. "I've expected you to trust me with your true story, but of course you have no reason to do so. Perhaps if I tell you my own story of the war, that will help.

"After the First World War, as you know, Germany became a republic and we lost our position as the Kings of Bavaria. Bavaria soon fell into political chaos and it was in my own Bavaria—my own beloved Munich—that Hitler and his Nazi party began to rise. Hitler courted me from the beginning, offering a return to monarchy and regional control in Bavaria if I would but back him for national power in greater Germany."

Rupprecht sighed deeply and took another drink of wine. "I must admit I desired this greatly—the return of my position, I should say. But I could never consent to assist Herr Hitler. He was a crazed little monster and I could tell so from the start.

Hitler never forgot that I spurned him. After the war started in 1939, I was forced to flee to Italy. My wife and children were seized late in the war by the Nazis while they were living in Hungary. They were sent to a concentration camp at Sachsenhausen and eventually to Dachau. I had no news of them for months and feared the worst, but by some miracle, they survived and they were freed at the end of the war and returned to me."

He finished his wine. "As you can see, my friends, I am no ally of the Nazis or former Nazis, or whatever they are calling themselves these days. So, my friends, I would love to hear your real story. I know you are Jewish, Herr Portnoy, as was your brother. I know you came to Munich hunting Heinz Hoffman for some reason. I know you contacted our illustrious citizen Adolf Alderbricht at his beer hall, and what he demanded. I also know about your visit there this morning and what transpired. As a matter of fact, that event is what brought this entire affair to my attention."

"How so?" asked Sara.

"Well, your friend here and his brother created quite a stir. Jewish lads breaking into a house and beating a prominent former Nazi. Word spread quickly and Odessa mobilized to handle the problem—if you know what I mean. Fortunately, one of their members is what you might call a double agent. He reported the details to me and I sent a few of my retainers to try to rescue you. In fact, I understand there were two cars starting to turn down the little road toward your cottage when my men arrived on the scene. Thankfully, the Odessa team turned around and retreated quickly. Fearing the worst, Jacob and his men approached the cabin with guns drawn and kicked down the door. I'm sure they gave you a nasty shock, but we had to be certain." He leaned forward. "That should answer some questions for you, but you still haven't told me the truth. Why are you hunting Heinz Hoffman?"

Max still looked as if he wasn't going to answer. But Sara had watched the prince carefully while he told his story. She'd heard of his troubles during the war, and she believed they could trust him. "Tell him, Max," she said at last. "I think we must."

Max looked at her with a questioning expression. She smiled at him, willing him to believe in her. He studied her for a few moments and then turned to Rupprecht. "I'll tell you what you want to know. The whole truth."

An hour passed in the dining room while Max told his story. Rupprecht listened with rapt attention, interrupting only now and again to clarify some detail or another. When Max was finally finished, the prince took a deep breath, sat back in his chair, and drained the rest of his wine.

"Your story has moved me," he said. "Of course I've heard so many tragic tales from the war—but hardly any worse than yours. To be frank, I've known that Hoffman was skulking around in Bavaria for some time, but I'd been rather content for him to just slip away. I know his family—at least slightly. They've lived in Bavaria for a long time and his ancestors served as minor retainers to the family, before his family fell on hard times. I knew he'd done something in the sciences for the SS during the war, but I didn't know it was nuclear research. That by itself doesn't add up to much—that was a legitimate war aim for Germany, as it was for the United States and England—but the slave labor is another thing. And worse, to send everyone to a concentration camp when the work was no longer useful." He shook his head. "I'll never understand what happened to my people when they let a powerful man convince them to allow hate to take the place of reason."

"I know I'm not the only one who suffered," said Max. "Sara here did, you did, everyone was scarred by this war one way or another. But there was something beyond the normal horrors of war that the Nazis did to so many people—particularly the

Jews—and Hoffman was part of that. He should be brought to justice. Although now I'm afraid we've lost our chance. I doubt he'll come above ground again."

"Perhaps he won't," said Rupprecht. "But perhaps he will. I've made some inquiries. If he or Otto contact Odessa, I'll hear about it. I can also furnish you with money and a vehicle. Unfortunately, I cannot lend you any of my people. As much as I might be tempted, we can't afford to get involved in this sort of thing, as you might imagine."

"There is something else you can do for me," said Max.

"What is that?" asked the prince.

"Bring my brother's body here," he said. "Make sure he has a proper burial."

"We've already taken care of that," said Rupprecht. "Jacob brought the body back. Your brother is nearby at a local funeral home. We can make sure there is a proper burial and a marker, here on the estate, or you can direct me where you would like him to be laid to rest."

"That's very kind of you," said Max. "I'd like to think about that a little. Perhaps when this is all over, I can let you know."

"And if—"

"And if we're killed as well?" asked Max. "Well then, please just do what you think is best."

"I will," said Rupprecht. "Do you want to see the body again?" he asked. "I've had him cleaned up."

"That's very kind of you," said Max. "Perhaps in the morning."

"Just let my people know," said Rupprecht. "For now, I'm sure both of you would like to get some sleep. It's near two in the morning already. We'll break our fast at ten tomorrow, to give you, and of course our overworked staff, a chance to rest."

"Thank you so much for everything," said Sara.

The prince rang a bell and a servant appeared, leading Max and Sara back upstairs to their individual bedrooms. When Sara was alone again, she sat down on the bed and let the tears wash over her. The day before had been the most intense of her life. She had felt genuine terror at the gunshots and feared the sniper was going to kill her and Max as well. When nothing happened, she'd feared frostbite. Then the abduction and the prospect of a horrible ordeal of torture. She wondered how Max was doing. He'd dealt with worse, and she felt a tinge of guilt that she was feeling sorry for herself. Just then, there was a light knock at her door. She rose and stepped cautiously over, leaning her head against the wood. "Who is it?" she asked.

"It's me," said Max.

Feeling a new surge of emotions, she opened the door.

"May I come in?" he asked.

She opened the door farther and he stepped into the room. She closed the door behind her. Max looked over the furnishings and whistled lightly. "Well, they don't want for much in this place, do they?"

"Do you know what this place is called?" she asked.

He nodded. "It's called the Schloss Leutstetten, it's just twenty miles or so outside of Munich. We are fortunate we were brought here, and that Rupprecht's men scared off Odessa. We might have met our end out there in the snow after all."

He was standing close to her. He'd put some cologne on and the scent stirred her. She had difficulty concentrating on his words. "Are you all right?" she asked at last.

"Of course not," he said, taking a step closer to her. "But it gives me great comfort that Prince Rupprecht has taken care of Karl—that he will be interred in an honorable place. I'll have somewhere to visit—to mark his life. If we survive this thing. I can't say the same for my family."

"You did the right thing telling him," she said. "I feel we can trust him."

Max shrugged. "Time will tell. It is encouraging that he was in opposition to the Nazis during the war, and his family was persecuted. That would seem to make him an ally. Although

I'm sure he's playing his own game now. We can trust him to a point—but we must be wary."

"Is that why you came to see me?" she asked, her voice trembling a little.

He smiled at her. "Partially. But then there was this also." He stepped forward and kissed her. She resisted for a moment and then fell into his arms, kissing him passionately in return. "We never finished our interrupted business from the hotel," he whispered. He led her over and laid her down on the bed. He reached over and turned out the light, letting the darkness fill them. He was tender and loving. She tried to keep her grip on reality but she'd been so lonely the last year—she allowed herself to be swept up in the moment. For tonight at least, there was just her and Max.

Sara woke up the next morning feeling rested and more alive than she had felt in a long time. Max was gone. He'd prudently snuck out sometime in the early morning to return to his room. But his smell was still on the sheets and she wrapped herself in them, closing her eyes and remembering their time together. After a while there was a knock at the door, and the maid from the night before was there, announcing that breakfast would be served in a half hour. Sara took another luxurious bath and put on the dress and stockings from the night before. There was also a warm wool jacket and gloves. She brought these down with her, assuming that when their meal was over, they would be departing.

Max was already there when she arrived. He gave her a knowing grin and she blushed as several staff members looked away. She was certain there were no true secrets in this house that never truly slept, and she felt a little embarrassed at their reactions.

Prince Rupprecht appeared and they were served breakfast. He inquired about their night's sleep and Sara thought there was a twinkle in his eye as he asked that question. They worked through some pastries and tea, with light conversation. When the plates were cleared, Rupprecht asked them if they were ready to continue their journey.

"Have you found out anything about Heinz's whereabouts?" Max asked.

"As a matter of fact, I have," said Rupprecht. "At least I've found something out. It may be nothing. It seems that after Otto and Heinz fled the scene near the cottage, they were spotted at Otto's home."

"How would you know that?" asked Sara.

"He lives in a cluster of houses at the end of a long road just off the highway," explained Rupprecht. "It's almost a compound really. Full of ex–Skorzeny commandos. But not everyone in that group has adhered to the Nazi ways—even if they seem to have. I'd put the word out to my network, you see, and a friend in that compound telephoned about their arrival. That got me thinking," said Rupprecht. "Otto knows that Heinz is being hunted. He may not know who or why—but he knows this package won't be delivered quietly. That makes a man nervous and apt to move quickly. I contacted the American authorities and the West German police. They are putting up roadblocks and watching the borders. But I realized they might try to slip through on a train. I called around to some of the stations and discovered to my surprise that there is a Herr Hoffman listed as a passenger out of Kaufbeuren to Switzerland at noon tomorrow."

"Would he be crazy enough to reserve a ticket in his own name?" asked Max.

"It may just be a coincidence," said Rupprecht. "If Otto is in a rush, he may have made a mistake here. He would know that travel by train is a tricky business; if there's a careful search it could be more dangerous than crossing the border by car. But by the same token not every train is checked, and Otto would know this too. It's too cold to cross the border over the mountains by foot right now. He has to get there by land or air. I think there's a good chance this is your man."

Max slammed his hand on the table. "It's him, I know it." He looked at his watch. "Is there time for us to get there?"

"Plenty of time," said Rupprecht. "And I have even better news for you."

"What's that?" asked Sara.

"Only that we've been reunited," came a new voice.

Sara felt the chill running down her spine.

"The American authorities were delighted to hear from me," said Rupprecht. "I understand your commander had been inadvertently left behind. I was able to locate Mr. Scott and bring him here."

Sara looked up to see the smiling face of Jeffrey standing at the far end of the table.

"What a lovely reunion," said Jeffrey. He looked at his watch. "Shall we get started? We have so much to talk about."

Chapter 16
Dead Americans

Thursday, October 14, 1948
2:45 a.m.
Bavaria, Germany

Heinz tossed and turned the entire night. His room was too stuffy, for one thing, and his mind raced about tomorrow. He knew it was going to be *the day*. The day when everything came together. He thought of Elsie and Hannah and wondered where they were and if they were safe. He was thankful they were captives of the Americans and not the Russians. He both admired and sneered at the softness of the Americans. He knew only too well what would have happened to his family if the Russians had captured them.

The hours passed slowly as his mind imagined what today would bring. He hoped all would go well, but there were no guarantees. Mistakes could be made and he might end up dead — particularly with this lumbering, unpredictable oaf by his side. How much could he trust that the day would play out as was planned?

Finally, the first inklings of dawn crept around the shutters, casting a pale light into his room. Not long after, he heard the pitter-patter of little feet and the sound of laughter in the other room.

He stumbled out of bed and opened the door to find Otto already up and fully dressed, with both children on his lap. He was reading them a story out of a fairy-tale book and they were listening with rapt attention. Otto used all the voices in the story, including the high-pitched squeaking of a princess and the deep rumblings of a monster who held her captive. Heinz stood at the door watching and listening, his eyes filling with tears—he knew it would be so very long before he would see his little girl again, no matter what happened today.

Aafke was in the kitchen preparing a breakfast for them, whistling softly to herself. She was a lovely creature and Heinz couldn't help thinking of his wife doing the same for him and little Hannah in their tiny apartment at the monastery. Strange, he thought, the happiest family times of his life weren't in fancy villas like those he possessed during the war, but instead the time that he'd spent at the monastery in their tiny apartment, in tranquil peace with his family.

They ate breakfast soon after, both children on Otto's lap as he fed them spoonfuls of oatmeal.

"What time is your train today?" Aafke asked as they were nearing the end of their morning meal.

"It's at noon," said Otto, checking his watch.

"It's nearly ten now," she said. "You can spend a little more time with us."

"Unfortunately we must go soon," said Otto. "I'll want to look around before I let our little doctor go. Do you have your papers, Heinz?"

The former scientist nodded. "The papers in my name. Much good that will do me. They'll likely seize me at the door."

"We shall see," said Otto. "I think all will go well." He patted his boy on the head and set him down on the ground. "In some ways I envy you, Heinz. You have quite an adventure ahead of you."

"As long as all goes well," said Heinz.

They packed up their things a few minutes later and Otto stepped outside to warm up the car, returning a few minutes later. Otto kissed his wife goodbye and the children rushed forward, hanging on to his legs.

"Don't go, Daddy!" they chimed in unison.

"Don't you worry, you two," he said, laughing. "I'll be back by dinner. But if I'm not," he said, wagging a finger at his son.

"Then I'm the man of the family until you return," his son finished.

Heinz saw a flash of worry on Aafke's face. He realized that she knew exactly what Otto did for a living—and perhaps worried that one day, her husband would never return again. She turned to Heinz. "I wish you the best of fortune," she said. "And that you will be reunited with your family soon."

"Thank you," said Heinz. "But even if all goes well, it will be at least a year or two before I see them."

"I was parted from Otto during the war," she said. "For almost a year. And I was newly pregnant. It was hard, but look at us now. Don't you worry, Heinz, you will see them again."

He squeezed her hands. He hoped she was right.

Otto gave his wife a final kiss and they were soon back on the road. Heinz saw that Otto had placed chains on the tires sometime that morning and they were able to drive up to the top of the steep hill with no problems. They reached the highway a few minutes later and after Otto stopped and removed the chains again, they turned and soon were motoring their way toward Kaufbeuren.

"Your family is lovely," said Heinz. "It reminds me of my own."

Otto smiled. "*Ja*, Aafke is a treasure," he said. "Without her and the children I . . . let us just say I am glad they are in my life."

"It seems strange," said Heinz, and then he stopped himself.

"*Ja?*"

"Well. Just strange to see you with them, acting that way, on the same day that you killed a man." He looked over at Otto and he could see the flush in the man's face. "I'm sorry, I presume too much."

"No, it is all right that you said that. You must understand, Heinz. Killing is my job," he explained. "For me, it is like delivering the mail. When the day is done the mailman returns to his family and is a postman no more. The same is true for me. Still," he said, "there are times when it is very hard."

"What about those Americans? Was that hard?" Heinz blurted the words out before he could stop himself. He thought he might be on very dangerous ground now, but he was so curious about the rumors.

"What Americans?"

"Well, I've heard the stories about—"

"*Ach, ja*, the tale that I executed a squad of captured Americans? Is that the story you're asking about?"

"Is the story true?" asked Heinz.

"Does it matter?"

"Perhaps you're right," said Heinz. "I'm sorry I brought it up."

"I'll tell you about it," said Otto. "It was a few days into what the Americans call the Battle of the Bulge. I was part of Skorzeny's commando group behind the enemy lines. I was dressed in an American uniform and I'd been trained to speak English fluently. My orders were to infiltrate a gasoline depot thirty miles behind enemy lines. It was one of the main refueling stations for their panzers. Their tanks, you know? I was about halfway there, walking along through the woods, when I was stopped by a squad of American soldiers. They'd apparently heard about our operations and the sergeant was skeptical. He started quizzing me about Hollywood actors and actresses and some nonsense about baseball. I knew the answers, of course. I'd prepared for my role.

"I thought I was in the clear, but then to my surprise the sergeant detained me. Apparently, I made one mistake. You see, I trained with an expert on the English language from England instead of the United States, and when I told them my Jeep was out of petrol he grew suspicious."

"I don't understand," said Heinz.

"They don't say *petrol* in America, they say *gasoline*. Before I knew it they had me surrounded."

"What did you do?" asked Heinz.

"Well, I only had my one pistol with eight rounds. There were twelve of them. I drew my weapon out slowly to turn over to the sergeant but then I flipped it on him, killing him and the man next to him in two shots.

"There were still ten of them though, and I only had six shots left. I rolled forward, landing on my feet again in a crouched position near the sergeant. I ripped a grenade off his chest and fired with my pistol at the same time, killing another one. I rolled to my right, barely missing a bullet fired at me. I pulled the pin out of the grenade and tossed it, firing a moment later and killing another chap. The grenade killed four more.

"I took off running into the woods. There were still four more GIs chasing me. I took two rounds in the back and hit the ground. I played dead until they surrounded me, then I flipped over and shot the last four with my pistol. I was sure they would kill me before I finished, but they just stood there with their eyes wide-open as if I was a ghost, and I dispatched them one, two, three, four. The last fellow turned just as I shot him, and I only wounded him. He ran off, screaming for help. I knew I had to get out of there before I was captured or killed, but I was losing blood fast. I lost consciousness."

"What happened to you?" asked Heinz, electrified by the story.

"I was fortunate," said Otto. "The one wounded man who ran must have died somewhere else, or he was too terrified to return. I was picked up by American medics a few hours later.

They didn't know who I was. I was in American uniform so they took me to their hospital and operated on me. I was allowed to recover there, and they had no idea I was one of the famous Skorzeny infiltrators."

"Weren't you worried they would catch you out?" asked Heinz, amazed at the story.

"*Ja*," said Otto, nodding. "I assumed at some point they would start asking questions. But I was there for a month and had aroused no suspicions. But I knew my luck could only last so long. The Battle of the Bulge was long over by this time and the Americans were advancing rapidly into Germany. One morning, a kindly nurse told me she'd received word that I would be taken back to England the next day. So, in the middle of the night I managed to take some food and a weapon and escaped. I made my way back to the front lines posing as a replacement soldier. A few nights later I escaped into the forest, dodging patrols until I found the German lines.

"That one American who survived had told his story about me though, claiming I captured them and then shot them in cold blood. That was the end of the war for me. I guess my own people wanted to make an example of me—because we were losing the war and they knew the Americans would control their destiny soon. But Skorzeny never abandoned me, nor did my mates."

"Then the rumors about you are wrong," said Heinz. "You didn't kill American prisoners at all."

"Yes."

"Why didn't you clear your name?"

"Ah, my little scientist. Rumors have a power of their own. I'm 'The Demon' now, a killer of prisoners and someone not to be trifled with. That has a value all on its own."

"What's that ahead?" asked Heinz, looking up the highway.

Otto slammed on his brakes, slowing down, but it was already too late. There was a police vehicle parked at an angle, blocking the road. Two German police officers were standing outside, pistols at the ready. Otto hesitated for a brief moment, then pressed his foot to the pedal again and moved toward the roadblock.

"What are you doing?" demanded Heinz.

"It's too late," said Otto. "They've already seen us."

"But they'll arrest us," he said.

"It's difficult to say what they are here for," said Otto. "This may have nothing to do with us." They pulled up to the barrier and Otto stopped the car, casually rolling down his window as if he was asking for directions. One of the police officers stood several yards away, his pistol aimed inside the car. The second officer stepped up, looking at the two of them.

"I need your papers immediately," the policeman demanded. "We are looking for Heinz Hoffman."

Chapter 17
The Station

Thursday, October 14, 1948
9:17 a.m.
Bavaria, Germany

Sara was stunned as she was led back upstairs by the maid to collect her things. She wanted desperately to speak with Max alone, but Jeffrey accompanied them to the top of the stairs and then perched himself at the landing, preventing any opportunity for her to consult with Max.

She quickly gathered her things along with an additional set of shoes and stockings provided by the prince. He'd also given her a suitcase to carry her things. When she was finished, she sat on the edge of the bed, collecting her thoughts and wondering what Jeffrey's arrival meant to their mission. After a few minutes, she realized she would have to return, so she stepped out of the room with her things and back into the corridor.

Max was already present at the top of the stairs, standing with his back to Jeffrey. His face was red and she could see the anger and frustration in his eyes, but there was no way for them to talk privately at this point. The three of them went back down the stairs together. Rupprecht was waiting at the bottom with some of his staff. Sara realized she could not show her emotions now and she did her best to compose herself, stepping up to the crown prince, who was oblivious to the chaos he had inadvertently caused.

"I want to thank you for everything you've done for us," Sara said. "If you would not have intervened, I'm sure we wouldn't have survived yesterday."

The prince smiled and bowed slightly. "Think nothing of it," he said. "I was glad to help out and I wish you the very best in bringing Dr. Hoffman to the justice he deserves."

Without further ceremony they departed the palace. Sara turned around in shock and amazement at the ornate architecture of the structure, the bright yellow contrasting with the red roof and white windows, all surrounded by a gray stone wall.

A car was waiting for them and Jeffrey gestured for Sara to drive. Max took the front seat and Jeffrey stepped into the back. Sara started the vehicle, her hands pressed tensely against the wheel.

"At least we aren't in that ridiculous Jeep anymore," said Max.

"Yes, you saw to that," said Jeffrey.

"Where are we going?" Sara asked.

"Ah yes," said Jeffrey in a silky voice. "I wondered when you would ask that." His voice lilted musically—he was obviously enjoying himself immensely now that he had caught up to them. "I was thinking the airport might be an appropriate destination. How about you?"

"You can't mean it," said Sara. "Jeffrey, we know where he is. At least I think we do. This is the chance to get him."

"Why on earth would I want to let you do that?" asked Jeffrey. "After everything you put me through. Imagine my embarrassment to be left behind, in direct violation of your orders."

"It's my fault, not hers," said Max. "I demanded that she take me without you."

Jeffrey laughed. "Nice try, Maximilian. You should've at least had the good sense to blame your brother. He was the one without a sense of humor."

"Don't you dare talk about Karl," said Max.

"I'll do that and more," said Jeffrey. "You're both deep in the stew. Confiscating government property. Disobeying direct orders from me. At the best, Sara, you'll lose your job and nothing more. But stealing that Jeep is a crime, and I wouldn't doubt it if the two of you ended up spending some time in jail, which you both richly deserve."

"Do what you want," said Sara. "But we can't go back to the airport. You have to give us the opportunity to try to catch Hoffman."

"I suppose I might consider that," said Jeffrey. "However, I do have one or two conditions."

"And what are those?" asked Sara, a prick of fear boiling up inside her.

"First, when we capture Hoffman, I will be given full credit," he said. "Even if Max identifies him, that will be left out of the official report. You will tell the authorities that after Karl's death you wanted to return to the airport and home, giving up the mission, but that I talked you out of it. You will both praise me in the official report and indicate that I continued our mission over your collective objections, and that the mission would have failed except for my direct intervention."

"And what if we don't?" asked Max.

"If you don't agree, then we are heading home now. And just in case you consider breaking your word later, it will be my word against yours, and on top of that I have absolute evidence of you taking the Jeep and its destruction at the cottage. This can be verified by Prince Rupprecht and his men. You will be prosecuted for theft and destruction of US government property, and given your involvement in that action, I hardly think they'll take your word over mine—a prominent US citizen with connections at the highest levels of the government."

"You're a real bastard, Jeffrey, do you know that?" said Sara.

He bowed slightly. "Call me what you will," he said. "What I truly am is a man moving up in the world and you're not going to stop it. If you do everything I've said I will recommend you keep your position at the agency and I'll assure there are no charges pressed related to the Jeep. We will chalk it up as a mission expense. Who knows," he said, "perhaps after that incompetent Varberg is fired, I will take his spot and we can continue to work together." He moved his hand back and forth on her shoulder. "Wouldn't that be a delight."

"Get your dirty hands off her," said Max, reaching up and ripping Jeffrey's hand away.

"Violence? That seems like the wrong decision." Jeffrey shook his head in mock disgust. "I guess you've decided to go home after all."

"I'm not going to let you touch her," said Max, his voice shaking. "Whatever the consequences."

"Well, that settles it then," said Jeffrey. "Sara, if you'd be so kind as to take us back to the airport."

"No," she said. "We will agree to your terms, but I have a condition of my own. You won't touch me again."

Jeffrey laughed. "Fine," he said. "I'll accept that. You've been soiled now, so I've lost interest." He unfolded his map and started scanning it. "Start driving," he ordered. "I'll give you directions once we hit the highway again. Make sure you follow them for once."

Sara drove them away from the palace, her hands shaking on the wheel. She forced herself to remain as calm as she could. A frosty silence settled into the car. She tried to make eye contact with Max, but he was staring ahead, as if refusing to look at her. The only person who vocalized anything during the drive was Jeffrey, who periodically shouted directions from the back seat.

Sara was fuming. Still, they were now so close to achieving their objective. She had to get Max to Hoffman. After that she would deal with Jeffrey one way or another.

It took over an hour of tense driving to finally arrive at the station in Kaufbeuren. The station was a modern structure with four tracks, an island platform, and two side platforms. Sara was surprised by the number of vehicles parked out front and the busy to-and-fro of passengers entering and leaving the building. She had hoped this location, outside Munich, might be relatively quiet, which would allow for a much easier identification of Hoffman—assuming the man truly showed up and this wasn't merely a wild-goose chase.

"It certainly is busier than I anticipated," she said out loud. "Will we be able to find him here?"

"I don't see why not," said Jeffrey. "The authorities have already been alerted to apprehend Dr. Hoffman when he checks in. Failing that, we have our good friend Max here, who can identify him on the spot." Jeffrey checked his watch. "It's still more than an hour until he is supposed to check in." He shifted himself in the seat, resting his head against the window. He lowered his hat over his eyes. "Wake me in half an hour," he ordered. "And don't bother trying to plot against me. I'm a very light sleeper."

Sara and Max sat there in the cold and the quiet, searching each other's eyes. They tried to mouth some communication back and forth silently, but Sara could not read lips and Max seemed to be just as frustrated. Finally, he shook his head and reached out his hand, taking hers and giving her a squeeze and a comforting smile. They sat that way as the minutes ticked away, Sara watching the passengers entering the building and keeping an eye out for Hoffman. But she saw nobody who matched the man she'd glimpsed in the beer hall, nor his massive protector. She spotted a police officer walking along. He was twirling a baton and strolling along as if on a Sunday walk. She was surprised there were not more officers about, and she wondered what that meant, since the police were supposed to be on alert for the Nazi scientist.

Finally a half hour had passed and she nudged Jeffrey awake.

She wasn't sure if he'd really been asleep, but he made a great show of rubbing his eyes and yawning, checking his watch and inquiring if they had seen anything. When they didn't answer he stretched and then looked at the two of them. "Well, I suppose it's time we go. Time to assure my future," he said, chuckling to himself. "You two just remember our agreement and remember it well."

He opened the door and they had no choice but to follow him, the three of them stepping away from the car and into the station itself. The inside of the building was a clutter of chaos. A long line stretched back from a ticket office while others passed to and fro, heading to the restrooms or out onto the platform.

Sara was again surprised to see only a single police officer walking amidst the busy crowd. She wondered if there was a squad in the back somewhere, waiting for Heinz to show himself at the ticket counter. Jeffrey swaggered in front of him, marching right up to the police officer and barking at him in English. The officer only spoke German, and Sara was forced to step in so that he could be understood.

"I'm Jeffrey Scott with the US Department of Public Affairs," said Scott, flashing his ID into the officer's face. The German stared at him, waiting for Sara to finish her translation before he responded.

"So what?" said the officer.

Jeffrey huffed in obvious frustration. "But certainly, you were expecting me. I phoned ahead of time. Weren't you waiting for Heinz Hoffman?"

"For whom?" asked the officer.

"For Heinz bloody Hoffman!" shouted Jeffrey, annoyed now. "Good God, man, he's a wanted Nazi." Sara could see that while the officer might not speak English or at least was pretending not to, there were others around who did. They were now staring at Jeffrey, some with hostile looks on their faces.

"I don't think we should have this conversation here," whispered Sara, taking his arm.

"Nonsense," said Jeffrey. "This man is playing stupid with us. He probably wants the arrest to himself. I want to get to the bottom of this right now." He turned back to the German officer. "Now stop playing games, man. Surely you have been informed that Heinz Hoffman is heading this way and reserved a ticket at this very station."

"I have no idea what you're talking about," said the officer, looking down his nose at Jeffrey. "Perhaps you should check with the ticket office?"

"But this is a security issue!" said Jeffrey, exasperated. "The police should have been briefed!"

"It's not my job to hunt Nazis," said the officer, stifling a yawn. "My job is to keep order inside the station, which if you look around, you'll see is difficult enough. I suggest you check with each ticket station and leave me to my duty." With that, the officer deliberately turned his back to Jeffrey and strolled away, whistling an off-key tune.

"Fine!" said Jeffrey to the air, throwing his arms up in exasperation. He turned and strode toward the ticket office, barging up to the front of the line and interrupting the sole attendant. Sara hurried to catch up but she could already see the German behind the window pointing to the back of the line. Jeffrey was flashing his ID again, pointing it at anyone who happened to be nearby. However, the person behind the counter seemed entirely disinterested and kept gesturing for Jeffrey to join the back of the queue. Jeffrey, ignoring her, took several steps to the left and attempted to open a door into the ticket office. It was locked. He banged on the door several times but nobody answered. Finally, his face red in anger, he stormed to the back of the line.

"I've seen toddlers behave themselves better than he does," said Max, stepping up to Sara, who was standing a distance away from the line. He put his hand on her back.

She felt his touch, immediately calming down. She realized this was the first moment they had been together alone since Jeffrey surprised them this morning at breakfast.

"What are we going to do?" she whispered. "I can't let him get away with this. You deserve the credit for catching Hoffman," she said. "If you hadn't told us about him, Mr. Varberg would never have allowed this trip, and Jeffrey would've known nothing about it."

"It doesn't matter," said Max. "I don't need the credit. I just want Hoffman. Now more than ever."

She looked at him, taking his hands, ignoring the crowd around them. For a moment it was just her and him.

"Of course you do," said Sara. "For your brother. I'm so sorry, Max. There has been so much that has happened in the past twenty-four hours. I've been so insensitive to you."

"You have been nothing of the kind," responded Max. "Yesterday there was no time to do anything but survive. And then last night," he said, smiling, "we had better things to do."

She blushed. "I know, but we have to take time for Karl too."

"Don't worry about that right now," said Max. "There will be time enough to mourn him when this is over. For now, I just want to get Hoffman, whoever gets the credit."

"But what if we can't find him?" she said. "There's been no sign of him or of that monster Berg."

Max nodded. "But I'm not surprised about that. They would want to arrive late, just before the train arrives. Either that or they're staying well out of sight for now. I'm not giving up hope just yet, unless that young idiot over there scares the game away."

Sara glanced over at Jeffrey, who was now halfway up the line. He was stomping his feet and staring around impatiently, waving his arms at some woman behind him in line. His commotion was drawing the attention of the crowd. "Isn't there anything we can do about him?" she asked.

"Nothing I can think of right now," said Max. "Too bad he wasn't with us yesterday, perhaps the bullet would've found him instead."

"That would've been a blessing," said Sara. "Somebody needs to do something about him."

"Well, for now, despite his idiocy he managed to get us to this train station," said Max. "If we catch Hoffman, I'll forgive him. Hell, maybe I'd kiss him."

"Go ahead," said Sara, laughing. "Perhaps that would take his attention off me."

Jeffrey finally reached the front of the line again. He was shouting at the attendant. The woman must've understood English or been able to muddle through Jeffrey's German, because Sara was not summoned to translate. After a few minutes Jeffrey returned, his face pale.

"What is it?" asked Sara.

"It looks like we may be heading home after all," he said.

"What do you mean?" asked Max.

"His ticket was canceled."

"Canceled?" said Sara. "Was it in person or over the phone?"

"I have no idea," said Jeffrey. "But I'm not going to sit here and waste my time. Look," he said, gesturing toward the platform. "His ride is already here."

Even as he spoke the building began to rattle with the sound of the approaching train. Sara heard a whistle and the slow chugging of a steam engine, hissing and coughing as it slowed down for the station.

"There's still a chance he's here somewhere," said Sara. "We just need to keep our eyes sharp." But even as she said that, she knew the task was well-nigh impossible. As the train arrived the crowd sprung out of their seats and started to press in a mass jam toward the doors. There were hundreds of people, all facing away from them. Unless there was some way to delay the train and search each individual, she realized they weren't going to be able to spot him.

The crowd gradually sifted through the doors, onto the platform, and began boarding the train.

"Let's go," said Sara, unwilling to just give up without trying something.

"Sturm, get back here," demanded Jeffrey. but she ignored him.

"I'm with you," said Max as they pushed their way into the crowd. They were crammed in the back part of the mass still shoving its way toward the doors to the platform. They swarmed in the jumble for several minutes before they were able to push their way through and out onto the platform. Max pulled her aside and located a bench where they could climb up and look out over the crowd. Her eyes darted this way and that, searching for Hoffman or for *Der Dämon*. Max did the same. The minutes ticked by, the platform emptying until there were just a few people left. Soon a conductor walked up the platform, calling out for anyone else to board.

The train was gathering steam and the platform was clear except for a few passengers who had disembarked and were waiting for friends or family to arrive.

The train started to shift into motion. "Sturm, let's go!" shouted Jeffrey. The American had stepped out onto the platform and was staring at the two of them, his hands on his hips. He gestured at them impatiently to join him.

Sara didn't want to leave. But the train was already picking up speed. There was no point in waiting further. Max stepped down from the bench and turned to help her, an immense look of sadness creeping over his face.

"Max, I'm so sorry," said Sara.

"Don't worry about it, my dear," he said. "This is not the end." But the tremor in his voice told her something different.

"We've missed our best chance to find him," muttered Max, as if talking to himself.

"Something will come up," she said.

Max shook his head. "We don't have any other leads and he knows we are after him. Perhaps this is the end after all."

"I said let's go!" shouted Jeffrey, barking the order at them.

The doors behind the American opened and a figure sprinted through them, dressed in a suit and a gray striped fedora. The man rushed toward the train, running alongside it for a few moments before hopping onto the stairs into the space between carriages.

There was a sharp intake of breath from Sara.

"What is it?" asked Max.

"That was Hoffman."

Chapter 18
The Barricade

Thursday, October 14, 1948
11:20 a.m.
Bavaria, Germany

"I said I need your papers." The West German police officer leaned into the window, looking them both over. Heinz stared directly ahead, trying to take deep breaths and control his heart rate, which felt like it might soon explode out of his body.

Otto sat next to him in the driver's seat and appeared completely relaxed, lifting a ceramic mug and taking a last sip of tea.

"Put that down and give me your papers!" The officer's right hand moved down to rest on his holster.

Otto reached into his jacket and removed documents that he handed the officer. The policeman reviewed the papers for a moment, staring at the driver. "Otto Berg," said the officer. "That name rings a bell. Have I met you before?"

"I doubt it," said Otto. "I don't normally travel this far southwest."

"What are you doing here then?" asked the officer.

"Escorting my friend to the train station," the commando explained.

"Let me see your friend's papers," demanded the soldier. Otto nodded at Heinz, who reached for his papers, his hands trembling. Otto gave Heinz a reassuring nod and then handed the documents over to the policeman. The officer took the papers and glanced at the name.

"Get out of the car!" he demanded, fumbling for his pistol.

"Any chance you'll just let us go by?" the commando asked.

"Get out!"

Otto shook his head. With lightning speed his left arm flashed out and grasped the front of the officer's uniform; he whipped his arm back toward him and the man crashed into the car, his head cracking against the top of the window frame with a thud. The policeman's body sagged and Otto released him, as the body crumpled to the ground.

The second officer stared in wide-eyed surprise at Otto. He raised his pistol. "Out of the car!" he ordered.

Otto glanced at Heinz, shaking his head slightly. He reached down with his right hand, picked up the ceramic mug, and hurled it at the officer, using his left hand to open the car door at the same time. The mug hit the officer in the chest, and in the fraction of a moment that he flinched from the attack, Otto was out the door and charging him, crashing into the officer with his shoulder and bowling the man over. Otto fell with him, landing hard on the policeman. He placed his elbow on the officer's neck and pressed down. Heinz was horrified as he watched the man's legs kick and flail under him. The struggle lasted for long moments, and then he was still. Otto rose, dusted himself off, and returned to the vehicle.

"You killed him," Heinz said.

Otto shook his head. "No. He's asleep. He won't feel well when he wakes up though. Neither will his partner."

"But won't they alert the authorities when they wake up?"

"I would think so."

"Shouldn't we . . ." Heinz let the thought hang there in the car.

"*Nein*," said Otto.

"But we'll be caught."

"I don't think so," said the commando. "They'll be out for a while, and you'll be long gone by the time they wake up and get their bearings. Besides, I don't kill Germans. At least not for free."

"I'm sure Odessa will pay you more. You're supposed to get me to the station," said Heinz.

"You're in enough trouble as it is," said Otto. "Now you want to kill fellow Germans? Really, Heinz, you're somewhat of a barbarian."

With that, Otto started the car back up. He reached into his glove box and removed a small brown paper sack. "Cookie?" he asked. "My wife baked these this morning." Otto took a bite and offered the bag to Heinz.

The scientist was stunned. How could he eat right now? He felt like vomiting. The adrenaline coursed through his body. He looked behind him, expecting another patrol car to converge on them in any moment. Finally, he couldn't take it anymore. "Are we going to go?" he demanded.

Otto's eyes were closed as he chewed the cookie. "My wife is an artist, wouldn't you say? Really, you must try one of her cookies."

"Otto, we must go now!" demanded Heinz.

"I don't know how she does it. But she told me once she likes to add a little extra butter and molasses." He took another bite, finishing the cookie.

"Otto! Please! They are going to wake up!"

The man nearest the car was already starting to move. His knees were swinging back and forth. Otto sighed, reached to the handle and whipped the door open again. The metal crashed into the side of the officer's head, and he slumped back down.

Otto stepped out of the car, stretched, and then placed the little bag of remaining cookies by the policeman, patting him gently on the chest. "Everything will be okay," he said. "When you feel a little better, eat these."

"Well, I suppose we should get going," said Otto, yawning and stretching his back again before returning to the car and closing the door. Taking a firm grip on the wheel, he pressed on the accelerator, slowly maneuvered his vehicle around the police car, and a few moments later they were up to full speed again and moving down the highway.

"I don't think you have what it takes," said Otto out of thin air. They'd been driving along in silence for the past twenty minutes. Heinz had been contemplating his future. He was jolted out of his thinking by this odd comment.

"What do you mean?" he asked.

"Where you are going, things are not easy."

"How do you know where I'm ultimately going?" asked Heinz.

"I know. I've been there. They don't like foreigners, especially Germans."

"I don't have a choice," said Heinz.

"There's always a choice," said Otto. "I know what you are capable of, little scientist. I wager the first time you're asked a tough question you will roll over and tell them everything. I've taken many fellow Germans many places to hide. I'm telling you, you're not going to make it."

"I'm going to have to," said Heinz. "I don't have a choice if I want to try to see my family again. This is the only chance."

"All this because of the Americans?" asked Otto. "I wouldn't worry about them. They are a pack of fools. Their oceans make them incautious and stupid. They think only of cars, houses, and their own comfort. They rule the world now but they are too messy, too divided. They won't last a hundred years."

"Well, they are here now, and because of them, I know what I have to do."

"I think you should reconsider," said Otto. "I have places you could stay here in Germany. The Americans won't hold your family forever. Before you know it, they'd be free again."

"And I'd still be on the run," said Heinz. "I have better options where I'm going. I appreciate your concern, Otto, but I must do this."

"I'm not concerned," said Otto. "I just don't know if I've ever seen someone more unprepared and foolish than you are. Still," he said, "I've said my piece." He reached toward the middle of the car and then sighed. "Perhaps I shouldn't have given them all of my cookies."

After this exchange they drove in silence for a few more minutes, the trees melting away to farmland, and then the houses and buildings of Kaufbeuren.

"Is that our town?" Heinz asked.

Otto nodded. "That's your place, all right. Once we get there, you stay in the car. I'll make sure things are all right and then pick up your ticket."

"What do you mean *my* ticket? You're coming with me, of course."

Otto shook his head. "I'm afraid not, my little scientist. My contract gets you onto that train. After that, you are on your own. But you'll be fine from there."

"But what if something happens?" Heinz asked. He was shocked by the news that Otto was not going to accompany him, and they were running out of time. Otto had pulled into the city and was already navigating the streets and heading toward the station.

"What's going to happen?"

"I might be shot or even killed," said Heinz. "You bought a ticket in my name. As a matter of fact, you bought tickets for both of us. Why did you do that?"

"I canceled your ticket after I made the initial call," said Otto. "I'm going to collect my ticket and give it to you. That throws them off the hunt, you see."

"But what if they check my papers before I leave, or at the border?"

Otto shrugged. "Same problem you already had. You either travel with my ticket and get arrested at the border, or you travel as Heinz Hoffman and get arrested here. But if they don't check too closely at the border, you'll be through."

"I can't do this without you, Otto!"

The commando checked his watch. "*Ach*, look at the time. I'm sorry, little scientist, but like I said, I've only been paid to the station. Take these," he said. "If you're asked for anything, just hand over these papers." He handed Heinz his own documents. "I promised Aafke I'd be home for the indoor picnic we are having this afternoon. Everyone is coming over from the neighborhood. I'm making apple strudel. Have I ever told you how I make it?"

Heinz glanced down at the documents. "I'm supposed to convince a border guard that I'm half a foot taller than I am, that I have an eye patch and a scar on my face? How can I use these documents?"

Otto shrugged. "Act natural. If you believe you're me, then the guard will believe it too. That's how I'm—"

"Invisible," finished Heinz. "I'll be honest, Otto, you're not that invisible."

"Trust me, I am." He reached out and offered his hand. "You'll be fine. I'll check out everything before I give you the ticket and we will wait out here until you are ready to get on the train."

Otto nodded as if that settled everything, then opened the door and headed into the station. Heinz saw he'd parked right in front of the station, even though there were spots in a less conspicuous location down the way on either side. *Of course the idiot parked here*, thought Heinz. *He thinks nobody can see him.*

A number of pedestrians were coming in and out, and a few glanced his way. He felt the hair rising on the back of his neck. What if one of them was a plainclothes policeman? He knew they must be waiting for him. Now that he thought about it, why had Otto bought a ticket in his name in the first place? If he knew he wasn't going to use it? *Idiot.*

He sat that way for long minutes, watching and waiting. Adrenaline was coursing through his body. He knew he was about to embark on the most dangerous part of his journey. He just hoped he had the strength and courage to face it. And where the hell was Otto?

Finally, the station door opened and the giant commando strolled out nonchalantly toward the car. Heinz was appalled to see the former soldier was finishing off a sausage and some sauerkraut out of a cardboard container, smacking his lips as if he was on a Sunday outing. He settled back into the driver's seat and reached up to pull an errant strand of pickled cabbage off his cheek.

"You bought food?"

"*Ja*, it's a long trip home."

Heinz turned away, fighting down his anger. "At least you could have got something for me."

"There's dining on the train."

"I'm hungry now."

"You should have had a cookie." Otto glanced at his watch again. "I'm going to be late, the strudel takes a while to make. You'd better get going."

Heinz was exasperated. "Did you at least manage to get my ticket?"

"Of course. You think I'm some kind of imbecile. Here it is." Otto reached inside his coat again and pulled out the ticket, handing it to Heinz.

He looked it over. "I still don't know how this is going to work," he said.

"Everything will be fine," said Otto. "Everything is going according to the plan. Just don't miss the train." Otto reached a hand out again; his other hand still held the last bit of sausage.

"That's it?" said Heinz. "That's all you have to say to me?"

"I'm out of time, little scientist, and so are you." He looked intently at Heinz. "Be careful. Remember what I said. Where you're going, this isn't a game. Be like Otto—or they'll flay the skin from your bones."

Heinz didn't want to leave the car. In the distance, he heard the whistle of the train and he could see the billowing smoke as the engine slowed down for the station.

"Well, that's it," said Otto. "Off you go now." He reached across Heinz and opened the passenger door.

Heinz stepped out of the car. He turned to Otto, but the commando slammed the door shut. With a quick salute he whipped the car out of the parking spot and tore off down the street, not even looking his way a final time.

Heinz opened the front door of the station and stepped into the busy waiting area. He was terrified by what he saw—there were people everywhere and many of them seemed to be looking at him with an appraising eye. He glanced to his right and saw the long line to the single window for tickets. His eyes darted toward the packed platform and saw many people were already at the train, and beginning to board. He started toward the platform when he heard a commotion to his right at the front of the line where a young man was standing. He was tall, thin, and well-dressed but busily shouting at the attendant in loud English. Heinz was shocked to hear his name come out of the man's mouth.

They must know he was coming. He stood frozen for a few moments, wondering what to do. Heinz turned and moved as quickly as he dared toward the men's room. He opened one of the stalls and sat down on the toilet seat. He locked the door behind him. His heart raced and he closed his eyes, trying to calm down. What should he do? He could leave the station immediately. If he did, he probably would not be caught. But he had no friends in this town, no contacts, and little money. The Americans had taken away his money when they took his papers. No, he had to get on that train.

Finally, he decided what he would do. He checked his watch, calculating how long the train was likely to stay at the station. He watched the second hand, letting a couple of minutes tick by. When he thought the time was right, he rose, took a deep breath, and opened the door, stepping swiftly out of the bathroom and moving purposefully toward the platform, his eyes straightforward and his head slightly bowed. He was sure a police officer would scream his name and he would be tackled to the ground. But he made it through the waiting area and through the double doors heading out to the platform.

That was when he realized he'd waited too long. The train was already moving, the platform almost deserted. He rushed across through the doors and toward the train, picking up speed even as the train did. He was going to make it! He grabbed a steel handle jutting up from the end of one of the carriages and leapt up onto the stairs. He was on the train! He turned to watch the station fade away. As he looked out over the few remaining pedestrians, he made eye contact with a woman who was staring at him with what looked like recognition in her eyes. He turned around and darted into the train. He was safe, for now.

Chapter 19

Hoffman

"That was Hoffman!" she repeated.

"Where?" demanded Max.

"He's gone now. He just sprinted through those doors and jumped on the train."

"How can you be sure it was him?"

"I'm not sure, but I swear it's the same man I saw in the beer hall."

The train was moving faster. "Come on!" she shouted, starting to move. "We've got to get on board before it's too late."

"What about Jeffrey?" asked Max, running after her.

"Forget him!" she huffed, rushing toward the train. It was moving quickly now and the last few carriages would soon pass them. She reached the end of a carriage and, running as fast as she could, she grasped the bar and pulled herself up and onto the train. She turned to help Max. He was a few feet behind her, running as fast as he could. She stretched her hand out, holding on with the other hand. She caught Max's wrist. They ran that way for a few steps and then she shouted: "Now!" Max leapt and she wrenched his arm. He crashed into her and they fell hard against the metal steps, tumbling down. She felt sharp throbbing pain in her back, and her head crashed against something, sparks flittering across the insides of her eyelids. But they had made it!

They lay that way for a few moments, holding each other. She heard a noise coming from Max and she realized he was laughing. "What's so funny?" she demanded.

"All I could think about the whole time is that we don't even have any tickets."

She laughed now too. She knew she would be terribly sore from the impact, but it didn't feel like anything was broken. Max was still lying on top of her. She put her arms around him, kissing his neck. "No," she said at last. "We'll have to get by without tickets."

"Poor Jeffrey," said Max. "He's going to be rather miffed with us, I'd imagine."

"We will have to do our very best to get over Jeffrey's disappointment," she said.

"So now what?" he asked, kissing her on the lips, a wry smile on his face.

"Well, this is certainly not the proper place for *that*," she said. "Much as I might want you. I suppose we ought to get up if we are able, and find out whether that really was Heinz, or if I've got us in worlds of more trouble for no reason at all."

"Yes," he said. "Although I don't want to get up. I want to stay here with you, forever."

"You're not the one with stairs in their back," she said, grimacing a little. "We'll have to find someplace a little more comfortable, *after* we catch Hoffman."

"Let's go find him then," said Max, pulling himself to his feet then helping Sara to stand. "That's quite a strong grip you've got, by the way."

"There's more to me than you see on the surface," she said, giving him a smile.

He smiled back, giving her a final kiss. "Well now," he said. "What's next?"

"Well, we should just move car to car and see if we can find him," she said.

"And hope we don't find any conductors in the meantime. If we find him, we grab him and we don't let go, no matter what," said Max. "We don't turn him over to the conductor, and we certainly won't turn him over to the German police. They can't be trusted."

"What will we do with him then?" she asked.

"Let's worry about that when we have him in our custody." Sara and Max made their way up to the very first car in the train, glancing this way and that at the rows of passengers on both sides. Excitement coursed through her veins. With Jeffrey out of the way, she was so close to her goal now. They just had to apprehend Hoffman and then let things play out as she knew they would.

They reached the front of the train and then turned back, moving much more slowly now and carefully scanning each passenger as they went. They moved through the first two cars with no success. There was nobody who remotely matched Hoffman's description. The third car was a dining car and again they did not spot Heinz. Unfortunately, they did attract the attention of an overeager waiter, who pressed them to take a seat and order something from the menu, pointing out there was free champagne. They declined and continued on, but Sara noticed the man was watching them closely.

"That man was staring at us after we left," she said to Max as they traveled between the third and fourth cars.

Max shrugged. "Why should he? Nobody knows us or knows we are here. In fact, we are nobody," he said, laughing. "The world may be looking for Heinz Hoffman but I can't imagine anyone looking for us."

"That's just it though," she said. "What about Odessa? What about *Der Dämon*? I didn't see him board the train with Hoffman. What if he got on earlier and they met up together?"

"I didn't see him," said Max. "It's not like the man is invisible. He's a giant with an eye patch. The Matterhorn would attract less attention if it walked through the station." Max patted the weapon under his coat. "Let's assume that Hoffman is by himself, but if he isn't, we'll be prepared."

The next car they came to was a sleeper car with closed compartments. They passed through this one quickly since they could not see into the compartments, and moved on to the next car. In a few more minutes they'd made their way all the way to the back of the train, but they had not spotted Hoffman.

Sara felt her heart sinking. "Maybe I was wrong," she said. "Maybe that wasn't Heinz after all. Or if it was him, maybe he didn't get on the train."

Max looked flustered but forced a smile. "It's all right," he said. "Jeffrey didn't make the train either and will probably search the platform. If Heinz was there but jumped off the train or never got on, there's a good chance he'll spot him. We'll go through one more time and if we don't see him, we'll get off at the next station and ring Jeffrey."

"Jeffrey can't catch Hoffman himself," said Sara. "That would be a disaster."

Max nodded. "I agree, but there may not be anything we can do about it."

Suddenly it hit Sara. "What about the sleeper car?" she asked. "We didn't check those compartments."

"I don't know how we could," said Max. "They lock from

the inside, and besides, why would Hoffman take a sleeper? The trip into Switzerland is only a few hours. Unless of course he did it to stay out of sight."

The more she thought about that, the more she was sure that's where he was hiding. "Let's go back and see if we can find a way inside them," said Sara. "If we are wrong, what could possibly happen?"

"We could be arrested and thrown off the train," said Max lightly.

Sara laughed. "Jeffrey is probably going to arrest us for leaving him anyway. I don't think we can get into more trouble."

Max nodded, smiling at her. "All right," he said. "Let's give it a try." They made their way back through several of the cars, heading in the direction of the sleepers. But in one of the sections between cars, a conductor was perched, apparently waiting for them along with the waiter they'd seen earlier. The waiter pointed to them and whispered to the conductor. He stepped forward, eyeing the two of them sternly. "May I see your tickets?" he demanded.

"What is this about?" demanded Max.

"My waiter friend here told me that you came to the dining car and refused his offer for free champagne. Several passengers also have complained about a couple tromping through the cars and ogling all the passengers in a rude and suspicious manner. I need to see your tickets and your papers."

"Well yes, let me retrieve those," said Max, reaching into his pocket. He whipped out the pistol, aiming it at the two men.

"Max, what are you doing?" Sara demanded.

"I'm getting us entrance to the sleeper cars," he said.

"Max, you can't do this," said Sara. The last thing she wanted to have happen was for the two of them to be arrested by the German police. However, Max ignored her and continued to point his weapon at the two men.

"Let's get going," he said. "And I warn you. If you do anything I don't ask you to do, you won't live out the day."

The conductor turned slowly and opened the door into the next carriage, which fortunately held the first sleeper car.

"Open the first door," Max ordered.

The man stepped forward and knocked on the door. A few moments later the door opened and Sara saw a blonde woman holding a baby peeking out. She was wearing a bathrobe and she was obviously flustered by the interruption.

Max kept his weapon hidden against the conductor's back as the man smiled, making up an excuse about the interruption. Max whispered for him to continue. They moved on to the next door and the next, working their way down the line of doors until they reached the final one. The conductor knocked on this door but there was no answer.

"The occupants must be in the dining car or walking about the train," said the conductor.

"Open it," demanded Max.

"We are not allowed inside when the occupant is not present," said the conductor.

"I don't give a damn," said Max, jamming the pistol harder into the man's back. "Open the door."

The conductor fiddled with his keys, his hands shaking nervously. The man finally found the right key and opened the door into the sleeper car. Sara peered over Max's shoulder and saw a man sitting on the bed, dressed in a suit and looking up in surprise. It was Hoffman.

"Everyone inside," said Max, pushing the waiter and the conductor into the compartment.

"What is this about?" asked the gentleman within.

"It's about justice," said Max. "I am Max Portnoy and I'm taking you into custody."

"You are who?" said Hoffman. "What is this about? I have a

ticket and I'm a German citizen on legitimate business to Switzerland."

The man's composure and calm raised a seed of doubt for Sara. What if they had the wrong man? Then again . . .

Max, however, pressed on. "I know you're a German citizen. I know it too well," said Max. "Dr. Hoffman, you may not remember me, but I certainly remember you. My family worked for you during the war. Well, *work* is a liberal term. We were slave labor, constructing your laboratory for your precious reactor."

Sara saw a flicker of fear as the man's eyes widened. She had no more doubts. Now she was certain that Max had found the right man. Elation ripped through her. They'd done it! They'd found Hoffman!

"What is all this about?" said the conductor, his hands in the air now.

"Dr. Hoffman here is a wanted war criminal," said Max. "Because of him, I lost most of my family during the war. And because of him, my brother was murdered yesterday. We are taking him into custody and we will make sure justice is done to him!"

"Who are you?" asked Hoffman. "Are you with the German police?"

"No," said Max, shaking his head. "I'm a private citizen and a Jew."

"That's it," said the waiter, spitting on the ground and glaring at Max. "I knew there was something wrong with you the moment I set eyes on you."

"Enough of that," said Sara, grabbing the waiter by the back of his collar and giving him a jerk. "There will be no Jew baiting today."

The train lurched and it was clear they were starting to slow down for the next station.

"Here's what we are going to do," said Max. "We are going to step off this train and I am going to escort Dr. Hoffman. You will not try to stop me or I'll shoot you," he warned the conductor and waiter.

"You'll do no such thing," said the conductor. "Shoot me if you want. I'm not letting you off this train until the police are here and they can sort this out. I don't know you except that you've waved a gun in my face and made threats. I'm not letting another German citizen leave in your custody until the proper authorities are here!"

Max aimed the gun at the conductor's head, pressing the barrel against his temple. "I warn you," he said. "You don't know how much I've been through to find this man. We are taking Dr. Hoffman off this train, whether you are alive or dead."

The conductor shook and closed his eyes.

"Just let them go," said the waiter, still held by Sara. "It's not worth your life. They'll get what's coming to them when the police find them."

Max pushed the gun harder against the conductor's head. The man finally nodded.

"You two will stay in this compartment until we've left the train," said Max. "If you follow us you know what will happen."

The train lurched to a final stop in front of a busy platform. "Sara, get the door," commanded Max in a tone of authority she had never heard from him before. She paused for a moment and then moved forward, opening the door to the corridor outside.

"Let's go, Hoffman," said Max, and the slight scientist rose reluctantly, following Sara to the door and into the hallway, which was already busy with passengers coming and going.

Max kept the pistol tight against the scientist's back and the three of them maneuvered through the bustle of passengers until they reached the stairs at the end of the carriage. Sara expected to hear the shouting of alarm behind them from the conductor or waiter, but Max must have cowed the men, because nothing happened. They paused at the stairs, looking out at the platform.

"What are we going to do now?" asked Sara.

"We'll figure it out," said Max. "We can't go to the German police, they can't be trusted. Let's see if we can get a cab and go to a secure place like a hotel. If we can make it there, we'll have more time to figure out what to do next."

"Should we try to call Mr. Varberg?" asked Sara.

Max shook his head. "Not now. We need to get somewhere safe first. If we don't, I'm afraid our friends back there on the train will alert the authorities and we'll be arrested before we can do anything else. No, it's best to do it my way."

She nodded, not knowing what else to say.

"All right," continued Max. "You lead the way. I'll be close behind you with Hoffman. When we get outside the station, hail a taxi."

"All right," she said.

"And you," said Max, turning to the scientist. "You might be tempted to call out for help, but I promise you I'm not going to let you free. If you alert anyone to what's going on, those will be the last words you will ever say."

Hoffman nodded. Sara could see the fear in his eyes. She felt no sympathy for the man. He'd done terrible things during the war and it was only right that he should feel a tiny fraction of the kind of fear and suffering he perpetrated on his victims.

They made their way along the platform to the doors, entering into the train station. Sara saw a police officer at the door looking over the passengers as they moved in and out. She froze.

"Max, do you see him?" she whispered.

"Yes," he said.

"What are we going to do?" she asked.

"Go up and ask him some questions," said Max. "Flirt with

him a bit if you have to. Do anything to distract him until we've passed through."

Sara did as she was told, stepping up to the officer. "Excuse me," she said. The man looked down at her and she smiled, touching his arm.

The officer smiled back at her. "What is it, miss?"

"I'm wondering if you can help me," she said. "I just arrived here and I need to know where the nearest market is. I have family in town and I want to buy them a little gift before I arrive for dinner."

"It's not really my job to play tour guide," said the officer, a touch playfully.

"But please," she said, squeezing his arm. "You must know where I could find a gift."

"Very well," said the officer. He proceeded to explain directions on how she could get to the nearest market on foot. Sara smiled, not hearing a word. Her heart was beating out of her chest. Long minutes seemed to pass and she wondered what was going on but finally, out of the corner of her eye, she saw Max leading Hoffman through the door. The officer droned on and on and then changed positions, drawing closer to her and asking her if she had plans for later in the evening after her dinner. She blushed and smiled back. "I'm not sure," she said, feigning interest. "What time do you get off of work?"

"It's called duty, not work," he said. "I'm off at eight o'clock."

"Lovely," she said. "If I'm able to get away I'll meet you here near the front entrance."

"You'd better," he said.

"I'll try," said Sara, smiling again. She stepped outside and leaned against the wall for a moment. "Disgusting," she said to herself. That behind her, she looked around, trying to locate Max. For a few moments she panicked, worried that something had happened to him, but he was there, a few feet farther down the pavement, standing next to Hoffman. The two of them looked like a couple of business associates or perhaps distant relatives waiting for a cab. She made her way toward Max, admiring again his coolness in such a situation. She came up behind them and touched Max's back. "I'm here," she whispered.

Max reached his hand around and squeezed hers for a moment. "Let's go," he said. Sara moved in front of Max and Hoffman and led the two of them toward several cabs that were waiting twenty yards away. She stepped toward the cabs, her hand raised as she tried to get the attention of the first driver.

"Miss Sturm, how nice to see you!" shouted a voice she recognized immediately. She froze, turning her head slowly. There was Jeffrey hurrying up to the station, two American soldiers close in tow. He strutted up to them like a peacock, looking them over.

"Well, well," he said, whistling softly. "What have we here?" he asked. "Could this be the famous Dr. Hoffman?" He turned to Sara and Max. "Congratulations, you've helped me succeed in my mission after all."

Sara and Max had no choice but to turn Hoffman over to Jeffrey's custody. The Americans loaded the German scientist into the back of a waiting car. Jeffrey then motioned for Max and Sara to follow him and they were led to a second car nearby. They weren't able to talk. Sara watched Max carefully. She could tell he was stunned. They were shunted into the back seat of the second car. When they were settled in, she took his hand.

"I'm sorry," she said.

He did not look at her. He seemed angry or frustrated, perhaps both. After a time, he seemed to recover himself and he squeezed her hand back. Taking a deep breath, he turned to her. "It's all right," he said. "It's not your fault, Sara. Just bad luck, I guess. Besides," he said, lowering his voice, "this is not over yet." One of the American soldiers stepped into the front seat and started the car. He didn't speak to them and they in turn were content to stay silent, each alone with their thoughts of how this had come to pass. Soon they were following Jeffrey's vehicle through the streets of the small town.

"Where are we headed?" Max asked finally.

"We have a little building on the outskirts of town that serves as a station," the soldier explained. "We use it for military police business mostly, sometimes as overnight barracks if we are stuck on duty."

They arrived at the building twenty minutes later and the soldier whisked them out of the car and through the front door. He led them upstairs to a second-story office that contained a steel desk, a few chairs, and not much else. When he had settled them in two chairs across from the desk, he asked them if they would like some coffee or anything to eat.

"Where are they taking Hoffman?" asked Max, ignoring the question.

"I can't talk about that," said the soldier. He reached into his shirt pocket and retrieved a package of cigarettes, offering them. Max and Sara each took one and the soldier finished lighting them. "I'm Sergeant Roberts, by the way," he said, nodding to the two of them by way of introduction. He looked at them a moment longer and then he quietly withdrew, closing the door behind him.

"What are we going to do now?" Sara asked.

Max shrugged. "I don't know yet," he said. He seemed to be in deep thought, his mind racing for some kind of solution.

"Well, we caught him at least," said Sara, watching Max closely. "That's something."

"I don't trust Jeffrey," said Max.

"I don't either." She continued to watch him. She needed to know what he was thinking. "Come on, Max," she said at last, touching his arm. "Don't close up on me now. What are you thinking?"

"It's your fault," he said at last, shrugging her hand off his arm. She saw anger flash across his face.

"What do you mean?" she asked.

"You spent too much time flirting with that officer. I only needed a second to get by." He turned toward her, his eyes red. "Perhaps you enjoyed it a little too much."

"That's not fair," she said, her face showing hurt. "You asked me to distract him and you told me to flirt with him. I got you the time you needed to get Hoffman by. How was there any way I could know that Jeffrey would be at the station waiting for us?"

"You're right," he said. "I'm sorry. This just isn't turning out the way I had planned."

"Is there anything I can do?" she asked.

Max looked like he was fighting to control himself; he was so different from the commanding figure she'd accompanied as they'd moved through the train station. Finally, he forced a smile. "Just having you here is something. And like I said, this isn't over yet."

Sara was about to ask him what he meant but the door opened and Jeffrey strolled arrogantly into the office, taking the seat behind the desk and putting his feet up and his hands on the back of his head.

"Well," he said, smirking at the two of them. "All is well that ends well."

"You can't do this," said Sara. "I know what you made us agree to, but you can't take all the credit, Jeffrey. This was Max's idea. He took all the risks, he lost his brother, for God's sake!"

"You mean I can't take *yours*," he said. "The credit that counts for you and me is credit with our agency. But remember, I was going to take you home but you insisted on carrying on, under the condition, as I recall, that I would receive complete and total credit for this operation."

"You'll never get away with this," said Sara. "Mr. Varberg will learn what really happened."

Jeffrey laughed, his head going back violently as he held his sides in mirth. "I forgot about your reliance on Mr. Varberg. He's a fool and so are you. Do you think he will even have a job when this is over? You're not American, Sara, so I'll forgive you. You don't understand what it means to be from a family like mine." He leaned forward. "And you could have benefited so easily," he said. "I offered you the opportunity to spend time with me. I could have advanced your career, but you spurned me and instead ran off with this Jew. What a pity."

"I would have never been with you," she muttered through clenched teeth.

"And more's the pity," said Jeffrey. "Well, be that as it may. I'll leave Max to run his business, and there may even be a vacancy for you now that Karl is out of the picture. You certainly won't be coming back to work for me after your shenanigans at the station."

"You bastard," said Max. "Don't you dare talk about—"

"Be quiet," said Jeffrey. "The both of you have grown tiresome. I'll leave you and spend some time basking in my triumph. Sara, your job is over. You're fired. Be happy if that's the only thing that happens to you. If you want to run off with Max and if he can keep you, so be it. I'm off to bigger and better things. One last thing," he said. "Since you're not associated with an agency anymore, I'm afraid I can't offer you a ride back to Berlin in a government plane. You'll have to figure out alternative transportation."

"But there's no way in or out of Berlin with the blockade!" she protested. "What will we do?"

"The Jews are resourceful," said Jeffrey. "Max will figure something out."

"Bastard," said Max.

"Yes, you said that before." He rose and started toward the door. He was halfway out when he turned to them, giving them an even bigger smile. "I almost forgot," he said.

"What?" asked Sara.

"The best of all. I have news about Dr. Hoffman."

"What is it?" asked Max.

"Well, as you know, Heinz Hoffman is a wanted Nazi war criminal. However, he is also a nuclear scientist. As you might have also noticed, we are all but in a shooting war with the Soviet Union. The very existence of our way of life is on the line. So we aren't going to punish Dr. Hoffman—in fact, we are going to reward him."

"He's lying," said Sara.

"Shut your mouth, you little bitch," said Jeffrey. "The men are talking." He turned back to Max, reaching into his coat pocket and removing a folded document. "I have here Dr. Hoffman's orders, sent to me by telex this morning from the US government. Dr. Hoffman is to be brought into custody, then he will be flown to Washington, D.C., for questioning, before he is reunited with his family and begins his new life. He's being given a townhouse on a military base near the Capitol. He's going to spend the rest of his life there with his family, and a government pension, assisting us with our nuclear program."

"He's lying," said Sara again.

"I don't think he is," said Max.

"That's the smartest thing you've said since I met you," said Jeffrey. "I guess you'll never know what really happened. But I'm telling you the truth. Dr. Hoffman's family was already moved to their house in America. He will rejoin them in a few days. His children will be educated in American schools, and he will live a life free of consequences and retire with a US government pension. The American dream, really, wouldn't you say, my Jewish friend?"

Sara was sure that Max would charge Jeffrey, but he sat in the chair, glaring with a fierce anger and hatred at the American.

"You truly are the worst person I've ever met," said Sara.

"At what point, my dear, did you believe your opinion

meant anything to me? I was interested in what's under your dress, not under your skull. Now that even that has been irrevocably soiled by Mr. Portnoy, here, I'll have to respectfully decline any further interest. So we'll be here for a day or two while I interrogate the good doctor, then I'll be off to my future and the two of you can go do whatever you want with what is left of your miserable lives. Please excuse me, I've got to get to work making preparations for Dr. Hoffman's comfortable journey to the United States of America." He bowed slightly. "I'll bid you both a fond farewell."

With one last look at her, Jeffrey slammed the door behind him. She heard keys in the door and she realized he was locking the door behind him. They were trapped.

"My God," said Sara, turning to reach toward Max. He jerked away from her.

"I told you we couldn't trust the Americans," said Max. "Especially that one."

"I'm so sorry, Max," she said, reaching toward him again, but he ignored her.

"I've lost my family. I've lost my brother. And now I find out not only that I didn't bring Hoffman to justice but instead I've brought him protection forever."

She reached out and put her hand on his leg. She thought he would push her away but he didn't. "I'm so sorry," she said again.

He turned to her, tears streaming freely down his cheeks. "It's not your fault, my dear. I know I've said some unfair things to you. Please forgive me. You've treated me fairly the entire time. You trusted me and you believed in me. You've loved me."

"How will you go on?" she asked. "Will you come back with me to Berlin?" She watched him carefully, wondering what he was going to do next.

Max laughed. "Like we could even get back to Berlin. When will that be? A decade from now? No," he said, shaking his head. "I can never go back there. I won't face my smirking neighbors, knowing what they did to my store, and what happened to my brother. I won't have them laughing at me for the rest of my life."

"What are you going to do then?" she asked.

He turned to her. "The question, my sweet dear, is what are you prepared to do?"

Her face showed confusion. "What do you mean?" she asked.

"There is something we can try perhaps to set everything aright, but it's madness."

This was what she'd been waiting for. "Tell me," she said. "I'll try anything."

"Don't say that until you've heard it all," he said.

"Tell me."

"Somehow, we have got to get Hoffman out of here," he said.

"But how is that possible?" she asked. "There are at least the two soldiers here along with Jeffrey. There might be dozens more."

"I don't know what will happen," he said. "But we may be able to work something. They didn't search us before they dropped us off in here and Jeffrey has never known anything about this," he said, patting the pistol in his coat. "If we can get out of this office, we may be able to catch them by surprise and spirit Hoffman out of here before they can stop us. Remember, they've got two cars out front."

"But even if by some miracle we could get out of here and get Hoffman away from them, where would we go? What could we do? They would just track us down again and then we'd end up in prison for sure." She shook her head. "I want to help you, Max, but I just don't know what good it would do. We are in enough trouble already, and what you suggest is impossible."

"Not impossible," said Max. "Just very unlikely. But there is a chance."

"A chance for what?" she asked.

"To get him to the Russians."

Chapter 20
Trapped

Thursday, October 14, 1948
1:47 p.m.
Kaufbeuren, Bavaria, Germany

Sara stared at Max in complete shock. "The Russians?" she asked. "What do you mean?"

"These Americans are too soft on the Nazis," said Max, his face contorted in agony. "Look what they are doing with Heinz. How can I let him leave here and go to the United States to a comfortable job and a retirement? I lost my entire family because of this bastard, and your employers want to reward him just because he has some knowledge of nuclear physics?" He sat down hard on a chair, his face white. He turned back to Sara. "Does that even make any sense?" he asked. "The Americans already have an atomic bomb. What could Heinz possibly help them with?"

"You're right," she said. "You're right, Max, but what can we do? The Americans have him, they have us. And whatever would the Russians have to do with this?"

"The Russians aren't soft. They are the opposite in every way. They killed most of the Nazis that they caught."

"Usually without a trial," said Sara.

"They'll give him a trial, even if it's a short one," said Max. "Does he deserve more? I was there. I watched him destroy my family. And it wasn't just my family either. He stomped out the lives of dozens of people. All for his science."

"Maybe you're right," she said at last, "but you still haven't explained how the Russians could help us now. And frankly, why aren't you just proposing we kill him right here and now?"

"Karl and I disagreed on that point," said Max. "I won't have his blood on my hands. I want proper justice for Hoffman, from a nation state. But if we won't get that from the Americans, we've got to get Heinz out of here. We have to take him from Jeffrey and get him to Czechoslovakia."

"That's madness, Max. We're in an army facility. We're locked in this office. You and I are civilians. We can't even get out of this room, and if we could, what would you propose that we do, kill the guards and Jeffrey? There could be dozens of Americans in this building. And then what? If we somehow made it out of here, they'd be looking for us. We wouldn't make it ten miles before they found us. Then we'd be in prison for the rest of our lives, or worse."

Max stepped over to her and took both of her hands. "You must listen to me, my dear. We just need to take one step at a time. First, we need to get out of this office. Then we need to see how many people are here and what the obstacles are. If the house is full of soldiers, then who could blame us for wanting out of a locked room? We haven't done anything wrong. If there is a chance to get Heinz out of here, then we take it. If we're stopped somewhere, I'll take the blame. I'll tell them I kidnapped you as well, as a hostage." He bent down and kissed her forehead, smiling at her. "Nothing will happen to you, I

promise. But I'm asking you to please give me this chance to re-
deem my family's honor and have justice. If we make it, the
Russians will make short work of Hoffman. If we don't, well,
I'll have done my best, and you won't be in trouble at all."

Sara shook her head. "It's madness, Max."

"It's a mad world."

She looked down, closing her eyes. She didn't speak for long
moments.

"Well?"

"I guess we can try to get out of this office, although I
haven't the slightest idea how you plan to do even that."

"Leave that to me, Sara," he said. He stepped around to the
desk and started opening drawers, shuffling his hands around
inside them. "Aha," he said after a few moments, retrieving a
thin nail file from the desk. "This should do nicely."

"What do you intend to do with that?" she asked.

"Pick the lock, of course."

"But how on earth would you know how to do that?"

He chuckled as he bent down to the lock. "A misspent
youth," he said. As Sara watched, he fumbled back and forth
with the instrument in the lock, moving it left and right and
then in a circular motion. He removed the tool periodically and
glanced down, peering at the lock before returning to his work.
He tinkered with the mechanism for a half hour. Sara expected
him to quit at any moment, but just when it seemed impossible,
she heard an audible click and Max turned the handle, pulling
the door slowly open.

Sara started to say something but Max gestured for her to be
silent. He tiptoed back to the desk, setting down the file. He
reached into his coat pocket and drew out the pistol, motioning
for her to follow him. Then he slowly opened the door, peeking
his head out into the hallway and glancing both ways before
stepping out into the corridor. Sara followed him, her heart in

her mouth. There was real danger here. The soldiers could react without thinking, killing both of them in the hallway. Even Jeffrey could do something stupid. But she had to move forward and let things unfold.

Sara stepped out behind Max. To her relief, there were no soldiers nearby. The hall was poorly lit, with bare walls and tile floors. Max started toward the end of the corridor, where a door was open to their left. He moved cautiously, placing each foot on the floor before lowering his weight on it. He was completely silent, like a stalking cat. For agonizing minutes, he moved this way, gradually nearing the door, Sara close behind him. When he arrived, he peered inside, again moving his head at a glacial pace to glance around the corner. He moved back and turned to Sara, leaning in until his lips were against her earlobe. "The two guards are in there," he said. "They are playing cards. It's the same two that apprehended us. I'll bet there aren't any more in this place."

"How do we know?" she whispered back.

"We don't, but it's an encouraging sign that I've spotted the same two men. Let's go the other way and see if we can locate Jeffrey and Heinz."

Sara followed Max again as he made his way slowly back the other way, past the office that had held them captive and toward the other end of the hall. There were twin doors at this end, both closed, along with a set of narrow stairs at the extreme end. As they drew nearer the doors, Sara heard muffled voices coming from the door to their left. Max tiptoed on until he could gently place his ear to the door. Sara stepped up behind him. She could not hear the words spoken, but she recognized Jeffrey's voice and was sure the other person in the room must be Heinz.

Max listened for a few moments more, then looked up to Sara for confirmation. She nodded. Max raised his pistol and reached for the handle.

Raucous laughter spilled out of the door at the other end of the hallway. Sara jolted and twisted her neck around. She could already hear the clomping boots on the wooden floor and she knew they had seconds to react. Hoping against hope, she grabbed Max's hand and pulled him with her across the hallway. She gripped and wrenched the doorknob, praying it was unlocked. It was, and the door opened into a darkened room. She shoved Max past her and dived in after him, slamming into something hard that crashed against her head. She reached with her foot and shoved the door closed, even as the boots thudded down the hallway. Sara closed her eyes, praying the soldiers hadn't seen or heard them. The boots banged and thundered past them and down the stairs. In a few moments, they were fading away.

She could breathe again. "Max," she whispered into the darkness. "Are you all right?"

"I've smashed my knee on something," said Max through gritted teeth. "I don't know how badly. But at least we're safe. That was quick thinking."

Sara felt her head where she had hit it. There was a nasty lump. She rubbed her fingers together, checking for blood. There was none. Her ears were ringing and she felt sick to her stomach. She kept her eyes closed and counted to ten, taking a few deep breaths. When she felt ready, she groped her way back toward the door, fumbling in the darkness. To her relief, she found a switch and flicked it on. Light filled the room. Sara blinked a couple of times and looked around. They were in another office, although this one looked unused. There were boxes everywhere. She'd crashed into the side of a wooden chair near a desk. Max was facedown in a jumble of boxes, his arms flailing as he tried to right himself. She couldn't help laughing and she bit the neckline of her dress, trying to fight back the sound.

He looked up at her, anger in his eyes, but when he saw his

own situation Max began laughing too, and both of them struggled to stay quiet. "What a pair of adventurers we are," said Max at last. "We've managed to capture a storage room."

"Not without casualties," she said.

"Indeed."

"What should we do now?" she asked.

Max limped toward the door, pressing his ear against it. "I don't hear anything," he said. "I think the guards have gone."

"What if there are others?" she asked.

"We will have to risk it, I suppose. Think of it, though—this is the most dangerous part of what we are trying to do. If we manage to get away with Heinz, we stand a good chance of making it to the border."

"But how will we cross even if we make it?" asked Sara. "All of the borders are guarded now."

Max smiled. "One problem at a time, my dear." He reached for the knob and turned it slowly, pushing on the wood. The door swung slowly open, creaking loudly. Sara winced, but soon Max had it open enough for the two of them to squeeze through. The muffled talking across the hallway continued unabated.

They crept across the hallway and once again moved up to the door. This time Sara pressed her ear to the door along with Max. She could now make out the words.

"I don't think you understand," said Heinz, speaking to Jeffrey in English with a thick accent. "I can't go to the United States."

"You don't have a choice," said Jeffrey. "You're my prisoner and you will do as you're told."

"You don't understand," said Heinz, "I—"

Sara reached down and tore the door open, shoving her way past Max and into the room. Jeffrey was sitting behind a desk with Heinz across from him. The two men were smoking cigarettes, a tray of sandwiches and coffee on the desk. If she hadn't known better, she would have thought they were two business-men having a casual meal and discussing a new venture.

"What the hell are you doing!" demanded Jeffrey. "How did you get out of that office?" He started to rise but then slumped into his seat with his eyes wide-open when he saw Max storm in behind her. Sara glanced back and saw that he had his pistol drawn and was aiming it at Jeffrey's head.

"Don't move," said Max, moving his pistol back and forth between Jeffrey and Heinz. "You're both our prisoners."

Jeffrey laughed. "Let's stop this charade," he said. "Sara, this coffee is cold. Go make a new pot." He turned to Max. "Portnoy, if you know what's good for you, you'll drop that weapon now before you get yourself killed."

"You're coming with me," said Max. "All of you."

"Coming with you where?" said Jeffrey, still laughing. "To the restroom? Seriously, Max, enough joking around. Put that damned thing down and let's talk like men."

Max took a step forward, aiming right at Jeffrey's head. "Get up right now, you bastard. You are coming with me."

Jeffrey only now seemed to realize that Max was serious. He looked at Sara. "Stop him," he ordered.

"She can't," said Max. "She's my prisoner too. You all are. Now raise your arms in the air and get to your feet, slowly. Both of you."

As Sara watched, Jeffrey and Heinz both complied with Max's directions and moved gradually out of their chairs. "You're mad," said Jeffrey. "You'll never get us out of here. Help!" he screamed suddenly.

Max laughed. "Nice try, Scott. Your guards left a little while ago. Maybe they wanted some dinner or something. There's nobody else here. We are all going out to the car." He waved his pistol. "Get going—Sara first, then Jeffrey and Heinz."

Sara put her hands up too. She tried her best to look scared, to play the part of a prisoner. She scooted slowly around Max and then turned down the hallway toward the stairs. She heard the men following behind her. Her mind reeled, and she fought to keep her pulse from tearing through her eardrums. They were committed now, and the next few minutes would be dangerous. If the guards came back, they might shoot first and ask questions later. That would ruin everything. She smiled to herself, hazarding a glance back at Jeffrey. At least that bastard was getting his. She relished what must be going through his mind right now. So close to triumph and now all of his dreams crushed before his eyes. Where were his contacts now? What could they do for him?

Still, they had to get to the car. She didn't know where the other two Americans were. Worse yet, there could be others. What if the downstairs was full of guards? Her mind reeled, trying to come up with an alternative plan—but she couldn't think of one. She arrived on the ground floor. The corridor was identical to the one above, except in the center there was a larger opening to the right, from which natural light was emanating. That must be the front door, she realized. She stopped for a moment there, listening for voices, sounds, anything. But she could hear nothing. The building was either empty except for them, or anyone down here was remaining silent. What if soldiers were waiting for them? If so, there was nothing she could do. The plan would be ruined. At least for now.

Sara risked a glance back at Max. He was still limping and his pistol bobbed up and down as he lurched along, a few feet behind Jeffrey and Heinz. She could see his features grimace in pain with each step and she wondered if he would have the strength to make it out to a car. There was nothing to do but keep moving forward. She reached the wide opening to her right and turned to see a double set of glass doors at the end of a short hallway. There were a couple of seats shoved against the wall, forming a small waiting room. She blinked at the stabbing daylight. She paused for a moment, gathering her courage. They would be at risk when they went outside. There could be pedestrians or even citizens in cars that might notice Max and the gun and try to stop them. What would they do if they were confronted by a police officer? she wondered. Would Max kill a German to assure their escape? Could she prevent him? If she could not, would she still go with him, even then?

She reached the double doors and pushed outward, shoving her way through them and out onto the sidewalk. Her eyes darted to the left and right. They were fortunate, the street was deserted except for the two cars parked parallel to the curb. The others made their way through the doors, Jeffrey scowling at her with hatred rippling along his mottled features. Finally, Max was through. "Give Sara the keys to one of these cars," he directed Jeffrey.

"I don't have any," the American said. "The soldiers have them."

Sara felt her blood freeze. An unexpected problem. "Where are the keys?" she asked Jeffrey.

"Search me," he said. Smiling, he looked at her. "Aren't you supposed to be a prisoner too?"

"Shut your damned mouth," she said, flustered. "Max, what now?" she asked.

"Go back inside and search upstairs for the keys," said Max.

"But what are you going to do?" she asked. "You can't stay out here."

"I'll bring them back into the waiting room. Hurry!"

Sara rushed back inside and up the stairs. She sprinted down the hallway and into the room where they'd heard the Americans talking. She looked around in utter exasperation. A sofa was crammed into the small space along with a coffee table and several dressers. Newspapers and documents were spread out all over the table and there were boots and articles of clothing everywhere. The room was a disaster. Taking a deep breath, she waded into the flotsam and started upending items, looking under everything in search of the keys. Five minutes passed and then ten. With each tick of a clock that hung above the sofa, she felt her fear rising higher.

Finally, she gave up. There were no keys in this room, or if there were, they were so well hidden she would never find them. She hurried back down the hallway and down the stairs. Max was waiting. He had sat down on one of the chairs. His face was pale and he looked like he might pass out. The pistol was hanging loosely in his hand and Jeffrey was moving toward him.

"Max, look out!" she shouted.

He jolted and his body shook. He looked up at Jeffrey and pointed the pistol firmly at the American. "Step back, sir," he commanded. "Do you have the keys?" he asked Sara.

"No."

"What?" She could hear the panic in Max's voice.

"I searched everywhere," she said. "The GIs must have taken them when they left."

"And now what are you going to do?" asked Jeffrey, a hint of amusement in his voice. "Walk us to your destination—whatever or wherever that might be?"

"Quiet!" said Max, obviously trying to think.

At that moment, the two American soldiers appeared at the door. They each had a brown sack and were smoking a cigarette. They had stepped through the door and taken a step into the waiting room before they both froze. Sergeant Roberts dropped his bag, and a sandwich and some fruit spilled out onto the concrete floor.

"What the hell is going on?" the sergeant asked. At that moment, he must have spotted Max's gun, because he took a step back. "Drop that weapon immediately," he ordered, reaching for his own sidearm.

Max whipped his weapon toward Roberts. "Don't move," he said. The sergeant stopped midmotion. "Sara, take his weapon."

Sara stepped over and took the pistols from both soldiers. She shoved one into a pocket in her dress and took the other weapon in her hand. Now they were both armed.

"Give her the keys to the car," Max commanded.

"What is going on?" the other soldier demanded.

"It seems that our Jewish friend here and my secretary have betrayed us," said Jeffrey. "They have some other plans for Dr. Hoffman, it seems." He scowled at Sara. "This is your last chance," he said to her. "You have a gun now. Point it at the Jew and stop this nonsense while there is still time. Do that and I'll restore your job. There will be no further consequences for your prior actions."

"I won't," she said. "We are leaving, and you're coming with us."

"That would be a mistake," said Max. "He's too slippery. Let's leave him behind."

"If we do, they'll be after us the whole way."

"The whole way where?" asked Jeffrey.

"You just never mind," snapped Sara. "Trust me, Max, we need to take him."

But Max shook his head. "I'm hurt," he said. "And these soldiers already know we've kidnapped Heinz. No, it would do no good to take him now."

"Please, Max, I'm begging you," said Sara. "It's a huge mistake to leave him behind."

"Very well," he said. "If you insist. But let's hurry. Get the keys."

Sara searched Roberts and found a set in his pocket. "Do

these keys start one of those cars?" she asked. The sergeant wouldn't answer at first so she jammed the pistol into his stomach. "Tell me!" she ordered.

"Yes," he said, his voice calm and more irritated than fearful. "The one on the right."

"Thank you," she answered. "Now you two go upstairs and wait thirty minutes. If you come back down here we'll shoot!" She knew they probably wouldn't follow her directions, but she hoped she and Max at least got a head start. The soldiers hesitated, then followed her direction and started down the hallway. She could hear their heavy boots on the stairs. "We've got to go right now," she said. "They could be getting weapons and coming right back down. We have to get away while we have a chance."

Max pulled himself slowly to his feet. He seemed hardly able to put weight on his swollen knee. "All right," he said. "Let's go."

Sara led the way through the doors. She stepped over to the car. Heinz and Jeffrey were a few feet behind her, with Max in the back. She reached out with the keys and started fumbling through them, looking for the right one. There were a dozen keys and she had to try several before she found the right one. She unlocked the door and then reached around to open the back one. She motioned toward it. "Max and Heinz in the back," she said.

Max hobbled forward while she kept her pistol on the other two. He lowered himself down, grunting from the pain. Once he was sitting, he pulled his legs into the car and then scooted to the far side. "Now you," Sara ordered Heinz. The scientist looked at her for a moment and then sat down in the open seat. Sara moved around to the driver's side, her pistol never leaving Jeffrey. She opened the door and stepped in.

In the fraction of a second it took her to find her seat, Jeffrey bolted for the glass doors. Max shouted at her and she tried to pull herself back out but it was too late. He was already through. Jeffrey had escaped them.

She made to go after him.

"Sara, leave him!" Max shouted. "We've got to go!"

"We can't," said Sara. "He's too dangerous!"

"There's no chance to get him now," said Max. "If we are ever going to get away, we've got to go now!"

She nodded, knowing it was a mistake. She shifted the car into gear and pressed the accelerator, tearing down the street toward an impossible future.

Chapter 21
To Poke a Demon

Thursday, October 14, 1948
2:12 p.m.
Kaufbeuren, Bavaria, Germany

From the confines of the waiting room, Jeffrey watched the car peel out. He'd never been angrier in his life. He'd had Heinz in his possession—a wanted Nazi! His future had been assured. And instead that German whore and her Jew boyfriend had ruined everything.

He stomped up the stairs, calling out to the two sergeants until he had their attention. They were back in their room, each holding an M1 Garand rifle aimed at the door. They lowered their weapons when they saw Jeffrey.

"What in the hell were you thinking!" he demanded. "You go off for a snack while I'm interrogating a prisoner! Now you've let them get away! You'll be court-martialed for this!"

Sergeant Roberts stared at him for a moment before he answered. "You remember that you aren't in charge of us, right, Scott? Your department asked for a favor from us, which we granted, but nobody said anything about you giving orders. If you'd told us we couldn't trust the two people who *were* under your command, who you locked in an office and told us we didn't need to worry about, we'd have stuck around, but we figured you weren't dumb enough to let them get free. Isn't that right, Sergeant Duchesne?" The taller soldier nodded in agreement.

"We are going after them, and we'll need more men. Where can I find them?"

"Now listen here, there's no way we're going on some wild-goose chase," said Duchesne. "We don't have one clue where they've gone off to. You'd better—"

"I'll use your phone," said Jeffrey. He stepped back down the hall to the office where he'd interrogated Heinz. He picked up the phone and made a call to his father, who in turn called a US senator friend. An hour later, he had the authorization for more men, and a critical piece of information—he had an address.

Jeffrey waited in the office for an hour until he heard the roaring and lurching of a truck out front. While he sat he stewed about Sara, cursing the girl. He remembered back to his days at Harvard and even before that at the privileged preparatory school he attended. No girl ever said no to him, at least once they knew who he was. But Sara, this stupid working-class German girl, didn't seem to care about any of that.

There was so much he could've done for her. Cigarettes, chocolate, dinners out. They could've had a grand old time until he had tired of her. When that happened, he always bought the girl a gold bracelet as a parting gift. Then he could move on to the next flower that caught his interest. And yet Sara was different from any woman he'd ever met. She'd said no over and over. She had instead run into the arms of some poor Jew. It made no sense. Weren't the Jews the enemy of the Germans? There must be something wrong with her, he realized. It certainly could have nothing to do with him, he told himself for the thousandth time.

That should have made him feel better, but for some reason it never did. But, he promised himself, what was about to happen next would make things right. He realized in some ways his situation was improved. As long as he was able to track them down, not only would he still get credit for capturing a Nazi war criminal and a significant asset for the US government, but also he would have his revenge on Sara and Max. They wouldn't get off now with a slap on the wrist. If he caught them, they'd be going to jail for a very long time.

Or perhaps something even worse might happen, he thought to himself. These captures could be tricky and fatalities tended to happen. What if Max died in the scuffle? He smiled to himself. Yes, that was exactly what should happen. He would get his revenge on Max, and Sara would be distraught.

Jeffrey could almost imagine her face in a jail cell when he came to visit her. Yes, that was something worth looking forward to. She'd be begging him for help then, but none would come. But for now he wasn't even sure any of this would come to pass. He would have to be a little lucky if he was going to track them down. Then again, wasn't his entire life based on luck? Being born into an important family was the luckiest event of all. No, he was certain that at the end of the day he would get exactly what he wanted. He always did.

Sergeant Roberts knocked on the door. "The other men are here, sir," he said.

Sir now, is it? thought Jeffrey, smiling to himself again. The sergeant learned fast. A couple of calls and now he was truly in charge of this operation. Now the soldier was following orders, but he should have listened in the first place. Well, he would have his revenge on these men as well. When the operation was over he would write up a negative report and he would make sure it found its way into both men's permanent military files.

A letter of condemnation from a US senator. Yes, that should do plenty to hurt their careers. This would be the last time anyone presumed to treat him like this. After this operation, he would be in a position so that none of these little people would ever treat him with anything but respect again.

"Sir, are you ready?" asked Roberts, pulling him out of his daydream.

"Why yes, Sergeant, I am, thank you," he said. No harm in being polite for the time being. He rose from the chair and followed the man downstairs. There was a truck out front now—what the soldiers called a *deuce and a half*, he thought he remembered. Was that because it weighed that much or carried that much? He wasn't sure. The vehicle had two doors in the front and a long bed in the back, covered by a green canvas top like the old wagons in the west.

"How many?" asked Scott.

"A full squad," said the sergeant.

"How many is that?" He saw the knowing smile on the sergeant's face. He'd known Jeffrey didn't know the answer to that. Another reason to squash this man when all of this was over.

"Twelve men, sir, including us."

He looked down at the note card he carried in his hand. He scanned the address again. This was his only chance to find Heinz. He jumped into the car with Sergeant Roberts at the wheel. Sergeant Duchesne was driving the truck. He sat in the back seat as was his due. He handed the card to the sergeant, who glanced down at it.

"I'll give you directions," said Jeffrey, looking down at a map. "Drive on, man." The sergeant moved the car out onto the street, the truck rumbling into motion behind them.

There wasn't much talk along the way. Jeffrey kept his eyes on the map, giving periodic commands to the sergeant. They reached the highway after a few minutes and began following it back toward Munich. After a half hour Jeffrey told the sergeant to turn right down a narrow side road that was covered with a thick layer of snow.

"We've got to put chains on, sir," said the sergeant, slowing the car down.

"Nonsense," said Jeffrey. "Drive on."

"But, sir."

"I said to drive on! Do it!" He was tired of the whining incompetence of these men.

The sergeant shook his head but didn't say anything else. *Good, he's learning his place.* They moved on, the car slipping and sliding in the snow as it struggled up a slight incline. After a mile or so they crested a hill and began a long, steep drive down the narrow road toward a cluster of houses a half mile away nestled in a valley.

"We need to put on chains, sir," the sergeant said again. "We can't go down this thing without them."

"I told you to drive on. We don't have time for that kind of nonsense."

The sergeant started to say something else, but apparently changed his mind. He started down the hill, tapping on his brakes and shifting into a lower gear. Despite his efforts, the car picked up speed. The sergeant started to grumble. Jeffrey, who hadn't been paying attention, looked up from his map again.

"What in the hell are you about, mister?"

"We've lost control," said the sergeant.

Jeffrey swore he saw a smile on the man's face in the rear-view mirror.

"Fix it, Sergeant!"

"Nothing to do now, sir. I told you we needed those chains."

They were speeding down the hill now. The sergeant was still pumping the brakes, trying to slow their descent, but he couldn't do so radically without crashing the car into the fences on each side of the narrow road. Jeffrey saw in horror that the road abruptly ended in a "t" at the base of the hill, and there was a tall wooden fence directly across the road at the bottom.

"We're going to hit it," said the sergeant, his voice a little shaky. "You'd better crouch down and hold on to something."

"Save me, Sergeant!" shouted Jeffrey, terrified now. He crouched down on the seat and closed his eyes, praying for his life.

The car crashed through the gate, slamming Jeffrey against the front seat. The vehicle tumbled and jerked, sliding sideways, slowing down as it spun. It came to rest, still upright, a few seconds later. Jeffrey opened his eyes. He was still alive. He checked his arms and legs. He seemed unhurt. He rose up, looking around. They had crashed through the gate, and came to rest fifty yards or so into an open field. The sergeant turned around, looking at Jeffrey. He had blood on his face from a wound on his forehead.

"You okay, sir?" he asked.

"Yes, no thanks to you, you idiot. Why the hell did you bring us down this hill with no chains?"

"But, sir, you—"

"Don't you question me, Sergeant." He looked around. "Where is the truck?"

"Still at the top of the hill, sir. They weren't about to try that thing without chains on."

"Well, that's something then," said Jeffrey. "How are we getting this car out of here?"

"No chance of that," said Roberts. "We'll have to come collect it later, if you want to keep going, that is."

"Yes, yes, we must keep going. Go get the men down here, Sergeant, and be quick about it."

"Yes, sir."

The sergeant stepped out of the car and trudged slowly through the snow. It was almost knee deep here. He reached the fence and started his way back up the hill. The man was taking his time, Jeffrey noticed, growing angrier by the moment.

He felt sore all over. He looked himself over again carefully, searching for any injuries. There were none. He'd been lucky. Lucky again, he thought, smiling. Just like he would be on this mission. He waited impatiently for the men to make their way down the hill. The car grew cold. That numbskull should have left the engine on, he thought. He probably shut it off on purpose. He rubbed his hands together; he needed some gloves and a thicker jacket. No matter, he wouldn't be here long.

The men were making their way down the hill now, rifles at the ready. *His men.* They would do what he told them to do. When they were about halfway down the hill he opened his door and stepped into the snow. His feet were covered with the frozen stuff immediately. He had shoes on, not boots, and he could feel the snow seeping into his socks and the bottoms of his trousers. He ignored the unpleasant feeling and trudged through the field, wobbling toward the broken fence and the road.

Jeffrey met the squad at the base of the hill. "Roberts, do you know which house we are going to?"

The sergeant nodded. "Based on prior intelligence reports, I think it's this one here," he said, motioning to a small house to their immediate left.

"Well, let's get this over with," said Jeffrey. "Follow me."

"Sir, is it smart for us to just walk up to the front door?" asked the sergeant.

Jeffrey scoffed. "We are Americans," he said. "Nobody would dare touch us. Now let's go!"

Jeffrey tromped down the road and then took a right into the driveway of the house. He reached up and patted the inside of his coat, feeling the pistol there. It never hurt to be prepared, just in case. "Spread out," he ordered the men as he approached the front door. The men stood and stared at him, none of them moving.

"Sergeant Roberts, make them do it."

The sergeant turned to his men. "Take positions," he said.

The squad scattered, the men taking individual spots around the yard, some squatting behind trees and a few behind the occupant's automobile. In a few moments, Jeffrey was satisfied and he turned and approached the front door. He took a deep breath and rapped his knuckles on the door. Nobody answered. He knocked again, harder this time. He pressed his head against the door but he didn't hear anyone inside. There was nobody home, he realized, or perhaps they were hiding from him. He was about to order the sergeant to break down the door when he realized he could hear sounds, but not coming from the house. He cocked his head, listening. The noises were coming from behind the house. He stepped off the porch and moved back toward the driveway. Behind the house, perhaps fifty yards away, there was a large square outbuilding. He listened again. This was the source of the noise—which sounded like many people talking at the same time.

"They must be in there," said Jeffrey. "Let's go." He marched down the driveway, Sergeant Roberts by his side. He was halfway to the building when he realized that the rest of the squad had not followed them. No matter. As they drew closer he saw the footprints of many people, not only coming from what appeared to be the house but also from the left and right through the fields from the other houses. There must be some sort of gathering going on, he thought. Well, they were all in for a surprise.

He reached the door, which contained a small square window. Jeffrey glanced inside and sure enough, there was a party of some kind going on. Long tables were full of food of every description. Men and women milled about, visiting with each other while a few children ran about the space, playing. There was classical music playing in the background. Jeffrey saw that the building must usually serve as a shop. At the far end there were a number of expensive tools lined up along benches, including a drill press, a table saw, and a giant planer.

Jeffrey thought about knocking but decided against it. He tried the door handle and found it was unlocked. He pushed the door open and strode into the building, the sergeant coming in behind him.

The crowd looked up and Jeffrey could see the looks of surprise as they glanced at the American uniform on the sergeant. The pleasant chatter died away quickly and soon only the children's playing could be heard. A woman stepped over to the record player and lifted the needle. In moments they were in dead silence.

One of the men stepped forward, a giant with an eye patch and a bald head. "What is this all about?" the man asked in perfect English.

Jeffrey drew himself up. "I'm Jeffrey Scott from the US government," he said. "I am looking for Otto Berg."

"Otto Berg?" whispered Roberts. "*Der Dämon*? Why didn't we bring the rest of the men?"

Jeffrey turned around. "Quiet, I'm in command here."

He turned back to the giant. "Are you Otto?"

"Who wants to know?" asked the man.

"I'm Jeffrey Scott with the Department of Public Affairs," he said, flashing an identification that nobody looked at. "I'm on a mission to find Heinz Hoffman and I understand you were protecting him until recently. I have questions for you—questions you are required to answer."

There was laughter behind Otto and the commando smiled, placing his arm around a blonde woman. "I'm sorry, but we are currently having a party," he said. "Come back tomorrow and I'll try to fit you into my schedule." Otto turned back toward the crowd.

"I demand that you speak with me now," said Jeffrey, "or you will be immediately arrested."

Otto turned back around. "You are threatening to arrest me in front of my wife and my children, in front of my friends?"

His voice was deadly quiet. Jeffrey felt a prick of fear. Even though they were more or less the same height, this monster of a man must outweigh him by a hundred pounds—all of it muscle. Jeffrey glanced around and realized for the first time that the other men in the room were all about the same age, and they all seemed fit and attentive. Several of them were moving around behind Jeffrey and the sergeant. Men and women were staring at him with what very much looked like hatred. Why had he left the rest of the men behind?

"I have a squad of men right outside this door," he announced loudly, his voice cracking a little. "Otto, you will come with me now," he said, snapping his fingers.

"There's only twelve of you? Or are you lucky number thirteen?" Otto asked. "That's not so many graves," he said, shrugging. "I told you, Mr. Scott, we're having a party. I'll talk to you tomorrow. Unless you'd like to join us and have something to eat?"

Jeffrey reached into his inside pocket and retrieved his pistol. He tore it out, his hand shaking a little as he aimed it at Otto.

"Jeffrey, don't do it!" warned the sergeant.

"Shut your mouth," he said. "I mean it, Otto."

The commando glanced at the pistol and laughed. "What are you going to do, shoot me in front of my friends?"

"If I have to," warned Jeffrey.

"If you fire that weapon we are dead men," warned Roberts.

"I told you to keep quiet!" He focused back on Otto. "I said now and I mean now," said Jeffrey.

"Very well," said Otto, setting down a plate of food he was holding and starting toward them.

"Move slowly," ordered Jeffrey.

"Whatever you command," said Otto, his face unreadable. He raised his arms and took cautious steps toward Jeffrey. When he was a couple of yards away he stopped. "Now, what do you want to talk about?" he asked.

"I—"

Otto leapt forward; his right foot flashed out with lightning speed, kicking the pistol out of Jeffrey's hand. He squared up again and punched Jeffrey in the throat, knocking him to the ground. Roberts raised his rifle but two men stepped up behind him, putting hands on his shoulders. Otto looked at Roberts and shook his head. "You don't want to do that," he said. "And my business is not with you."

Jeffrey was staring at the ceiling, his hands around his neck. He was choking from the severe pain in his throat, and he struggled to catch his breath. Otto stepped over to him, reaching down and wrenching him to his feet with the front of his shirt. He lifted Jeffrey over his shoulder like he was a sack of flour and marched him through the crowd and over to the nearest table, shoving some of the food out of the way.

Otto smashed Jeffrey's face hard against the surface of the table and held the back of his neck so the American couldn't move. Jeffrey heard the commando unbuckling his belt and pulling it through the loops of his pants. "Now," said Otto, "I will show you what I do to bad little boys who don't listen." He whipped the belt down, cracking it against Jeffrey's buttocks. The pain was searing and Jeffrey called out, but Otto wasn't finished. He hit him again and again, counting as he went. When he reached ten, he stopped. Jeffrey's backside was on fire; he felt hot tears streaming down his cheeks. Jeffrey squirmed and fought but Otto held him with an iron grip. "Have you had enough?" he asked.

Jeffrey could hear the mocking laughter coming from behind him. He looked to his right and there was a group of young children watching, their mouths open in shock. He was furious and humiliated. All he could think of was killing this man. But there was nothing he could do; he stayed silent for a few more seconds until Otto pushed his face harder onto the table surface.

"Yes, I've had enough," he muttered through gritted teeth.

"Excellent," said Otto. "A good lesson learned then. Now, let's talk." He seized the back of Jeffrey's shirt and jerked him up again, dragging him through the crowd and over to the end of the building toward the machine tools at the back of the shop. Otto shoved Jeffrey's head under a huge drill press, reaching down to turn the machine on. Jeffrey could see out of the corner of his eye the one-inch-thick drill bit spinning a foot above his head.

"Now," said Otto pleasantly. "You understand who you're dealing with." He flicked a switch and the drill bit sped up. He moved it down a couple of inches.

Jeffrey tried to fight it but Otto held him in an iron grip. He felt warm liquid running down his legs and he realized to his humiliation he had pissed himself.

"While that's rather unpleasant," said Otto, glancing down at the wet spot spreading over Jeffrey's trousers, "now I've properly paid you back for embarrassing me in front of my friends. You were rude and you did not accept my invitation to speak politely to me like a gentleman." He pulled the bit down a couple more inches. "So, what is it you want from me that is so important that it can't wait until tomorrow?"

Jeffrey struggled to speak. He was white hot with fear and anger and his eyes kept darting up at the spinning drill bit that was only about six inches away now.

"Spit it out," said Otto. "I've got guests."

"Heinz Hoffman was captured by me today," he managed to say. "He . . . he escaped our custody with the help of two German traitors."

"Do you mean that woman and Jew?" asked Otto, laughing. "You let them take Heinz away from you? You must be a bigger fool than you already seemed to me."

"Shut your mouth," said Jeffrey.

Otto shook his head. He reached up and moved the bit down another four inches. It was a bare two inches above Jeffrey's head now. Otto leaned in and whispered into his ear. "I'd be careful what you have to say now. What do you want from me?"

"You must know where Heinz is."

Otto shrugged. "How would I know—my work with him is done. I was paid to get him to the train and to the train I delivered him."

"That's right," said Jeffrey. "You helped a wanted Nazi escape. If you don't want to spend the rest of your life in jail, you better tell me what you know right now."

Otto moved the bit down another inch. He reached down and retrieved a marker from the bench. Still holding Jeffrey's head perfectly still with his other hand, he drew a big "X" on the American's temple. "It's not smart to threaten me," said Otto. "Yes, I helped a Nazi escape. I've helped many, many Nazis escape. But nobody is coming to arrest me. Certainly not a little whelp like you. Now I've got a nice mark on your head, just where I want the drill to go. So I'll ask again, what do you want from me?"

"I want you to help me track down Hoffman."

"Sure," said Otto. "I'll do it. For ten thousand dollars in gold."

"You have to be kidding," said Jeffrey.

Otto reached up again to the drill press.

"Okay! I believe you," said Jeffrey. "I'll get you the money."

"Today."

"I can't get it for you today," said Jeffrey. "But I promise you from the US government."

"Ten thousand dollars. In gold. Today. Otherwise, you get no help from me. I've half a mind to run this bit through your brain instead, but since you do work for the US government, and likely have access to resources, I'll repeat my request. I want gold for the information I have about Heinz, and I want it today."

"I'll get it," said Jeffrey.

"Good, we have a deal," said Otto. He shut off the drill press and whipped Jeffrey up to his feet. "Now, silly little boy, clean yourself off and go get my gold. We have two more hours for our party, then I'll be ready to leave with you. But only if you have the money in hand."

Jeffrey leaned against the workbench. He looked around at the women and children who were all staring at him, many of them glancing down at his trousers. He wanted to kill Otto right then, but he knew that was impossible. No matter. He would get his revenge soon enough.

"I'll get your ten thousand dollars if I can borrow your phone," he said.

"All right. You can use the phone in my house. But don't touch anything. There are fresh cookies in there. Don't touch. Aafke would be mad. Once you're done with the phone, get out and don't come back here until I'm done and you have the money. And remember, in gold."

"And also," said Otto, "I'll have a neighbor bring you some pants. Fritz here has a ten-year-old boy, his trousers should fit you fine."

Chapter 22

To Passau

Thursday, October 14, 1948
2:13 p.m.
Kaufbeuren, Bavaria, Germany

"We have to go after him!" shouted Sara from the driver's seat. She was a few blocks away from the American building now and she started to look around for a street to turn around on.

"No time for that!" shouted Max. "The soldiers will be armed now and Jeffrey is too. We would be caught if we went back." Max kept his pistol aimed at Heinz but he moved his other hand and placed it on Sara's shoulder. "It will be all right," he said. "He doesn't know where we are going."

Max was right, of course. Their plan was madness, but because of that there was no reason for Jeffrey to believe they would head toward Czechoslovakia. If anything, he might suspect they would take Heinz out into the woods and shoot him. There was no way he would think they would deliver him to the Russians for justice. Sara approached the next cross street. "I don't know where I'm going," she said.

"We need to head northeast," said Max. "Try to find the highway. We are probably three hours away."

"Don't we have a map?" she asked.

"I don't think so," said Max, "but check the glove box." Sara kept one eye on the road and with her right hand groped the passenger dash. After a few tries, she managed to open the handle. She felt around and was happy to feel the thick folded paper of a map. She pulled it out and handed it into the back seat to Max.

"Be careful," she said, nodding toward Heinz.

"Where are you taking me?" asked Heinz. Neither of them answered as Max fumbled with the map with one hand while keeping his other on the pistol. Eventually Max was able to open the map and scan the contents. "It's a map of all of Germany," he said. "It's not going to help us with city streets or side roads, but I see the highway we need to take."

"Where is it?" she asked.

"It looks like it springs from about the center of town. Head left here," he ordered.

Sara continued to speed through the town. They were definitely heading toward the downtown now though, she thought, as storefronts and three-story structures popped up in front of her. Finally, Max shouted at her to turn left again, and she did so, spotting a sign that said MUNICH as she did so. She kept on this road and fifteen minutes later they were out of the town and back into the farmland. Sara felt comfortable about where they were headed now, and she could use the Alps to her right to make sure she was going in the right direction.

They headed almost due north for some distance, until they came to the city of Buchloe, where they turned right and passed the sparkling blue waters of the Diessen am Ammersee before arriving at Gilching and then into the suburbs of Munich.

"Why are we going back to Munich?" Heinz asked. "Can you please tell me where we are going?"

"Perhaps you should be asking why we are taking you anywhere," said Max.

"Fair enough," said Heinz. "Why are you taking me somewhere? Is it possible you are part of Odessa?" he asked, his voice hopeful.

Max scoffed. "We are the farthest thing from Odessa," he said. "But you already know that."

"I thought perhaps you were lying," the scientist said. "So you really are—"

"A Jew, yes, I am."

"I don't know you," said Heinz.

"No, you wouldn't, I'm sure," said Max. "You wouldn't recognize me or my brother. We were just insects to you. We were slave labor working in the caves—working for you along with my parents, my sister, and my brother."

Sara continued to watch Heinz in the rearview mirror. He had grown noticeably pale. She enjoyed the moment, watching a little justice transpire, watching a Nazi get his due.

"I don't know what to say," Heinz muttered at last. "Surely you must understand that—"

"What?" said Max. "That you were merely following orders?" He scoffed. "Don't you dare say that. You have to know by now that excuse doesn't work. Taken to its logical conclusion, the only responsible person in Germany would have been Adolf Hitler."

"All right," said Heinz. "I won't claim that. But still, you're here," he said. "You've survived the war. What do you want from me?"

"Yes, I survived," said Max, his voice beginning to shake. "But you sent us all to a concentration camp. My parents and sister died there. Karl and I were starved, beaten, left for dead. It was all your fault. We suffered, we died, because of you."

"I didn't send them anywhere," said Heinz. "You have to understand, none of this was in my control. When the project was completed, we were placed in hiding. I didn't know what happened to the labor force."

"The project wasn't completed," said Max. "The Americans were coming for you so you ran like rats while you sent my family to their deaths. You knew what was going to happen to us."

"There's nothing I could've done," Heinz said. "I'm sorry for your loss, but you must understand it wasn't my fault. I was just pursuing science. You don't understand the pressure we were under and we had no control over the labor."

"And that bastard friend of yours killed my brother," said Max.

"What are you talking about?"

"At the cottage," said Max. "My last relative, the only thing left to me, and your friend killed him."

Sara was watching more closely now as Max grew agitated.

"My friend?" asked Heinz. "Are you talking about Otto? That man's not my friend. He's out of his mind. He was assigned to me by Odessa. I had nothing to do with it. I've never killed anybody in my entire life."

"So it all comes back to you not being responsible for anything," said Max. He cocked the hammer on his pistol. "It was everybody else's fault and had nothing to do with you. The death of my entire family, the death of my brother."

"Max," said Sara, interrupting him. She had let this go on for a while, because she felt it was good for Max. She'd even taken some joy in it, but things were starting to get out of hand. Max was working himself up into a furor. She was afraid he might do something crazy. She remembered her concerns about Karl. "You cannot shoot him," she said. "He has to be brought to justice. We agreed on that."

"I know," said Max. "But he deserves to die."

"He will die," she said. "When we get to the Russians and he has a proper public trial. But not before. You promised me. I put my entire life at risk for you, my entire future."

"The Russians," said Heinz after a moment. "Ah yes, I am—"

"You are going to the Soviets, who will make sure that justice is done to you. If I don't shoot you before we get there."

Heinz stared at Sara with imploring eyes.

"Max, put the weapon down," she said. "There is no place for him to run. And I need your help getting through Munich."

They navigated through the city, Max giving her directions now and again in a quiet voice. Soon they were out of the city and heading northeast. Sara continued driving but kept one eye on the back seat, which had now devolved into a stony silence. That had been too close. She hadn't trusted Karl but she'd thought Max could control himself to get what he wanted.

They drove that way in silence for another hour and a half, passing Landshut, Landau, and various other towns along the way. Soon they were only a few miles out of Passau. Max kept his pistol on Heinz, who sat rigid and staring straight ahead.

It was dark and they were getting low on petrol, but Sara could already see the lights of the city in the distance. "It's getting late," she said. "What are we going to do next? We can't simply drive up to the border and ask to pass through, the guards would stop us and I'm sure our friend Heinz here would not cooperate. We need some time to rest and eat, and we need to look at your knee."

"I don't know what we should do," said Max. He reached into his pocket and pulled out his wallet, thumbing through the contents. "I have a little bit of money but I don't think enough for a hotel or even a decent meal. Jeffrey had the money Rupprecht gave to us."

Sara hadn't thought through all of this. They'd been on the fly since Jeffrey showed up in the first place and disrupted their plans. She'd thought they would get information from the beer hall owner and apprehend Heinz shortly thereafter. She'd never imagined they would be on the run or that they would need enough money for multiple hotels and days of meals. This was supposed to be a straightforward operation.

"I have a friend in town," said Heinz. "A fellow scientist

from the war. He would give us a decent meal and we could attend to Max's injury."

Max laughed. "You're kidding, right? We go visit your friend so he can turn us in or kill us where we sit?"

"He'd more likely have me shot," said Heinz. "He never agreed with the Nazis, or what we were doing. He resigned his position during the war and was arrested for his troubles. Besides, you have a gun and he most assuredly does not. You might think I'm trying to escape or get help, but right now, all I can think about is eating."

"Okay," said Max. "We will go to this friend for dinner. But that's it. We won't be staying the night. We'll have to cross the border tonight somehow, no matter how tired we might be. And remember," he said, "I'll have my pistol on you the whole time. If you say a thing to the family I'll kill all of them. Do you understand?"

Heinz nodded. He gave Sara directions into the town. As they drove, Sara considered the border problem. She knew nothing about the geography around here. She'd never been to Czechoslovakia. How would they get past the German border guards? Even if they did, why wouldn't the Czech border guards just shoot them on sight for invading their country? Well, one problem at a time. They did need something to eat, and it would give Max and her a little more time to think about what to do.

She drove into Passau and Heinz gave her directions. They crossed a river and headed into the downtown part of the city.

"This is the old city," he explained. "We just crossed the Danube. And there is the Inn and the Ilz. Three rivers come together here. It's beautiful during the day, and you should see the university. One of the nicest in Germany."

"We don't have time for a tourist trip," said Max. "Get us to your friend's house so we can eat and fix my knee."

Heinz continued to give them directions. They passed the

old city and made their way into the eastern suburbs. Ten minutes later they reached a block, much like the others they'd seen. Heinz directed them to stop halfway down the block. "That's his place there," said the scientist, pointing to a three-story townhouse. They stepped out of the vehicle. Max placed his pistol in his coat, but his hand was inside his pocket on the weapon.

"Remember what I told you," said Max. "One step out of line and I'll kill your friend and his entire family."

Heinz nodded without answering. He knocked at the front door. Max stood next to him, watching his face closely to ensure Heinz didn't try to communicate his situation with facial expressions. The door opened and a slender man in his fifties with peppered gray hair and gold-rimmed spectacles stared out at them. He looked back and forth at them, obviously surprised that a trio of people were standing at his front door uninvited. Finally, his eyes settled on Heinz. "Dr. Hoffman, is that you?" he asked.

Heinz nodded.

The man smiled. "But whatever are you doing here?" he asked. "And who are your friends?"

"This is doctoral candidate Sara Sturm and Doctor Max Portnoy. They are fellow scientists," he said. "And this is my old friend and political dissident, Doctor Peter Lutz. Peter, we are here for a conference at your university."

Peter seemed a little surprised by this and looked again at Max and Sara. "You're taking me aback, Heinz. What kind of conference would you be invited to that I wasn't? Should I be offended?"

"No, no, my friend. Sara here is finishing her doctorate and working directly for Max. The conference is for students. Max is supervising her and I just came along for the ride."

"But," said Peter, looking around and leaning in, as if someone might be listening, "I thought you were in hiding, my old friend."

Heinz laughed. "That old nonsense? No, I'm in the clear now. Aren't you going to invite us in?"

"Of course, of course. Please, by all means."

Sara had watched Dr. Lutz the entire time. He seemed very suspicious about what was going on. Her fears were confirmed a few moments later when he turned to them again.

"I find this all very peculiar, my friend. Why would you visit here without phoning ahead? Are you sure you aren't in some trouble? Are you being followed?"

"No, of course not," said Heinz. "I've been safe and secure for years now. Sure, there was some interest in me earlier, but all of that is passed now and I've been able to return back to work and to the university."

"I hadn't heard any of this," said Peter, looking suspiciously at all of them. Sara was watching him very carefully. She hoped Max was paying as much attention as she was.

Peter was quiet for a few moments and then clasped his hands together. "Well, in any event, here we are. You've come right at dinner time, so I hope you'll join us. Brita will be so excited to see you again." His face blanched for a second. "Of course we don't have much in the way of food. A little soup and some bread. But we will share all we have. I think I have a little wine as well. We'll make a proper reunion out of it."

"Excellent," said Heinz. "That's very kind of you. We would love to have some food and get a chance to catch up. I'd love to hear what you've been doing since the war."

Brita stepped into the front room just then. She was a woman in her midfifties, stout with gray hair. She wore her hair in a tight perm and eyes peered out through thick glasses. But she was smiling warmly and she was delighted when she was reintroduced to Heinz and introduced to the others.

"And where are the children?" asked Heinz. "Won't they be joining us?"

Peter laughed. "Unlike you, my friend, my children are

grown. Helmut is at the university and Trude is married with a little one on the way."

"You're going to be a grandparent?" said Heinz. "Well, we do have something to celebrate. I wish I'd known, I would've brought you a present!"

"Please excuse me for a few minutes while we get dinner together." Peter led them to the dining room and then his wife and he disappeared into the kitchen, coming back carrying plates to the table. The scientist stared at the wine. "Perhaps I have something better." The phone rang and Peter scurried off to answer it. He returned a few minutes later, a bottle of brandy in his hand. "Here we are," he said, filling all of their glasses with a little of the amber liquid. "A proper welcome."

They sat down to dinner shortly thereafter. Peter told Heinz all about his experiences during and after the war. The Germans had held him for about a month after he resigned his position. The Gestapo had interrogated him, fearing he might be a spy, but they seemed to lose interest in him quickly and Peter was allowed to return to Passau and resume his post at the university.

When the Allies arrived, they had arrested him and he'd faced questioning again, but he was released and he'd returned to his position yet again. "That seems to be my lot in life," said Peter, smiling. "People seem keen on arresting me, but they quickly figure out I'm rather a dull fellow with not much to add. I'm not an innovator like my friend Heinz here. I'm almost a lab assistant, really. Just retesting the theories of others."

"That's not true," said Heinz. "You're a fine scientist."

"I appreciate the sentiment, but I would point out who was wanted for years by the Americans and Russians, and who on the other hand they didn't care about at all."

"Well, in any event, all of that is behind us now," said Heinz. "How are the two of you doing here?"

"Well enough," said Peter. "It's hard to come by fuel sometimes, and as you can see our table is somewhat a more humble affair than it was before the war. Still, we make do with what we have. We are alive and we are safe. We've been luckier than most."

Peter turned his attention to his other guests. "Max, I don't think I've ever heard of you." Sara noticed that Peter was eyeing Max closely. "I find that rather odd," said Peter. "I thought I knew all the nuclear scientists in Germany."

"I only recently finished my doctorate," said Max, a trifle uncomfortably.

"And yet you're already serving as the supervisor for another candidate? How odd. What is your field of specialty?"

Max blanched at the question.

"He can't tell you," said Heinz. "He's working on something specifically for the Americans."

"Come now," said Peter. "Surely among friends we can share a little information."

"Well, I suppose it's all right for you to know if you keep it to yourself," said Heinz, leaning in. "He's working on a two-stage bomb."

"The hydrogen bomb?" said Peter, taken aback. "But surely the Americans wouldn't let Germans in Germany work on such a thing?"

"I told you," said Heinz. "It's a very secret research. The Americans are trying to stay ahead of the Soviets in the nuclear game. And Max here is their best hope among the Germans."

"A hydrogen bomb will never work," said Peter, crossing his arms. "It's nonsense."

"I think you said the same thing about the one-stage atomic bomb," said Heinz. "In any event, we can't tell you any more about it than that."

"And Max is the preeminent German scholar on thermonuclear devices, even though I've never heard of him?" said Peter, looking at Max again.

"He's young," said Heinz. "A prodigy."

"You have a lovely city," said Sara to Brita, trying to change the subject. She wanted to steer things before Heinz uttered something that would make Peter realize they were lying to him. "Have you always lived here?"

Brita looked over at Peter, almost as if she needed permission to answer. "Yes," she said finally.

"Were you able to stay here even during the war?" Sara asked.

"Yes," said Brita. "There was some bombing but we were very fortunate. Even when they took Peter away, first the Germans and then the Allies left me alone. We've been very blessed indeed." With that, Brita cleared the table and Peter poured a little more brandy, handing out cigarettes to all of them so they could enjoy an after-dinner smoke. The cigarettes were American.

"Let me get the evening paper," said Peter, excusing himself to step outside.

"I'm impressed you have American cigarettes," said Max to Brita, "these are very hard to come by."

"One of the perks of the university," she said. "But you're right, we don't have very many."

"Then we shouldn't take yours," said Sara, starting to return hers. "That's very kind of you, but no, please. Besides, we must be going."

"But surely you can stay longer," protested Peter, returning with a copy of the evening paper. "Stay the night, we'd love to stay up and visit with you more."

"We have a hotel in town," said Heinz.

"Which one?" said Peter. "I know all the best ones."

"I . . . I can't recall," said Heinz, "the name escapes me."

"That's rather odd too, my friend. So many mysteries tonight. Still, if you haven't registered, you haven't paid. I insist that you stay here instead."

"That's very kind of you," said Max. "But we have to leave early and it would be too much of an imposition on you. Thank you again." He stood and so did Sara. Peter again eyed them with a suspicious look. He turned to Heinz.

"Why don't you let the two of them go and you stay here with me, my old friend," he said.

Max glanced meaningfully at Heinz.

"Ah, no, I'm afraid I must go with them."

"Well, all right then, but it's a missed opportunity," said Peter, shrugging slightly. "At least let me escort you to the door."

Brita went into the kitchen and Peter walked them the short distance to the door, opening it for all of them.

"Well, it's been a pleasure to meet you all," he said.

"The pleasure was all mine," said Max, reaching out his hand.

Peter waved them all goodbye and closed the door behind them. He walked into his sitting room, taking a seat in his favorite chair and stoking his pipe. He lit it and closed his eyes, taking a couple of deep breaths. After a few minutes he reached over and picked up the receiver of his phone, slowly dialing out numbers he had memorized long ago. He waited a few moments and someone answered on the other end.

"They just left," he said. "They are heading for the Czech border." A voice responded on the other side, then asked him a question. "Yes," said Peter. "I took care of it."

Chapter 23
Closing the Net

Thursday, October 14, 1948
5:50 p.m.
Bavaria, Germany

Otto stood in his house. The picnic was over except for the cleanup, which he'd asked Aafke to do since he had business to attend to. That also kept her out of the house while he handled this idiot American.

"Hurry up!" he shouted at the bathroom door. There were some rustling noises and then the door opened. Jeffrey was standing there, wearing borrowed trousers that looked two sizes too small. They were skintight and three inches too short.

"That will do nicely," said Otto.

"These are ridiculous," said Jeffrey. "You have to have something better."

"They will do," said Otto. He noticed that the American sergeant was having a hard time holding in his laughter. Otto looked at the man and winked before returning to Jeffrey with a neutral stare.

"Fine," said Jeffrey at last, apparently giving up. "Your gold is on the way. It will be here in the next few minutes. So what is your magical help you are going to bring us?"

"I'll make a phone call," he said. Otto picked up the phone and made a call. He talked for a few minutes with someone, and then hung up.

"Well," said Jeffrey.

Otto shrugged. "I had a contact but it was a dead end." He stepped over and picked up a piece of apple strudel. "Do you want some?" he said, offering it to Jeffrey. "I made it myself."

"I wouldn't mind," said Roberts.

Otto cut him off a piece, and placed it on a plate. He started to take it over but then stopped himself. "I forgot the cream," he said. Returning to his icebox, he retrieved a covered bowl. "I made this fresh this morning," he said. "Fresh from my neighbor's cow. She is a miracle cow—always providing the best cream."

"Will you be quiet about the stupid dessert and tell me what we are doing next!" demanded Jeffrey. Otto stared at the American for a moment and Jeffrey looked down. "I apologize," he said at last.

"I have another call I can make. It might be a long shot, but I will try." He called the operator and asked for a number. He was patched through and he talked for a few minutes on the phone. He hung up.

"How do you like the strudel?" Otto asked the sergeant.

"It's phenomenal. Best I've ever had."

Otto smiled with pride. "My mother's recipe. It was hard to get ingredients during rationing, but I can make it now and again. It reminds me of home, before the war, before everything became sad."

"Can you please, for the love of God, tell me what your phone call was about?" asked Jeffrey through gritted teeth.

"I know where they are," he said.

"Where?" asked Jeffrey. "Let's go."

"Gold first," said Otto. "Now, who would like some tea?"

"Your gold is on the way!" said Jeffrey. "Damn it, this is our only chance. We have to go now!"

"Have some strudel. We're waiting for the gold."

"Damn it!" shouted Jeffrey, but under the stern glare of the commando he quickly looked down and didn't say anything else. Otto served him some pastry and cream but Jeffrey refused, with a pouting stare out the window.

"Did you serve during the war?" Otto asked the sergeant.

"Yeah," said Roberts. "In the Big Red One."

"*Ach*, the First Infantry Division. You were at the Bulge. So was I."

"So I've heard," said the sergeant, his face hardening.

Otto nodded. "You've heard a version of the story at least."

"Killing prisoners is no good."

"I agree," said Otto. "But—"

At that moment the front door opened and Aafke stepped in, the children in tow. The kids ran to Otto, throwing their arms around his legs. "Mutter told us you are leaving us again," said the little boy. "Don't go, Vater, please don't go."

Otto's face fell and he reached down, tousling his son's hair. "It will only be for a little while," he said. "I should be back in a few days. Then we'll take a nice long vacation."

"There's a truck pulling up," said Aafke, a look of concern on her face. "Is everything all right?"

Otto stepped over to her. "It's the payment I asked for," he said. "The ten thousand dollars in gold."

"Why gold?" she asked.

Otto smiled, whispering in her ear. "I just wanted to make it difficult on this snot little boy. Now listen, after I leave, get some of the boys together and have them take the money over to widow Schoener's house. Tell Frau Schoener she won't have to worry about how to make ends meet anymore."

Aafke took his hands. "I love you so much," she whispered.

"I love you too," he said. "But not in front of our guests now." Otto turned back to Jeffrey. "This gold will pay for another two or three war criminals to make their escape!" he barked loudly.

The phone rang and Otto stepped into the other room to answer. He returned a moment later. "Let's get going!" he barked.

"Where to?" asked Jeffrey.

"To Passau, of course."

Chapter 24

Flight

Thursday, October 14, 1948
7:37 p.m.
Passau, Germany

Sara maneuvered through the streets of Passau, trying to find her way back to the eastbound highway. Max was in the back again, guarding Heinz. The Nazi was quiet, staring out the side window.

"I don't understand you," said Max at last.

"Why is that?" the scientist asked.

"You made no attempt to betray us at dinner."

"I guess I've accepted my fate."

"You must have told him something," said Max. "Sara, we have to hurry."

She nodded. "Look ahead," she said. They were coming down a hill and the highway spread out before them to the left and the right. She weaved down the decline and took a right, heading toward the Czechoslovakian border.

"How far away do you think we are?" asked Max, staring at the map.

"It can't be much more than twenty miles," said Sara. "You still haven't told me how we are going to get over the border."

"I thought about that during dinner," he said. "I think we stop a mile or so before the border and then make our way on foot. If we can dodge any German patrols, we should be able to get over the border."

"And into the hands of a Czech patrol that will shoot us on sight," said Sara.

"We'll have to trust to our luck," said Max. He reached forward and squeezed her shoulder. "I'm sorry I've involved you in this," he said. "It's a fool's errand, I know. But I'm glad you're here with me."

She reached back and squeezed his hand. "I'm glad too," she said. "Whatever is about to happen, I'm glad I met you."

They drove along for another fifteen minutes. A sign announced the border was five miles away and to be prepared to stop. "Almost there," said Sara. "How much farther should we—"

The car shook and rumbled, the engine sputtering. "Something's wrong with the car," said Sara. She pressed on the accelerator and the car jerked, the engine coughed and died. Sara pulled over to the side of the road. "What's happened?" she asked.

"I don't know," said Max. "Here, take the pistol and I'll try to check things out." He handed the gun to her and she trained it on Heinz. He stepped out of the car with a flashlight, and opened the hood.

"Sara," said Heinz, "I want to—"

"Quiet!" she ordered. She watched Max tinkering with the engine, then he moved back to the gas tank. Finally, he stepped around to the driver's window.

"I think I know what's wrong," he said, holding up a finger. There was clear liquid on it.

"What is it?" she asked.

"Water in the gas tank," he said.

"But how?"

"Peter, I'll bet anything," said Max. "He excused himself to go get the evening paper, remember." Max turned to Heinz. "You did warn him, didn't you."

"I don't know what you're talking about," said Heinz.

"Don't lie to me!" said Max, pointing the pistol at the back window.

"Max! Enough!" ordered Sara. "I told you, he's not to be hurt."

"Well, what the hell are we going to do now?" Max asked. "We are still five miles from the border. I could limp maybe a mile through the woods, but not five."

"What about finding a ride from someone else?" she asked.

"And do what," said Max, sarcasm lacing his voice, "ask them to drop us off a mile from the border? We'd be in a German jail cell before midnight."

"We're going to have to try to make it on foot," she said.

Max shook his head. "I can't," he said. "No way."

"Look, Max, we have all night," said Sara. "We'll go fifty yards at a time. We can rest in between." She stepped out of the car and put her arms around him, kissing his cheek. "We've come so far," she said. "I know you can make it the rest of the way."

"I'll try," he said. "But I don't know how we'll make it."

"One step at a time," she said. "But for now, we've got to get into the woods and get moving before a police car spots us and pulls over to help."

Max looked at her. "You're braver than I ever imagined," he said. "Thank you for trusting me, and for believing in me."

"Let me take the pistol," she said. "You concentrate on walking and I'll keep an eye on Heinz."

He nodded, handing her the weapon and the flashlight. Sara

stepped around and opened the door, helping Heinz out of the car. He looked at her meaningfully but she turned her head, motioning for him to walk ahead of her. They took a few steps into the forest. Max reached down, picking up a serviceable branch he could use as a cane. He broke off the shoots and leaves as best he could and then nodded to Sara. The three of them moved off into the darkness, heading east.

Chapter 25
Closing the Ring

Thursday, October 14, 1948
10:13 p.m.
Passau, Germany

Otto left the townhouse, checking his watch. He stepped back to the truck. They'd been on the road now for almost three hours. He opened the passenger door of the deuce and a half and stepped into the seat. Jeffrey was there, wedged between him and Sergeant Roberts. Sergeant Duchesne was in the back with the rest of the men. "They headed for the border all right," he said. "I quizzed Peter and everything he told us before was true."

"Did you kill him?" asked Jeffrey.

"No," said Otto, his eyebrows furrowing. "Who do you think I am? I don't murder people for no reason. Honestly, Jeffrey, you need to reassess your views on people. The good news, our scientific friend in there knew enough that a few gallons of water would mess up their tank. He excused himself during dinner and poured a five-gallon drum in. With any luck, our friends didn't make it to the border."

"And if they did?" asked Jeffrey.

"If they did, then I'm sure the police would have arrested them on the spot. That's what you arranged for, isn't it?"

Jeffrey nodded. "I still don't like this. We're trusting this scientist friend of his far too much."

"Do you think he made up seeing Heinz tonight?" asked Otto. "Just for fun? And remember, Heinz thinks he's on his side. No, this is all too real."

Sergeant Roberts started the truck and maneuvered through the narrow residential streets and back down to the highway. They turned right and headed toward the Czechoslovakian border.

A few minutes later Otto spotted something. "Look, what's that?" he asked. "Pull over."

The sergeant eased the truck over to the right, parking behind an abandoned vehicle.

"That's ours all right," said Roberts, scanning the vehicle.

"So, Peter came through for us after all," said Otto. "I only hope we can catch them. They have an enormous head start. We'll have to run the whole way."

"What do you mean, run?" asked Jeffrey. "I can't run for miles."

"Then stay behind," said the sergeant, grinning at Otto.

"I'm coming with you," Jeffrey insisted.

"That's fine," said Otto, "but then you'll have to run."

"Sergeant, bring Duchesne and two more men with you," Jeffrey said. "Leave the others here to guard our equipment."

Roberts nodded and in a few moments they were ready.

"Let's go," said Jeffrey, darting into the woods. "We have them now."

Chapter 26

A Dance in the Dark

Thursday, October 14, 1948
10:53 p.m.
Czechoslovakian border, Germany

"I have to stop again, I'm sorry."

Sara halted, peering through the almost pitch-darkness at Max. He leaned against a tree, bending over to hold his knee. His breath was coming in rapid, ragged bursts. "I can't make it," he said. "I'm sorry, Sara. I just can't."

They'd been walking for hours, Sara hoped in the right direction. She was able to spot the stars now and again and she continued to orient them from the North Star. But they were making terribly slow progress. Max could only hobble about a hundred yards before he needed a break, sometimes as much as ten minutes. She calculated they still had at least another two miles, assuming they had more or less traveled in a straight line. How would they even know when they made it across? she wondered.

Every crack and unknown noise jolted her and fear coursed through her. Her biggest fear was coming across a German patrol that might shoot first and ask questions later. But now her attention was turning to Max. Keeping an eye on Heinz, she moved over to him.

"You've got to keep going," she said, taking his hands. "We only have a couple miles left."

Max couldn't even raise his head to look at her. "I can't do it," he said again. "I'm sorry, Sara. But I'm exhausted. I've got to rest."

"We can't rest now," she said. "Here, put your arm around my shoulder. We can walk together."

"What about Heinz?" he asked.

"I've still got my pistol," she said. "We will both keep an eye on him."

Max nodded his head and they moved on. He was pressing down on her shoulders heavily and she was quickly winded, but they were moving faster now and they made it a half mile before taking another break, then another half. They were only a mile from the border now. It was possible they'd even passed into Czechoslovakia already, since Sara didn't know exactly how far they'd had to go, or how far they'd traveled.

"We're going to make it," said Max, as they rested again. "I know I can make it now, because of you."

She kissed him on the forehead. "Yes. We are going to make it."

A flash of light caught her eye before them. At first she thought it was just her imagination but then she saw it again. She stared in the darkness, her eyes blinking as she tried to concentrate. She saw it a third time and there was no doubt. "There are men back there behind us," she whispered, "coming this way."

"We've got to go," said Max. "Take my arm."

Sara took his weight again and they moved out with Heinz

in front of them. They hobbled as fast as they could but she knew they were never going to make it. Max stumbled and fell, Sara falling with him. She hit the ground hard and the pistol flew out of her hand. Heinz had this chance to escape but he just stood there, staring down at them, his mouth open. A light flashed on his face and she heard shouting behind her in a voice she knew only too well.

She rolled over, staring behind her. The flashlights, for there were a number of them, bobbed in the darkness as the men approached. Figures appeared out of the darkness. She recognized Jeffrey first and then saw four American soldiers. She was surprised to see the bald man with the eye patch she'd last seen at the beer hall in what seemed a lifetime ago, lumbering out of the trees as well, a grim grin on his face.

Jeffrey's eyes were full of glee as he approached the three of them. The Americans fanned out, rifles raised. Otto stood directly behind the American leader, his face neutral.

Jeffrey clucked. "Well, well," he said. "Sara, you've been a very, very naughty girl. Trying to take this Nazi to the Russians? Why, I'd have to say that might be treason, my dear. And Max," he said, turning to face him. "You might have been given a lot of leeway because you're a Jew, but I don't think you're going to get away with this. It's years in prison for both of you, I'd fancy. If they don't just execute you. Of course it's a big promotion for me."

Jeffrey turned to Heinz. "Well, my friend," he said. "I'm sorry our conversation was cut short back at the office, but never fear, as I promised you, your family is safe and you're going to be well taken care of." He laughed. "What a funny world we live in where a wanted Nazi like Dr. Hoffman here is going to enjoy a dream life in the United States and at the same time the two of you are going to prison for trying to bring him to justice."

Heinz looked up at Otto. "Can't you help me?" he asked.

"Sure," said Otto. He drew a grenade out of his coat and pulled the pin, holding it up for everyone to see.

"Grenade!" shouted Sergeant Roberts.

"Well, yes," said Otto. "But it won't go bang unless I release my hand. Now, Miss Sturm, is it? If you'd be so kind as to collect Max there and also Dr. Hoffman, I'll hold these other folk for a few minutes until you can get across the border."

"What in the hell are you talking about?" demanded Jeffrey. "I paid you to help me catch them."

"True. But they are taking him across the border."

"Shoot him!" shouted Jeffrey.

"Sir, that's a really bad idea," said Sergeant Roberts. "Unless you want to visit Jesus today, I'd tell you we don't have any options here."

"Your men are much wiser than you are," said Otto. "Now, Miss Sturm, please be on your way."

Heinz looked at Otto as if he was going to say something, but he merely nodded and turned, his head down. Sara assisted Max to his feet and, leaving the pistol, they hobbled forward, back into the darkness. Soon they were lost from view.

"You son of a bitch," said Jeffrey. "You'll fry for that."

Otto ignored him, glancing at his watch now and again. When fifteen minutes had passed, he placed the pin back into the grenade but kept his hands together.

"Now shoot the bastard!" said Jeffrey.

"We can't, sir. He's still got the grenade."

Otto took a few steps back the way they had come. "I guess I'll bid you goodbye, Mr. Scott, for now." With a quick movement Otto pulled the pin again and lobbed it into the middle of the Americans; then turning, he sprinted into the darkness. Sergeant Duchesne fired a couple of rounds in the direction the commando was running, but then all of them were diving out of the way of the live grenade.

The metal ball hit the ground, right in the middle of the

group. Jeffrey landed hard a few yards away. He closed his eyes, wincing, waiting for death. A few moments later he heard laughter. He opened his eyes. The grenade was belching smoke into the forest, the white cloud wafting up to the sky, mocking him like some kind of genie. He yelled in animal rage, but there was nothing he could do. They were gone, and his dreams were gone with them.

Chapter 27
Across the Line

Thursday, October 14, 1948
11:18 p.m.
Czechoslovakian border, Germany

Max, Sara, and Heinz continued on in the darkness.

Max was struggling mightily now. He stopped, closing his eyes, his breath coming in ragged spurts. Sara, keeping an eye on Heinz, stopped to help him.

"Come on, Max, we're almost there."

He shook his head, leaning heaving against her. "I don't know if I can make it," he said.

"Nonsense," said Sara. "We've come so far. I know we're already in Czechoslovakia, we just need to find the border patrol."

"Why did Otto do that?" Max asked. He looked closely at Sara, his eyes searching for answers.

"How would I know?" said Sara. "You heard Heinz. The man is a lunatic."

"Jeffrey is going to be awfully disappointed," said Max, a wry smile creasing across his face.

"Yes," said Sara, smiling back. "The world is full of disappointments, and if anyone deserved a big one, it's the illustrious Mr. Scott."

"What do you think will happen to him?" asked Max.

"Who knows," said Sara. "If he's as connected as he claims, probably nothing. But he's not going to get some big promotion for what happened, and that's something at least."

"I still don't understand why Otto stopped him," said Max.

"You heard Sara," said Heinz. "The man is crazy." Heinz spat on the ground. "And he's left me in the lurch."

"What's that? In the distance?" asked Sara. She peered into the woods and she could make out flickering lights. It was a patrol for sure, but whether they were West Germans or Czechoslovakians, there was no way to know. "Have we made it far enough?" she asked.

"There's only one way to find out," said Max, grimacing as he took a step forward. "We'd better make some noise, or no matter who they are, they'll shoot us for sure," said Max. "Hey there!" he yelled in German. "We're coming out with our hands up!"

There was shouting in the distance and flashlights whipping through the woods. Sara's eyes were blinded by lights and there were harsh, screaming voices. Soldiers appeared among the trees, and for the second time that night they were surrounded in the woods by soldiers.

Max tried to talk to them in German but the men did not seem to understand. Sara smiled. They had made it.

The men shouted at them in what was obviously Czech, but she didn't understand what they were saying. They were roughly seized and searched, the soldiers pointing their weapons at them and screaming. Sara looked at Max and he smiled at her with a little sadness in his eyes. A soldier stepped forward and struck her on the head with a pistol, and the darkness swallowed her; she remembered nothing else.

Chapter 28
Questions and Answers

Tuesday, October 19, 1948
2:17 p.m.
East Berlin, Germany

Sara huddled in the corner of the cell, shaking in the cold. She hadn't eaten in days. She had no idea what time it was, how long it had been since the last interrogation. She raised her hand and ran her fingers along her lip. The cut was still there on her lower lip where the Russian interrogator had slapped her in her last session. Her head felt sore all over. She wondered if her face was covered in bruises.

She'd asked them over and over why they were beating her. After all, she'd helped bring Heinz to them. A real Nazi with blood on his hands. She kept trying to explain what it had cost her. She would be arrested and jailed, probably for life, if she ever returned to the American sector. She asked for Max over and over but the men ignored her, repeating their questions and beating her when she didn't answer.

She thought back to the last few days. They seemed as distant as her other life—her life before this pain. The Czechoslovakian guards had arrested them and taken them to a cell in Prague. They hadn't even bothered to ask her questions. They'd simply beaten her several times a day. But then the Russians had arrived. She'd been transported back to East Berlin to face questioning and, they told her, a future trial. She'd hoped she might be transported with Max—even to spend a few seconds with him would have given her comfort—but she was moved by car, wedged between two Soviet men with leather coats and stern faces. Her attempts to ask about Max had earned her a slap to the face and nothing else.

She'd arrived in East Berlin and been taken immediately to Stasi headquarters, the East German secret police. Since then, her existence consisted of endless hours in this bare cell, without even a bed or blanket, followed by torturous sessions with her accusers. Time would tick by in lonely isolation and then the door would be abruptly ripped open and a guard would drag her back to the interrogation room, where the questions would start all over again. Why had she come to Czechoslovakia? What was the nature of her work with the Americans? What true government agency did she work for? What was the real nature of her mission into Soviet territory?

She gave no answers they wanted to hear. She was a lowly secretary working for the Office of Public Affairs, she told them, over and over. She had violated the Americans' trust in every possible way to bring Hoffman here. Max and his brother were civilian Jews, motivated by justice. The Russians simply could not believe her. She didn't know what to do or how long she could last before, in desperation, she would admit to anything they wanted to hear, just to end the misery.

The door opened again. Fear tore through her. A grinning guard moved toward her, grabbing her by the hair. He dragged her to her feet and pulled her out of the cell and down the hallway. Her bare feet were torn and bleeding; she whimpered as she hobbled, trying to keep up with him. She tripped and fell to the ground, her head exploding in pain as her hair was torn out by the roots. The guard grimaced and screamed at her in Russian. He reached down and jerked her by the arm back to her feet. She cried out in pain. The guard slammed her against the wall, continuing to berate her. He dragged her back down the hallway another twenty yards until they reached an open door. He shoved her inside, slamming the door behind her.

Sara recognized the room immediately. It was the same size as her cell, but this space contained a bare wooden table and two chairs facing each other. This was the interrogation room. The only difference now was she was by herself. There'd always been an officer waiting for her before, seated at the table, a set of documents and a notepad set out before him. Always the same man, the same questions in German with his thick Russian accent.

She wondered what was different this time. She looked around in terror, expecting the man to rush out at her from the shadows. But there was nobody here. She stared at the chair. Her cell contained no furniture. She was forced to lie on the cold floor or slump against the wall. She hobbled toward the chair, hands shaking, and pulled it slowly away from the table. Painfully, she lowered herself into the seat. She expected the door to open at any moment, but it didn't. She had at least a few moments by herself. Taking a few ragged breaths, she leaned forward and put her arms and head on the table. She luxuriated in the chair, in a place to rest her head. In a few moments, she felt herself falling to sleep.

The door opened. She gasped and pulled herself up, preparing in fear for what she knew was coming. She stared in shock and surprise, as if she was looking at a ghost. It wasn't a guard, nor the officer. She was looking at Max.

Her lover was dressed in the same clothes she'd last seen him in. But he looked completely healthy. Even his knee was much better, and he walked with only the slightest limp. His face was full of concern and he smiled sadly at her. He rushed to her side and drew her out of the chair. She held him tightly, shaking in weakness and relief. His arms enveloped her and he kissed her head and face. "I'm so sorry," he kept repeating.

She held on to him for long minutes, her exhausted mind trying to grasp how he could be here. Was this real, or was she dreaming? She could hardly tell the difference anymore. But unlike the nightmares that had torn through her mind these past few days, here was strength and warmth. Here was love and security. "How can you be here?" she asked when she found the strength to speak.

"Don't worry about that right now," he said, pulling away from her and lowering her back into the seat. She could see the anger growing on his face. He marched to the door and tore it open. He stormed out of the room, returning a minute later. A guard appeared with a tray of hot food and tea. He placed the tray down on the table.

Sara was overwhelmed by the fragrance of warm bread and soup. She tore at the loaf, hands shaking, and stuffed some of it into her mouth. The food tasted better than anything she'd ever had before. She put more into her mouth. She heard herself growling and moaning in pleasure.

"Slow down," said Max, sitting down on the other side of her. "Take a few bites at a time. You're starving. If you eat too quickly, you'll be sick and worse off than before."

She could see the concern and the anger in Max's face. She was so confused, but her mind wouldn't work right now and all she could think of was the food in front of her. She forced herself to slow down, her eating and her mind. She closed her eyes, dipping chunks of bread into the soup and taking tiny bites, chewing a number of times before she swallowed. She felt something on her back and she jerked away, opening her eyes, but it was only Max. He was placing his coat over her shoulders. She closed her eyes again, letting the warmth envelop her, taking in the glory of the food.

After a time she was full. He poured her some tea and then he sat down across from her. His face had a strange expression she'd never seen, something mysterious, and expectant. She sipped away at her tea, trying to fight her exhaustion. She wanted to sleep but she was terrified that she would wake up and this would all be a dream. Besides, Max was here. Somehow, miraculously, and he was saving her, bringing her back to life. When her tea was finished, he asked her if she wanted anything more. She shook her head, pulling the coat more tightly around herself. As crushingly tired as she was, she felt better than she had in as long as she could remember.

Max cleared away the tray and took it to the door. He knocked and a guard poked his head in. Sara recognized the man. He was the one who had dragged her here in the first place. She whimpered, moving the chair back, bracing herself, preparing to face whatever was coming her way. Max looked sharply at her and then at the guard. He turned and waved the man out, before closing the door and coming back to her. "I'm sorry about that," he said. "You have no idea how sorry. If I'd known any of this was going to happen, I would never—"

"How can this be?" she asked, her face still broadcasting confusion. "How can you be free while they've done this to me?"

"I wasn't free," he said. "Not until this morning. I came to you straightaway." His face flashed anger. "They had their questions for me as well, which is unforgivable."

"What do you mean, Max?" she asked. She knew he was about to tell her his secret. "You say they held you as well, and yet you are untouched. You look healthy. You still have your regular clothes. Why did they leave you alone and yet do this to me?"

He reached across and took her hands. She started to pull away but his hands held her. They were so warm and she'd been cold for so many days now. She looked into his eyes. That look was there again on his features. A look of trepidation. "Why?" she asked again.

"This won't be easy for you to hear, but I need you to listen to everything."

"What's going on?" she asked.

"Sara. My dearest. I'm not who you think I am."

Her face flashed with fear, her hands began to shake. She tried to pull away but he wouldn't let her.

"I work for the East German government," he said. "For the Stasi. I was sent to West Berlin to try to gain access to Hoffman."

"But why would you want Hoffman?" she asked.

"Think about it," he said. "He's a nuclear scientist. My people, we are behind the Americans. We don't have our own atom bomb. Until we have one, the world is in imminent danger of a war, is it not?"

She tore her hands away. "Your people," she said accusingly. "You must mean the Russians."

He started to say something and then stopped himself. "Fine. The Russians. But they are our allies, we are all one people, with one socialist future together."

"You're the enemy!" she hissed. "And you led me to betray my people."

"*Your people?*" he asked. "You are a German. Your people were defeated by the Americans. They are your enemy, not me." He tried to take her hands again but she put them behind her back.

"What about Karl?" she asked, her mind playing through the past few weeks. "Is he even your brother?"

"Yes. He is my brother, and we are Jews."

"You lied to me about everything else though," she said.

"You almost cost me my life. You have cost me my future. I'm a criminal now to the Americans. I did all of that for you, for our love. But it was all a lie. You never loved me! You used me and destroyed my life!" She started to cry, the tears streaming down her face.

"You're wrong!" he said insistently. "So much of what I told you was the truth. We were slave labor under Hoffman. We did lose most of our family to a concentration camp. But our camp was liberated by the Russians, not the Americans. The East German government approached us soon after. They knew we had connections in the West. They knew about Hoffman. They asked us to train for a special mission, to find this scientist who was at large and bring him to the East."

"You lied about us," she said.

"No. Well, at first. I will admit, I started our relationship out of duty, but Sara, you must listen to me," he said. "Somewhere along the way, I did fall in love with you."

"That's another of your lies!" she shouted.

"No, it is not!" he shouted back. "You may think everything was a lie but it wasn't. When I first met you, I thought it was a miracle. Here was a chance to get through the blockade and into Bavaria. A chance to go after Hoffman. But as time went on, I saw your frailness, your love, your spirit. I did fall in love with you, Sara! It killed me to keep lying to you. But if I had told you, what then? I would have been arrested and I would have never seen you again. This way—"

"This way you've completed your mission and ruined my life in the process."

"No, Sara. This way we can be together forever."

"What do you mean?" she asked, wiping the tears with the back of his coat sleeve. Her face showed her pain, her confusion, but she wanted to listen to him, even if their time was coming to an end forever.

"You're right that I completed my mission. Hoffman will

help us immensely. I've been given a promotion, new duties."
His face darkened. "Although they had enough questions for
me before they told me the end result."

"Why would they have questioned you?" she asked.

"Because of you, my love," he said. "Right away I told
them that I was in love with you, that I wanted to spend the
rest of my life with you. They thought you'd cast some sort of
spell on me. They knew you worked for an American organization. They've spent the past week drilling me about that,
from every angle they could contrive, trying to get me to
admit that there is something more nefarious going on here.
Today they admitted they were satisfied with my answers,
and with yours. I had thought you were getting the same
treatment as me. Just daily questioning. If I had known what
was going on . . ." His fingers twisted, then balled into two
fists. "Don't you worry, my dear. There will be severe pun-
ishments for what has happened to you."

"But look what you've done to me," she said at last, not able
to think of anything else to say. "You've ruined my life."

"How?" he asked. "You were alone, working a secretary
job. You barely had enough to eat or coal to warm you. Here
you will be treated well. The Americans have lied to you," he
said. "People here are well taken care of. Every job is treated
with respect, women and men are equal. You will be respected,
promoted. You have invaluable information you can provide
the Stasi."

"What information?" she asked. "You just said it, I was a
secretary, at an unimportant department."

"You don't understand how much you know, my dear! You
worked for the Americans," he said. "You had access to their
technology, their record keeping, their processes. Knowledge
of transportation in and out of West Berlin. Trust me," he said,
reaching out for her hand again. "You have much that will be

invaluable for us. They will treat you well for it and someday you will be the wife of a senior Stasi official."

"Wife, then you mean . . ."

"I want you to marry me, Sara," he said, taking both of her hands in his. "I want us to be married right away. My promotion entitles me to a two-bedroom flat in the best part of the city. We will have plenty of food, plenty of heat. We will start building our life together. A socialist life, where everyone is taken care of. Please tell me you will say yes."

She stared at him in utter surprise, her mind reeling. Marry him? An East German spy? She sat there for some time, her eyebrows furrowed, her face flushed. "I need some time to think about things," she said at last.

"Of course," he said, taking a deep breath. It seemed her response was better than he had feared. "You'll have as much time as you need. Let me escort you to your quarters."

She froze, terrified. "I can't go back there," she said.

He laughed. "Of course not, my dear. You'll have a proper bed and as much time as you need." He took her hand and led her out of the interrogation room and past the guard, who now looked visibly nervous. *Good*, she thought. *You think you're nervous now* . . . He led her down the corridor, past more doors that she was sure led to other cells. They turned the corner and down another series of hallways until they reached a set of bars. Max barked at a guard and the soldier fumbled with his keys, unlocking the door and quickly opening it. Max continued on through another set of hallways and then up a couple of flights of stairs. Sara had to take the stairwell slowly, and he put his arms around her, pulling her up each stair gently.

Finally, they reached a new hall and Max stopped at a doorway to his left, pulling out a key to open it. "My quarters for the past few days," he said. She stepped inside. The room was bare and quite small, but there was a window and a bed. Next to the bed was a table with a lamp and a few books. Across the way was a chair and a standing rack with a few clothes hung up on it. "Here you are," said Max. "Get some rest. I'll check in with you tomorrow morning. Then we can talk some more."

"But if this is your quarters," she said, "where will you sleep?"

"I'll grab another room down the hall," he said. "These are temporary quarters for visiting officers. Don't worry," he told her, taking her hand. "I'll be very close and I won't let anything happen to you. Not ever again. For now, get some sleep." He reached in to kiss her but she turned her head. He started to say something then stopped himself. "I understand. Get some rest, my love."

He closed the door behind her. She wanted to process everything now but she was exhausted. She pulled the covers aside and collapsed into the bed. She drew the blankets over her and fell almost immediately asleep.

She woke the next morning feeling greatly refreshed. There was a tray on her table with breakfast and tea. Her clothes were also there, laundered and neatly stacked on the chair. She dressed and then sat at the little table by his bed, eating and drinking her tea. She felt completely awake now and was able to consider her situation. That didn't necessarily help things. There was so much to consider. Max checked on her after a little while and she told him she needed some more time. She spent the morning turning over all of the points, considering her options and her future. When he returned in the afternoon with a new tray of lunch for two, she was ready to talk to him.

He brought in another chair. They had the room to themselves. He started the conversation.

"Were you able to sleep last night?" he asked.

"Yes."

"You look much improved this morning."

"I feel much better, thank you."

He stammered for a few seconds, obviously struggling with his thoughts. "Listen, Sara. I know I threw a lot at you yesterday. I also know I deceived you, and you have every right to tell me to go to hell and to never speak to me again. But the last part of our conversation was completely the truth. I love you, more than anything. I'm ready to start a life with you. I will marry you today. I know we can build a life together here. I also know that you've been deceived by the Americans about what it is like here. Certainly, we don't have all of the flash, the capitalism, the glitzy lights. But we have something better than that. We have equality. Everyone here receives according to their needs. Everyone contributes according to their abilities. This is the way the world was meant to be, not with a few aristocrats or rich people hogging all the resources. In this system, you are judged on the merits, and you are rewarded based on your efforts, and your contribution to the whole."

"I don't know about all of that," she said. "I guess I'll see. I lived so long under the Nazis, the system you are describing could hardly be worse. But that's not what I've been thinking about this morning. I've been thinking about us."

He shifted in the chair and leaned forward. This was clearly what he wanted to hear. "Tell me," he said. "Tell me, please. Will you have me?"

"Yes," she said. "I will marry you, Max. It will take me a little while to trust you, to believe everything you have to tell me, but just like you, I fell in love. You are the man I've always wanted. I feel safe with you and protected by you. You only lied to me about the reasons we were doing what we did, but I don't think you lied to me about your feelings for me. Even your passion for this socialist system. I can tell how much you believe in it. How passionate you are about it. I want your passion in my life, Max, I want you in my life."

He took her hands, the tears filling his eyes. "I can't believe you are saying this to me," he said. "I hoped against hope that you still loved me, that you could see past what I had to do, why I did what I did."

"Tell me one thing, my love. How could you turn Hoffman over to them? Knowing he would be protected. Knowing he would never be brought to justice?"

Max shook his head. "That was the hardest thing I've ever done," he said, "besides lying to you. To be honest, I secretly considered killing him once I got my hands on him. I could have done so and explained it away to my superiors. Not every operation succeeds. Karl wanted to kill him even more than me. I think he would have if he hadn't been shot himself. But something changed for me. Something that made it impossible to take any action against Hoffman."

"What was that?"

"You," he said.

"I don't understand."

"If the mission failed, we would have remained in the West. You would have gone back to your job. There was no way I could have brought you here, to talk to you about a future, about our future. I wanted you forever, more than I wanted revenge on Hoffman. That was the choice I had to make."

"So you let me ruin my life? So you could keep me?"

"Of course not," he said. "But again, Sara. What was your life in the West? You had nobody, you had nothing. Here you will have so much more, and we will have each other."

She nodded at last. "There is one thing I have to ask of you," she said.

"Anything."

"I have to go back one more time."

"Back? Where?"

"To West Berlin. There are things in my flat. Little pieces of my past. A few keepsakes from my brother and my parents. I have to get those things. They are all I have."

"Impossible," he said. "I can't let you go. We wouldn't get permission."

"How did you get through in the first place?" she asked.

"Well, there are a few exceptions," he said. "If you have the right diplomatic papers. But I can't imagine—"

"I need you to do this for me," she said. "You can come with me. I promise, I'll marry you the second we get back. But I have to get my things. I need to say goodbye to my old life. I need this from you, Max."

He shook his head, raising a hand to scratch his cheek. "I don't know, Sara, I don't think you understand what you're asking of me."

"They'll do it for you," she said. "You're a hero now. They owe you something. Think of it as payment for what they did to me. Tell them you demand it. They'll say yes, I know they will."

"All right," he said at last, rising to his feet. "I'll make the request. But don't get your hopes up. This is not the West, where people do whatever they want on a whim."

Sara stood up and moved around the table. She reached her arms up around his neck and kissed Max deeply on the lips. He took her in a viselike grip and they held each other for long moments. "Thank you," she whispered. "I love you."

"I love you too, my dearest. You stay here, I'll go talk to my superiors. I should be back by suppertime."

He returned a few hours later, a smile on his face. "I tell you," he said, chuckling to her. "Maybe you understand our system better than I do. They approved. They are very excited about your decision. And excited to interview you, now that you will cooperate. Here are your passes," he said, waving some slips of paper at her. "According to this, we are members of the East German diplomatic corps."

"They will let us through?" she asked.

He nodded. "And we have some guards they are sending along with us . . . for our protection."

"When can we leave?" she asked.

"Right now," he said. "They want to start your interview in the morning. We will only have two hours. I apologize it can't be more."

"That's perfect," she said. "I don't need more than that." She rose. "So we can leave this second?"

He checked his watch. "Indeed, the clock is already ticking, we need to get going."

They left the room and hurried out of the building where a car waited for them. Max opened the door for her and then got in on the other side. There was already an East German soldier in the front seat, and another one at the wheel.

"Our escort," he explained.

"To keep an eye on us?" she asked.

"For our protection."

The car whisked them away from the building and into the snowy streets of East Berlin. There was virtually no traffic on the street. Sara was struck by how dark and dingy the buildings were. Even though West Berlin was still only half rebuilt from the war, there were cars everywhere and stores with bright lights and neon signs.

"It's so different here," she commented.

"Yes," said Max. "I told you there wouldn't be any of the flash of the West. But remember, that is merely shallow capitalism. There is no depth to it, no heart. You'll grow used to East Berlin soon enough, and before you know it the glitz of the West will make you ill."

She nodded, not sure she could believe that. The car turned onto a broad avenue and headed west. They drove for another few minutes. She could see in the distance a checkpoint, guarded by soldiers in two different uniforms. "This is the Friedrichstrasse checkpoint," said Max. "I believe your American friends call it Checkpoint Charlie."

She watched as the car slowed down and they approached the checkpoint. An East German soldier holding a machine gun stepped out into the street and raised a hand for them to stop. They pulled up near the gate and the driver rolled down the window. He spoke with the guard for a few moments and flashed his ID. The guard nodded and waved them through. They rolled into the neutral area between the two gates. A soldier in an American uniform was there, a rifle in his hands. He motioned for them to stop. The driver rolled the window down again and showed his ID. They spoke for a few moments in German and then the driver motioned to Max. Max handed forward his documents and the driver turned them over to the American. The soldier looked at them for a moment and then turned around, handing them to a West German policeman who reviewed the papers carefully for long minutes. Sara checked her watch. They'd already used up a half hour. If this took much longer, they wouldn't have time to reach her flat.

"Don't worry," Max whispered. "We're almost through."

True to Max's word, the policeman stepped forward and leaned into the car, looking them over. He looked at the paperwork again and then handed the documents back, giving a negligent wave for them to proceed. They had made it, they were safely into West Berlin. She sighed deeply in relief.

"Worried, were you?" Max asked, giving her hand a squeeze.

"If we were detained," she said, "they might have figured out who I am."

"I doubt that," he said. "Remember the blockade. They have far too much going on, to worry about little fish like us."

The car moved on, building up speed. They had to weave back and forth now among the traffic, stopping now and again for pedestrians to cross the street. The storefronts were lit up and the traffic lively.

"Garish really," said Max. "I've struggled these last few months putting up with it all. Although I didn't mind the restaurants too much, or the access to American tobacco."

The car continued on, moving through the streets of West Berlin. Fifteen minutes later, she started to recognize the buildings. "My neighborhood," she said quietly.

They pulled up in front of her building. Max looked up and down the street. "I don't see anything suspicious," he said at last. "Do you want me to go up with you?"

She shook her head. "I want to say goodbye to my old life. I will collect those few things and just spend a little time up there. I won't be long."

He reached over and kissed her warmly. "We'll be home again in no time," he said. "I'll have them drive you by my current flat. It's not much, but it's home. We'll move to something better very soon. Speaking of soon, when would you like to marry me?" he asked.

"Tonight," she said. "If it can be arranged."

His eyes widened. "I'll move mountains to make it happen."

She kissed him again and left the car. Looking around to make sure nobody was watching her, she entered her building and then climbed the stairs. She still had to take her time, she had not recovered from her ordeal, but she felt excitement now and renewed energy. Finally arriving at the door to her apartment, she pulled her keys out and let herself in. She tried to be quiet. She didn't want to draw the attention of any of the neighbors.

Sara turned on the lights when she was inside. The apartment was freezing. She thought about starting a fire in her stove, but what was the point? She would only be here for a few minutes. She stepped over to the little kitchen and ran some hot water. She splashed her face, trying to revive herself a little. Turning back around, she took a deep breath. She was ready for what was to come next.

A light flicked on. She gasped. Sitting on her sofa, a leering smile on his face, was Jeffrey.

"So nice of you to join me, Sara," he said. "Nobody thought you'd be foolish enough to return here, but then again, they don't know you like I do."

"Jeffrey, I can explain," she said.

He lit a cigarette and whistled. The door tore open and American soldiers rushed in, weapons in hand. "No, I don't think you can."

Chapter 29
The End Game

Thursday, October 21, 1948
3:47 p.m.
West Berlin, Germany

Another interrogation room. Sara smiled to herself. The chairs in here had padded seats at least. There was tea for her and cigarettes if she wanted. She hadn't seen her cell yet but she was sure it would be nicer than the one the Russians had provided her. There would probably be a mattress and a blanket. The Americans had a thing or two to learn about procuring information.

She thought of Max. What had they done with him and with the soldiers? What would become of him now? She wanted to talk to him. She wondered if she would ever see him again. The door opened and Jeffrey stepped in. He still wore the same sickening, arrogant smile he'd possessed in her flat. The same towering arrogance he'd lorded over her month after month. He was smoking too, as always. He offered her a cigarette but she declined.

He sat down at the table, settling in as if this was the moment he had waited for all his life. He leaned toward her. "I knew there was something about you," he said. "Mr. Varberg wouldn't listen to me, and now he's going to be even more in the hot seat, along with you. The old damned fool should have taken my advice and fired your ass long ago."

"Where is Mr. Varberg?" she asked. "I need to speak with him."

"I'll bet you do," he said. "So the two of you could try to get your stories straight. He'd probably like that too, but I'm not going to give either of you the chance. This is my arrest, and you are my prisoner. And I promise you, Sara, before I'm done with you, you're going to sing every song I've wanted to hear from you."

"I need to see Mr. Varberg," she said again, rising out of her chair.

"Sit down!" he shouted. He reached across the table, taking her by the shoulders, and shoved her down.

"Don't touch me," she said.

He smiled, wryly. "Ah yes. Don't touch me. That's the story you've always had for me, isn't it? From the first time I asked you out, you always declined. I thought there was something wrong with you, that maybe you didn't like me. But then Max came along. I didn't realize until then that you only had a taste for Jews."

"Shut your mouth," she said. "I advise you to stop right now and go get Mr. Varberg."

Jeffrey's forehead creased and an angry red vein appeared in the center. "And I told you there's nothing he can do for you! You're a traitor! You're going to rot in a federal prison for this—if they don't send you to the electric chair! But first you are going to tell me everything. You're going to spill the beans and there's one more thing you're going to do for me." He rose, stepping around the table toward her. "We're finally going to have that date that you've always denied me."

Sara felt adrenaline course through her body. This was getting out of control. "What are you talking about, Jeffrey? Come on now, I'm in your custody, you know you can't touch me."

He stepped closer, a wild look in his eyes. "So you'll let that Jew have you but I'm not allowed. You will deny me this like you denied my right to go on this mission! I'll be damned if you tell me no again!" He lunged at her, grabbing her hands.

Sara screamed for help, pulling away from him. He tried to drag her out of the chair but she kept her balance. She screamed again but nobody was coming. "I told you!" he shouted. "You're not going to stop me this time!"

Sara pulled her arms back violently, sending Jeffrey stumbling toward her. She head-butted him hard in the face. His head thrashed back and he shouted in pain, his arms flailing to gain his balance. She kicked him in the crotch, then brought her heel down on his right knee, shattering it with one hard kick. In the same movement she lashed out with lightning speed, grabbing the back of his head, and smashed it to the table. Jeffrey crumpled to the floor, knocked out by the blow. His right leg jutted out backward at a horrible angle and blood flowed freely from his nose and forehead.

"I told you, you don't get to touch me," she said, spitting on the still figure.

The door crashed open. Guards appeared, pistols aimed at her head. Mr. Varberg rushed in, his face mottled and eyes wide. He looked at Sara and then down at Jeffrey.

"What the hell happened?" he demanded.

"Your lecherous assistant tried to rape me," she muttered through clenched teeth. "I taught him a little lesson."

Mr. Varberg stared down at Jeffrey for a moment longer and then raised his face to Sara. "Come with me," he said at last.

The door opened to Max's interrogation room. He was seated at the table, drinking a cup of coffee. Sara entered the room and he rose. "My dearest!" he shouted, rising to embrace her.

"You need to have a seat," she said.

"But—"

"Please sit down, Max, we need to talk."

He was confused but he listened to her, taking his seat. "I'm so glad to see you. But how can you be here?" He reached out for her hands but she pulled them off the table.

"Max, I have to tell you the truth now."

His face morphed into shock. "What do you mean?" he asked.

"You said you're not who I thought you were. I have to tell you the same," she said.

She could see the distress in his face, but she launched on. "I don't work for the Office of Public Affairs. I am an operative with the Central Intelligence Agency. We knew who you were, who Karl was. We knew what your mission was. I was tasked with accompanying you."

"How can that be?" he asked. "How could you know?"

"We have our methods."

"But our store? How did you even meet me?"

"Two agents came into town and vandalized your store. They were pretending to be American businessmen visiting to invest in the city. You met them in the woods. Sergeants Roberts and Duchesne. They were keeping an eye on Jeffrey, and keeping up the chase on you, so you didn't think things had gone too easily."

He nodded. "I see. Clever." But then his eyebrows furrowed. "Wait a second," he said. "You let me bring a German nuclear scientist to the Russians. You are a traitor; they will never forgive you for what you've done."

"Hoffman is a mole," she explained. "We arrested him with his family at the monastery, just like you heard. But he didn't get away. He cut a deal. In exchange for US citizenship for his family, a house, and a pension, he agreed to allow himself to be *caught* by you and taken to the Soviet bloc. He is going to gather intelligence about the Soviet nuclear program, and get that information to agents we have in Russia."

"That's impossible," he said, shaking his head. "We almost lost him several times. He was working with Odessa."

"He was working for us, and so was Odessa. They do, now and again."

"I can't believe you," he said. "I was the one deceiving you."

"I know it felt that way, but I assure you, I'm telling you the truth."

"But what about us?" he said. "What I told you then wasn't a lie—not for me."

"Max, I don't want to—"

"Tell me," he said. "Tell me the truth! Was it all a fake? Did you ever love me?"

"Just like you told me, at first, it was all just a mission. But as time went on, I admired your courage, your humor, your sensitivity."

"But did you love me? Did you truly want to marry me?"

"Max, don't ask those questions. I had a mission to accomplish. Who knows? In another world, another time, maybe there could have been something between us. But do I love you?" She looked away. "I'm sorry, Max. These are difficult times."

"I can't believe it," he said. "You lied to me the whole time. About everything." She kept staring at the wall, not wanting to look at him, to think about their time together. She heard an unusual sound, and realized he was laughing.

"Outwitted by a woman," he said. He put his head back and laughed again. "Congratulations to you, Sara Sturm." After a while, his face grew serious. "What happens to me now?" he asked.

"That depends," she said. "And that's why I came to see you. You have two futures in front of you, Max. If you cooperate, you'll be given a home in the United States. You'll be able to work with us, provide information. You'll be taken care of."

"And freedom?" he asked.

She shook her head. "You'll have to live on a base. You'll be watched. It's not a perfect life, Max, but it's life after all."

"Will I ever be exchanged?"

"I don't know. That wouldn't be my decision. But so long as Hoffman is in the Soviet Union, there's no way that would happen. If there is a chance, it will be years from now."

"And if I don't cooperate?"

"They will still interview you. For many years I would think. They won't kill you, I think, but your accommodations will be rather less desirable." She leaned forward. "Please, Max, I implore you to cooperate. There is no escape for you. You have information about Stasi that would be invaluable to us. Isn't that the same offer you made to me?"

He smiled sadly. "I offered to spend my life with you as well."

She rose, stepping around the table. She reached down, taking his head in her hands. She kissed him softly on the lips. "I'm sorry," she said. "I wish you the best."

"I love you," he whispered.

"I know." She started to pull away.

"Will I ever see you again?" he asked.

She reached down and kissed his forehead. "I don't think so. Goodbye, Max."

"Goodbye, my love."

Sara knocked on the door to Mr. Varberg's office. His *real* office. "Come in," he said. She took a seat across from him at his desk. "How are you feeling?" he asked.

"I'm doing just fine," she said.

"Fully recovered?" he asked.

She smiled. "Recovered enough. What's going to become of Jeffrey?" she asked.

"He's getting a thorough talking-to."

"Is that all?"

"He won't enjoy it."

"But he knows I'm an agent now," she said. "He's a danger to—"

"That's all I can tell you on that subject. But don't you worry about Jeffrey revealing who you are. I've made arrangements so he won't be telling any secrets. Let's move on to the business at hand." Varberg reached down and flipped through a folder. "Sara, I can't tell you enough how proud we all are of you," he said. "For a first mission, this was one for the record books."

"Thank you, sir," she said. "It got a little messy along the way, but I'm glad it turned out all right."

"All right is an understatement. You've scored a major coup. You not only planted a critical mole that will bring us invaluable information, but you brought back a Stasi agent we can mine."

"He's cooperating then?" she asked.

Varberg smiled. "Not yet, but he will. We flew him out to Washington this morning. We'll show him the houses available. Then the cells. He'll figure it out."

She nodded. "I hope he'll be okay."

"You didn't get too close to the situation, I hope, Sara. Sometimes it's hard to separate the mission from fantasy."

She fought down any emotion, keeping her face neutral. "No, sir, no problems at all."

"Good. Well, you have a month off before you need to report back to headquarters for your next assignment. What are you going to do?"

"I'm going to go home."

"That's right, you told me about your home. It's in Washington State, isn't it?"

She nodded. "That's where my parents immigrated from

Germany before the war. They own a little bakery in a small town called Snohomish."

"They were lucky to get out when they did," he said. "So few were as wise as they were."

"I know," she said. "I lost my grandparents and most of the rest of my family to the Holocaust."

"Did you ever tell Max you are a Jew?"

She shook her head. "No point. I had enough trouble with him as it was—I didn't need another reason to bring us closer."

"And your brother?" Varberg asked. "Any word?"

"Nothing new," she said. "He moved to a kibbutz in Palestine right after the war. He was involved with one of the secret Jewish organizations. He disappeared during one of the actions against the Arabs. I'd like to go there and find out what happened."

"You may get your chance," Varberg said.

"What do you mean?"

"The Israelis heard about your exploits. They want to borrow you for a special mission."

Chapter 30

Justice

Thursday, October 21, 1948
8:55 p.m.
West Berlin, Germany

Jeffrey hobbled on his crutches up to the door of his apartment building. The doorman greeted him, glancing down at his cast. Jeffrey scowled at the man and limped in through the secure doors, making his way slowly to the elevator.

He couldn't believe what had happened. He'd been duped this entire time. Sara was an agent for the CIA and so was Varberg. Heinz had been working for them also, or agreed to work with them. He'd been made a fool of—everyone was laughing at him.

And that vicious bitch had crushed his knee. The doctor said it might never work properly. He stepped off the elevator and moved toward his apartment, his mind racing. He would call his father immediately. There would be hell to pay for what they did to him. So what if Varberg was in the CIA? That didn't make him immune to the rest of the government. He'd get his revenge on both of them. With any luck, they'd both be thrown out of Germany, if not the CIA, by this time next week.

He reached his door, smiling to himself. He wanted things arranged so he could be there when they were fired. That shouldn't be too difficult to arrange. He reached out and unlocked his door, hopping inside. He flipped on the lights and closed the door, heading toward the kitchen. He would miss this place. The flat was in the most expensive district of West Berlin. If Varberg had known he lived here, the man would have been red with jealousy. Sara could have come here, but she'd been such a fool. Did he have to leave? What if he still took Varberg's spot? Why couldn't he be posted in the CIA? It was no different from any other agency. The more he thought about it, the more he loved the idea.

"Hello, little American."

Jeffrey froze. He looked to his left. Otto was sitting on his sofa in the semidarkness. "How did you get in here?" he asked. "This is a secure apartment building."

"I'm invisible," said Otto.

"What do you want?" said Jeffrey. "I'm warning you, I have powerful connections."

Otto stood up, stretching. "Do you have any cookies?" he asked.

"What? No. What are you talking about?"

Otto took a step toward him. "Cookies. I like them. You should see the ones that Aafke makes. The very best. You met her, remember, at the picnic?"

Jeffrey hobbled backward, glancing at the door. There was no way he could reach it in time on his crutches.

"Listen, I don't know what you want here," he said, "but you know who I am, and who I work for. You can't harm an American."

"The Americans are paying me to harm an American," said Otto. He reached down and removed a knife from his belt.

"Do you see this knife?" he asked, showing it to Jeffrey. "I received this when I was officially indoctrinated into the SS. It's a badge of honor really—for a German at least."

Jeffrey's eyes widened. He stepped back against the kitchen counter, groping behind him to find something to defend himself. His hand came across a kitchen knife and he brandished it. "Stay back!" he warned.

"Or what?" said Otto. "You'll defeat me in a knife fight? I'm glad you have a weapon. It makes me feel better about this." The commando took a couple steps forward. He was only a couple yards away now.

Jeffrey screamed and lunged forward, aiming for Otto's chest. The commando hopped to the side and brought his knife up, clanging it against the American's weapon.

"That was a good attempt," said Otto. "Try again."

Jeffrey could feel the fear ripping through him. His hand shook, he could barely keep ahold of his knife. The commando gestured for him to come at him again. But he had an idea, a desperate hope. He faked a lunge and then threw his knife at Otto. The weapon spun through the air toward its target. At the same moment, Jeffrey whipped around and rushed toward the door. He reached for the handle, sprinting for freedom. The handle turned and he pulled on the door.

A flash ripped past his vision and a tearing, lancing fire burned his hand. He looked down and saw in horror that Otto's knife was buried to the hilt in his hand, which was pinned squarely to the door. He screamed in pain, turning to see the commando walking calmly toward him, the kitchen knife in his hand.

"Bravely tried, little American," said Otto. "But predictable, I'm afraid. Now, I have to finish this. I'm sorry, but orders are orders."

Otto stepped forward and drove the knife into Jeffrey's neck, jamming the weapon up into his brain. He twisted the knife once, and then whipped it out. Jeffrey's body collapsed to the floor, his arm still grossly held up by his hand, pinned to the door.

The commando stared down at Jeffrey for a few moments, shaking his head. He then stepped over and picked up the phone, dialing a number. "It's done," he said, listening to the response. "No, I made it quick, like you asked. He didn't suffer, at least not very much. Yes, I'll pick up the payment tomorrow. And I have your promise, I'll be taken off the lists? Is that correct? Thank you." Otto hung up the phone and then dialed another number, speaking to the operator to patch him through.

"It's me," he said. "My business is over. I miss you, my dear."

"I miss you too," said Aafke's voice on the other end.

Otto sat down, closing his eyes, his whole body trembling. "I don't want to do this anymore," he said. "The killing. I just can't do it anymore. The nightmares."

"I told you to quit," she said. "We have everything we need. Come home to the family. We have our little farm. There's plenty set aside for the children's future. You need to let the war go, my love."

"I should have listened to you before," he said. "I thought I could keep at it. But I can't take any more lives. I'm done with killing. I'm done with Odessa."

"Come home," she said.

Otto hung up the phone and stepped to the door. He carefully removed the knife from the door. Bending down, he lifted Jeffrey up and carried him to his bed. He placed his knife in Jeffrey's hands. Rising up, he gave the American a stiff salute, then turned and walked out of the apartment.

He walked past the doorman, giving the man an envelope of cash, and stepped into a waiting car. Roberts and Duchesne were there in the front seat.

"Is it done?" asked Roberts.

"*Ja*," said Otto. "I almost felt bad for him. Almost."

"Don't," said Duchesne. "It was justice."

"Anything we can get you before we go back to the airport?" asked Roberts.

"Can we stop by a bakery?" asked Otto. "If there's one open at this time of night. I want to pick up some cookies for Aafke and the little ones."

"It sounds like you have a lovely wife," said Roberts. "My Kiffen is waiting for me at home."

"And my Paula," said Duchesne.

"I'm getting too old for this," said Roberts. "I'm thinking about retiring, maybe doing some coaching."

"I've always wanted to be a teacher," said Duchesne, "or maybe a principal."

"I'm done too," said Otto. "Too much killing. I'm going home for good."

"What do you think will happen with Sara?" Roberts asked.

"Don't worry about that one," said Otto. "She's going to run the world."

Author's Notes

Early Cold-War Germany

Germany was a fascinating and tragic place in the immediate aftermath of World War II. The entire country was occupied by the former "Allies," with Russia (the Soviet Union), the United States, England, and France all receiving a section of territory.

The German people suffered from shortfalls in food and fuel for several years. Although the United States supplied significant resources to Europe after the war, the bulk of these resources came in the Marshall Plan, which was not enacted until 1948. In addition, there was some feeling, perhaps with reasonable validity, among the Allies, that other nations such as the Netherlands, Belgium, and France, which had suffered terribly under Nazi occupation, should have priority in goods.

Another unusual aspect of the occupation was the rapid decline of relations between the Western nations and the Soviet Union. Even during World War II, relations were at times strained, but after the war, the two sides separated into the eastern and western European blocs that would form the basis of the Cold War, with the West constituting England, France, the

United States, and the Western democracies; and the East, formed by the Soviet Union along with Eastern nations occupied by the Soviets, such as Poland, Czechoslovakia, Romania, Bulgaria, and the east part of Germany.

This split created a cynical double action on both the Soviet and American sides, where officially the nations punished the Nazis; but in reality, both sides rushed to grab resources such as rocket and nuclear scientists and even members of the SS and Gestapo that had significant contacts and influence.

The average German spent the postwar years trying to survive. They resented the guilt forced on them by the rest of the world related to the Nazi atrocities. Many Germans protected former Nazis or at least would just prefer to forget and get on with life. These attitudes, along with the increasing hostility from East and West, led to a complex situation in Germany.

Odessa

Odessa was an organization formed of former SS members (Organisation der ehemaligen SS-Angehörigen). The organization was created to assist SS members and their families to hide in Germany or to escape to other nations, often South America.

The organization had agents in many nations of Europe, and was assisted by the Roman Catholic Church, especially the Franciscan order of monks.

The CIA was also at times involved with members of Odessa. The focus of the US government after World War II switched quickly from bringing Nazis to justice, to protecting western Europe and the United States from the rising threat of communism. The SS was highly skilled and influential in Germany during the war, and their members had much to offer the United States in their new fight against the Soviet Union. The CIA and other US organizations walked a fine line in these circumstances, officially condemning and hunting down Nazis, while often secretly working with them to obtain information or even to employ them.

The entire NASA rocket program was riddled with former German rocket scientists, many of whom had employed slave labor during World War II. The CIA also worked with wanted Nazis like Klaus Barbie, the "Butcher of Lyon," who passed substantial information on to the CIA in exchange for protection and pay.

The German Nuclear Program

The Nazis worked on a nuclear program throughout World War II. The Germans made progress on nuclear research and work on an atomic bomb, although they were well behind the efforts of the United States and England.

Ironically, the Germans would have likely built a nuclear bomb far ahead of the United States if it was not for the Nazis' inherent racism. The Germans expelled many prominent Jewish scientists from their universities and government agencies in the mid-1930s. In addition, many, including Albert Einstein, fled to the United States and other countries.

Regardless, the Germans pursued a nuclear program. The program was hindered by a lack of focus. A number of competing agencies battled for limited resources and did not share information. There was also a lack of faith that a bomb could be built in time to assist in the war effort, and thus scientists were refocused on projects like the rocket and jet programs, in which the Germans were far ahead of the rest of the world.

The Nazis did work on a nuclear reactor, named B-VIII, constructed in a secret cave in southern Germany between February and April 1945. The reactor was constructed with hundreds of uranium cubes on long cables that would be dipped into heavy water. The reactor never functioned because they did not have enough cubes in place before the war ended.

The vast majority of the Nazi nuclear scientists were captured by the Americans or British, and were ultimately relocated to the United States to work in scientific organizations with no consequences for any wartime activities.

The nuclear cubes themselves were largely sold on the black market and disappeared, with only a few having been recovered in the last few years.

The Berlin Blockade

The Berlin Blockade could be considered the first significant open event of the Cold War. As discussed above, Germany had been split into four "zones" occupied by different countries. As the Cold War progressed, the three "Western" zones occupied by the US, England, and France became the country of West Germany and the Eastern or Soviet-occupied zone became East Germany.

Berlin was also split up into four zones, although the Soviet section of the city made up almost half the total territory. Berlin, however, was surrounded for many miles in each direction by the Soviet zone.

The Russians, in the summer of 1948, in an effort to drive the Western powers out of Berlin, cut off all access to the city. The Western sections of the city had no access to food or other supplies and potentially could fall at any time to the Soviets. The United States and its Western Allies decided to fight back, and supplied the city by a massive air operation. Hundreds of flights a day delivered food and supplies to the people of West Berlin and the Allied military forces occupying that section of the city. Thousands of tons of supplies were delivered each day. This effort was by far the largest air supply of goods in human history. By comparison, the German effort to supply the besieged army in Stalingrad during World War II was only able to supply a couple of hundred tons per day.

Threats and counterthreats of force were made by both sides, but the Soviets finally backed off and opened up the land routes to West Berlin again in May 1949, almost a year after the blockade began.

The success of fighting against the Berlin Blockade was a shining moment in American military and Cold War history.

The Bavarian Royal Family

The House of Wittelsbach is the Bavarian royal family. The family were kings in Bavaria from 1806 onward, and had served as counts and dukes and electors for many centuries before this.

Crown Prince Rupprecht was the head of the family during World War II. The crown prince served with distinction as a general and then field marshal during World War I, in the Imperial German Army. Between the world wars he was courted by the Nazis, as were many members of the German aristocracy.

Unlike a number of German aristocrats, who supported or even joined the Nazis, Rupprecht and his family refused to support the growing movement. He fled to Italy when World War II began and his wife and children were eventually captured and sent to concentration camps. They were starved and mistreated, but survived the war.

Rupprecht was treated well by the US after World War II, and returned to his family home, although his efforts to restore the monarchy in Bavaria were unsuccessful. He was mourned by many at his death and treated to a royal funeral.

Nazi Hunting and the Complications of the Cold War

After World War II, a number of individuals took it upon themselves to hunt former Nazis. Prominent Nazi hunters include Simon Wiesenthal and Serge and Beate Klarsfeld.

The Klarsfelds were the original inspiration for this book, although the story told here is very different from their own. At the same time, the themes are the same. Beate Klarsfeld was a German woman who met Serge, a Jewish individual of French and Romanian background, at a train station in Paris in 1960. Serge was passionate about justice against Nazis while Beate was typical in her initial attitude as a German who remembered her own suffering late in the war and just wanted to move on from World War II.

The Klarsfelds began by protesting former Nazis who had risen to prominent positions in the new West German government, including the chancellor. They then moved on to hunt down former Gestapo members who had committed atrocities in France, including Klaus Barbie.

Their story is inspiring, particularly Beate's actions, which for a woman in the 1960s and 1970s, with all the barriers and obstacles, are absolutely amazing.

But the story is complex, just like this novel. The Klarsfelds ran into barriers from the German, US, and French governments as they attempted to track down or expose these Nazis. They also were accused, as socialists, of promoting East German and Soviet values, and even of directly working for the East Germans.

No Nazi-hunting story can be told without addressing the messy complexities of the German national desire to move on from the war and also the rapid changing of alliances from World War II to the Cold War.

Otto Skorzeny and His Commandos

Otto Berg is a fictional character, but his commando group is not. Otto Skorzeny was one of the most colorful people in World War II. He served in the military branch of the SS, the Waffen-SS, and was involved in a number of significant special operations during World War II.

Skorzeny and his forces rescued the Italian dictator Benito Mussolini in 1943, after he was deposed and held by Italian partisans. Skorzeny executed a daring airborne raid with gliders that landed in a tight area in the mountains.

Perhaps his most famous, or infamous, action was Operation Greif during the Battle of the Bulge in December 1944. This action is referenced in the book. Skorzeny sent a group of English-speaking soldiers in American uniforms to infiltrate the Allied lines during the German offensive and sow chaos. Although only a few dozen men were involved, the operation had the intended effect, with rumors flying about their intentions, and men and supplies held up at checkpoints where nervous soldiers would quiz men about Hollywood stars and sporting events, trying to ferret out the Germans.

Twenty-three of his men were captured, and eighteen of them were shot as spies. Skorzeny was tried as a war criminal for Operation Greif and spent several years in prison. He escaped from a US camp in Darmstadt and hid for a while with the assistance of other former Nazis.

Skorzeny later assisted the military in Egypt and allegedly advised President Juan Perón in Argentina. He may also have worked for the Israeli secret service, Mossad. Skorzeny's life after World War II is illustrative of the complex web of alliances and approaches after the war, where he was first tried, then escaped, then lived first in hiding and then essentially in the open. After that, he served as an advisor for a number of countries, some of which were enemies of each other.

DISCUSSION QUESTIONS

1. Were you surprised to learn about US involvement with Nazis after World War II? Was this ethical? Was it appropriate to do so for the sake of national security and the advancement of nuclear and rocket technology?

2. The German people suffered after World War II from food and fuel shortages. The victim nations such as France, Holland, Belgium, and Denmark were given priority at times for resources. Was this an appropriate response to the Nazi wrongdoing during the war? Should it have applied to just Nazis and their families, or to all Germans?

3. Is Otto a hero, an antihero, or a villain in the story?

4. Jeffrey is killed by Otto at the end of the book, a death clearly directed by Mr. Varberg. Why was Jeffrey left out of the true mission? Because he didn't know, was he wrongly killed at the end? Did his actions and decisions, with imperfect information, warrant the taking of his life?

5. Sara is Jewish and an American. She had to lie to Max throughout their time together and cultivate a relationship with him. Did Sara fall in love with Max? Was she purely professional the entire time?

6. Germany was divided into West and East Germany by the Cold War. Many Europeans feared Germany ever being reunited, given World War I and World War II. Have those fears been realized? Is there any scenario where Germany could again be a threat to European security?